WORKING GIRL

Recent Titles by Graham Ison

DIVISION*
ROUGH DIAMONDS
UNDERNEATH THE ARCHES

* available from Severn House

WORKING GIRL

Graham Ison

severn House

This first world edition published in Great Britain 2002 by
SEVERN HOUSE PUBLISHERS LTD of
9–15 High Street, Sutton, Surrey SM1 1DF.
This first world edition published in the USA 2002 by
SEVERN HOUSE PUBLISHERS INC of
595 Madison Avenue, New York, N.Y. 10022.

British Library Cataloguing in Publication Data

Ison, Graham
    Working girl
    1. Detective and mystery stories
    I. Title
    823.9'14 [F]

ISBN 0-7278-5821-1

Except where actual historical events and characters are being
described for the storyline of this novel, all situations in this
publication are fictitious and any resemblance to living persons
is purely coincidental.

Typeset by Palimpsest Book Production Ltd.,
Polmont, Stirlingshire, Scotland.
Printed and bound in Great Britain b
MPG Books Ltd., Bodmin, Cornwal

'Hello, Charlie One, Charlie One from MP. Fourteen – one four – Talleyrand Street, an antiques shop. See a Mr Xenophontos re reports of believed blood dripping through ceiling. Ends origin Information Room two-three-four-one. To Charlie One over . . .'

One

S he'd been a good-looking girl. Once. But now the body, with its matted blonde hair – black at the roots – tangled and soaked in its own blood, had become just another piece of evidence for me to work on.

The room looked like an abattoir. There was blood all over the place. It had puddled on the sheets around the victim's head, and from there it had spilt on to the threadbare carpet. Which is how the antiques dealer downstairs had noticed it. Dripping through the ceiling. One day I'll come across a story-book murder: dead blonde spread decorously on the floor of the library up at the manor house and not a sign of plasma, entrails or brains anywhere.

I put my hands in my pockets – always a good place for a detective to put them: it avoids leaving accidental fingerprints all over the place – and surveyed the scene of carnage, wondering why the hell I did this job. What a way to make a living.

My brother Geoff is in the travel business – nine-to-five, Monday to Friday – arranging holidays for people who want to get away from it all, just like I did right now. They were pleased to see Geoff, went to him willingly, made a friend of him, threw money at him to make their dreams come true. Me, I made people's nightmares come true. The last person they ever wanted to see was me. I was the bloke who hammered on the door in the dead of night to confirm their worst fears.

I'm sorry, sir, but your daughter – or for that matter your wife, mother, sister or girlfriend – has been the victim of an incident. *An incident, for Christ's sake? She's been bloody well murdered.* No, sir, I'm afraid it's bad news, really bad news, I mean.

Then comes the counselling. Counselling's nothing new. Believe me, I know. It's just that a whole load of two-two psychology graduates have turned it into an art form. You can be counselled for everything now. Tell the police that some son-of-a-bitch has nicked the hub caps off your car, which you have to do or the insurance won't pay up, and the next thing you get is a call from some well-bred do-gooder with a plum in her mouth telling you she's from Victim Support. Terrific.

I learned counselling as a very young, trainee CID officer. An old detective sergeant took me out to a burglary at a seventy-year-old widow's terraced house in Victoria. I don't know what the bastard who broke in got – the woman didn't look as though she'd had much to start with – but the callous sod had wrecked the place. The sergeant was marvellous. Bald apart from tufts of grey hair sticking out at the sides of his head, and thick-lensed, horn-rimmed spectacles. And no hope of promotion. Didn't stop him from being caring though. Dusted the place with fingerprint powder. Everywhere. Window frames, doors, tables, glasses, crockery. Told me to make the tearful old girl a cup of tea.

'Are we going to catch this bastard, Sarge?' I asked quietly.

'No chance, son,' he said.

'Then why all the fingerprint gismo?'

'It'll make the old dear feel better, son. She'll think that right now she's the only person in the world the police care about.' He'd produced a Sherlock Holmes-type magnifying glass and made a full-length novel out of a short story.

But that's counselling, real counselling. Not some silly bitch asking if you were ever abused as a child – thus making you a natural victim – as a result of which some glue-sniffing infant has broken in to your house and purloined your video, your television, your computer, your camcorder and anything else he can lay his grubby little rubber-gloved hands on.

However, enough of this cynicism. Back to the present.

The body was on its back, naked, spreadeagled, wrists tied to the brass rails of the bedhead, ankles tied to the rail at the foot. Briefs stuffed in the mouth. A sex game that had gone wrong? Or made to look like it? Unlikely, I thought: no lone prostitute would ever put herself at the mercy of a punter, no

2

matter what he paid. But there again, strange things happen in Soho.

'Her name's Monica Purvis, sir,' said a uniform.

'How d'you know that?'

'I nicked her last month for tomming. She was a regular at Marlborough Street.'

'Well, that's saved a bit of time.' Marlborough Street was the magistrates court off Regent Street where most of the prostitutes who plied their trade in and around Soho finished up in front of the stipendiary. If they weren't quick enough to avoid the PC on the beat, that is. And with the state of the police today they had to be damned slow not to avoid him. Unless they'd got so used to not seeing any coppers on the street that they didn't look for them any more.

The pathologist arrived and put on his rimless spectacles. He peered at the human detritus on the bed. 'Hmm!' he mused thoughtfully, which seemed to sum up the situation. 'Dead,' he added.

'Thanks,' I said. I'd more or less come to that conclusion myself. What a bizarre sense of humour pathologists do have.

The technicians of murder arrived in their white boiler suits and latex gloves. Photographers, fingerprint experts and scenes-of-crime know-alls, humming and nodding like they knew all the answers, and muttering about exhibit labels and continuity of evidence.

'OK to remove the rope, guv?' one of them asked.

I looked at the pathologist and he nodded.

I stood around, still with my hands in my pockets, jingling my loose change, while they got to it. The pathologist created a macabre little cameo out of putting on his own, superior-quality, latex gloves and turning the cadaver. He always called a body 'the cadaver'. Me, I just called it a body.

'Well?'

'Looks like a single stab wound to the jugular, Harry, which would certainly have been enough to cause death.'

Funny that, the way he and I came to the same conclusions, over and over again. 'So?' I raised an eyebrow.

'If you're going to ask me the time of death,' said the

pathologist, 'you'll have to wait for the post-mortem.' He waved a rectal thermometer at me as if to emphasise the point.

'I know,' I said. We had this same conversation at every murder scene. The pathologist was called Mortlock, Henry Mortlock. It seemed an eminently suitable name somehow and we only ever spoke across a dead body, either at the scene or in the mortuary. I wondered what sort of dinner guest he'd make, what he'd talk about. Did he have a sense of humour, and was it as morbid as mine? Probably was. We didn't have a lot to laugh about in our respective trades.

But I was once a patient of a staid, apparently humourless, little Maltese doctor. It was only later that I learned he was a trad jazz enthusiast. He used to take a holiday every year in New Orleans, stay up half the night every night, and get smashed out of his brains on rum. And when he got back he'd tell me that if I drank more than twenty-one units a week I'd kill myself. Funny people, medics.

'We're about wrapped up here, guv.' The senior SOCO – they call them scenes-of-crime *examiners* now, but to me they're still scenes-of-crime *officers* – ambled up, peeling off his gloves.

'Find anything?'

'Apart from the body?' The SOCO grinned.

'Yeah, apart from the body, smart-arse.'

'What looks like the murder weapon.' The SOCO handed me a plastic-shrouded sheath knife, the sort Boy Scouts used to carry before they were deemed to be offensive weapons. 'Lifted a few dabs from round and about.'

'Any money?' I asked.

'No. Unusual that for a tom.'

Well, if robbery had been the motive, the murderer didn't have to kill the girl. Just the threat would have been enough; it had happened before, many times. No, if he'd taken the money it was an afterthought.

'There's an imprint of a shoe in the blood on the left-hand side of the bed,' continued the SOCO. 'Looks hopeful. Let you know, guv. And there's this.' The SOCO held out his hand. A solitary cufflink, now in a small plastic bag, complete with

4

obligatory exhibit label, stared up at me. The cufflink said NO. 'No discernible prints on it,' he added with a grim smile. 'And this.' 'This' proved to be a cigarette end and, as an exhibit, was entitled to its own little plastic bag and exhibit label. He scribbled a few notes on his clipboard and wrinkled his brow. 'DCI, er –?'

'Detective Chief Inspector Harry Brock,' I said. 'Haven't changed it since we last met. Can't seem to find the time to fit it in.'

'Yeah, right.' The SOCO wrote it down laboriously. If he'd been using a pencil, he'd've licked it, but ball-points make a mess on the tongue. 'Esso One Two, right?' he asked, a surly expression on his face. It was shorthand for Specialist Operations Department One, Serious Crime Group Two – in other words SO1 (2) – which covers the west part of the great metropolis.

'OK to shift the body, guv?' Detective Sergeant Dave Poole had worked with me on five murders now. He was a scruffy bastard. Tie slackened off, top button undone. Mix-and-match suit – which is another way of saying his trousers, with creases everywhere but in the right place, didn't match his jacket – and shoes that would have made Ken Clarke's Hush Puppies look the height of footwear elegance. He lived out Kennington way with a blonde virago called Madeleine. Fought like cat and dog, so I heard, and I think Dave got the worst of it. He turned up one morning sporting a swollen eye with a half-closed lid. I told him to apply for a self-defence refresher course at Hendon. He didn't laugh.

'Sure, Dave. And do your bloody tie up.'

The white-suits beavered around, making a big thing of taking the late Monica Purvis out of the room.

'So, what have we got, Dave?' It was a rhetorical question. I didn't know the answer and neither did he. Well, I knew some of it. A tom called Monica Purvis had been carved up in a sleazy room in Talleyrand Street, off Shepherd Market in the heart of London's West End. Outside – and unaware of the sordid little dramas being played out almost daily in their midst – unsuspecting punters nightly flocked to the bright lights just waiting to be ripped off by the sharks in the shadows.

'Live sex show, sir, just starting. Real girls.' Real girls, eh? What other sort were there in a live sex show?

Housewives, shop-girls and female clerks huddled in dark caverns and stared open-mouthed and screamed and had orgasms as male strippers leaped about a microscopic stage like hairless orang-utans, their panting audience hoping that these prancing poofs, who used gallons of baby oil a week, would reveal all, not knowing that they daren't because it was largely padding.

Perhaps I'm a cynic.

'What time d'you make it, Dave?'

'One o'clock, guv.'

'Great.' This was one o'clock in the morning, you'll understand. It is a fact of death that prostitutes are not generally found dead at one o'clock in the afternoon.

'House-to-house?' Dave pulled out a battered packet of cigarettes and offered it to me.

'I've packed it in,' I said. 'Remember?' I'd started smoking at school and once got a thick ear from a master who'd caught me at it behind the bike sheds. He told me that his brother had died from lung cancer. I've been trying to give up ever since.

'So have I,' said Dave gloomily and started his usual feverish search for his lighter. He found it and puffed smoke towards the ceiling.

'What houses?' I asked.

'What houses?' Dave looked blank, pulled his cigarette from his mouth and swore as it stuck to his lip.

'You just said house-to-house.'

'Yeah, well, isn't that what we always do, guv?'

'Not at one a.m. in an area that hasn't got any houses, you prat. This is Talleyrand Street, for Christ's sake. People don't *live* here. We'll start local inquiries later this morning and work through the day. At least you will.'

'Thanks, guv.'

'And get someone going on this.'

Dave looked at the cufflink called NO before taking it gingerly. He held the transparent little packet between forefinger and thumb. 'There are hundreds of these about, guv. See 'em in every shop window, every shirt catalogue. There's others, too. Like HOT and COLD, LEFT and RIGHT, MILD and BITTER, ABC and XYZ, and all that sort of stuff.'

'Good. You've just proved you're a cufflink expert.'

Dave didn't look happy.

There wasn't much in the room. But then Monica Purvis didn't live here. Any more than I lived at my place of work, even though my estranged wife Helga thought I did. Before we became estranged, that is. But Helga is very German and very logical. She just didn't believe I was working the hours I was. And that was because her uncle had some cushy number in the German police and was never late home for supper.

She hadn't always been like that, though. We'd met at Westminster Hospital, sixteen years ago on St Valentine's Day, but it wasn't as romantic as it sounds. A couple of weeks previously, I'd got involved in a punch-up with some drunken louts outside a wine bar in Whitehall, and finished up having to go for a course of physiotherapy on my shoulder. And it was Helga Büchner who did the business.

We'd hit it off straight away. She was a twenty-one-year-old, flaxen-haired beauty, with brief underwear clearly visible through her white coat, probably by design. That same night I took her dancing – all right, it was only a police dance at Caxton Hall – and over the next few weeks we went out to dinner, often, almost bankrupting myself in the process. And we slept together. I couldn't get enough of her and she couldn't get enough of me. It was idyllic. I was hooked and we were married within two months.

It was only later, much later, that the sour comments of a woman sergeant at the nick turned out to be prophetic. 'Marry in haste, repent at leisure,' she told me, and for good measure, added, 'Change the name and not the letter, marry for worse and not for better.' I was sufficiently arrogant to think that she was jealous.

However, that's a whole lot of water under several bridges. Right now, I had a murder to worry about.

I cast my gaze around Monica's 'workshop'. A double bed, a threadbare carpet and a washbasin.

And a pine chest of drawers.

Only the top drawer had anything in it. Some colourful underwear, mainly red and black. A couple of pairs of fishnet hold-ups, a packet of birth-control pills, a box of condoms, a whip and two pairs of handcuffs. So why did this maniac use rope or whatever to tie her up with? Because he came prepared and didn't know about the handcuffs?

There was a black skirt – more of a pelmet really – on the only chair, together with a shiny, skimpy, red top that would have left the midriff bare. And yet another pair of fishnet hold-ups. All tossed there hurriedly, by the look of them. But toms didn't waste time. Punter in, quick bang-bang and out again, looking for the next john.

There was a pair of stilettos underneath the chair, spindly and so high they must have been agony to walk in. But then Monica didn't do much walking. And sure as hell she wasn't going to do any more.

'What's the name of the bloke who called the police, Dave?'

Dave peeled back a page of his pocket-book. 'Xenophontos, guv. Frixos Xenophontos. Keeps the shop downstairs.'

'What's he? Maltese, Iraqi, Arab? Or none of the above?'

'Cypriot, sir.' Dave smirked.

'Let us pay a visit to this upstanding member of the community then.'

Dave glanced at his watch. 'It's nearly twenty past one, guv.'

'So? *We're* up. Members of the public cannot decline to assist the police in a murder investigation merely because of the lateness of the hour.'

We walked downstairs. There was a long pause before a small brown face peered nervously round the curtain covering the door of his shop and mouthed, 'What you want?'

'Police,' I said loudly, and felt it politic to display my warrant card.

He rubbed the glass with the sleeve of his woolly cardigan and peered closely at the ornate document. 'It's late,' he shouted.

'I know.'

A rattling of keys and a drawing of bolts, five probably.

'Mr Xenophontos?'

8

'Yes, sir.'

'You called the police earlier, I believe?'

'Yes, sir.' Mr Xenophontos, clad in cords with a grubby singlet peeping from beneath the cardigan, and red slippers with turned-up toes, moved reluctantly back into the shop. Reluctantly because he purported to sell antiques, and antiques dealers are by nature reluctant to allow policemen to look around their establishments. His eyes followed mine. For months I'd been looking for a coffee table. To buy, although God knows where I would put it; we've sort of lost interest in home-making, Helga and me, since the tragedy that caused the rift.

But Mr Xenophontos thought I was looking for stolen property.

I put his mind at rest. 'I want to talk to you about what happened upstairs.'

'Is it a murder?'

He knew damned well it was a murder. When hordes of police appear late at night, illuminating the area with their revolving blue lights, and carry out a body, it is not likely to go unwitnessed by interested parties. Or nosey ones. Of which Mr Xenophontos was, with any luck, one.

'Yes, it's a murder. Tell me what you know about it.'

'I am sitting here' – Mr Xenophontos waved a hand at a small desk towards the rear of the shop – 'doing my books. This self-assessment is giving me a headache.' He sighed. 'And I've got my books open here, like now.' He tugged at my sleeve, pulling me towards the desk and, coincidentally, distracting my attention from a rather fine set of candlesticks that I determined would later interest the Arts and Antiques Squad at the Yard. 'Suddenly I see blood dripping on to my books, there.' He pointed dramatically at a number of red splashes that defaced the pages of his large ledger.

'The Inland Revenue'll like that,' said Dave. 'They're bloodsuckers.'

'I sniffed it and I thought to myself, it's blood,' said Mr Xenophontos. Not only was he an antiques dealer, but a haematologist too.

'So then you called the police, yes?'

9

'Yes, sir. It's what every good citizen should do.'

'Absolutely. How well did you know Monica Purvis?'

'Is that her name?'

Not too well apparently. 'That's her name.'

'Hardly at all. I knew that she had a room up there, obviously.' Mr Xenophontos looked around furtively and waved vaguely at the ceiling. 'And I think I know what she did for a living. But it's not my property, you see. I rent. Like she does. Did.'

'Did you see anyone coming in with her this evening?'

'No, sir. No one. When my shop is shut, I pull the curtain over the window, like now. I don't see out and no one sees in.' Mr Xenophontos looked disappointed that he was unable to assist in this matter.

'Did you *hear* anyone coming in with her tonight? Or did you hear any noises from up there, like a fight?'

'All the time I hear noises. Of the bedsprings. I complained many times to the landlord, but he just shrugs.'

'But tonight, did you hear anything unusual? Apart from the bedsprings, I mean.'

Mr Xenophontos gave this great thought, at least I hoped that he did. 'No, sir. Not nothing. Apart from the bedsprings.'

'And how often did you hear the bedsprings, Mr Xeno-phontos?'

The small Cypriot grinned. 'From about six o'clock, maybe every half an hour, sir. But only for four or five minutes at a time. And then she's going out again and coming.'

'That reckons,' said Dave.

Two

The helpful uniform who had identified the body as that of Monica Purvis had spoken briefly to the police station via the plastic box on his shoulder and come up with an address. According to the records at West End Central police station she had a room in Charleston Terrace, Paddington. I decided, in view of the time, that I would delay calling there until early the following morning. That is to say, later today.

One day I will have the good fortune to chance upon a murder victim who resides in an elegant house in Chelsea. Who has a Rolls-Royce languishing outside in the street and whose immediate next-of-kin is a willowy thirty-year-old blonde who simply adores policemen.

Alas, that day is yet to come.

Charleston Terrace, within sight, sound and smell of Paddington railway station, was littered with elderly motor cars, most of which failed to display tax discs. And if, perchance, their owners actually possessed MOT certificates they would undoubtedly prove to be forgeries. But that was not my problem.

Monica Purvis's last known place of abode was Number 27, a gaunt Victorian dwelling half way down the street. The paint was peeling from the window frames and the doors, and great chunks of the concrete façade had broken away to reveal bricks whose one hundred and fiftieth birthday anniversary must be about due. The windows were filthy, some of the panes missing altogether, and tawdry curtains hung at them, some drawn, some not.

The front garden – a generic term, you'll understand – was a patch of asphalt upon which stood the rusting wreck of a 1959 Sunbeam-Talbot and several parts of sundry motorcycles and a

11

galvanised bath. All of which, apart from the bath – there again, maybe not – were too old to arouse the interest of even the most enthusiastic of the Stolen Car Squad's newest detectives. The basement area contained a number of bicycles, none of which appeared capable of being ridden.

I allowed Detective Sergeant Poole to precede me up the cracked and chipped stone steps to the front door. If they were going to give way at any point – and they looked as though they may – it was only fair that Dave should make the discovery and sustain the injury. Claims for injury on duty are much more likely to succeed if witnessed by a senior officer. Rank hath its privileges, as we say in the constabulary.

'Yes?' My repeated knockings were eventually answered by a squat, square man in filthy grey flannels circa Brighton sea-front 1929, and an equally filthy singlet. He was bald at the front but had a pony-tail at the back – where else? – that appeared not to have been treated to a shampoo in the whole of his estimated fifty-four years.

'Are you the owner of these premises?'

'I don't want no double-glazing, if that's what you're flogging.'

'I'm a police officer, sir.'

'So?'

'And I'm investigating the murder of Monica Purvis.'

'Who?'

'Monica Purvis. I'm told she lived here.'

'Oh, right. Lives upstairs. Blonde kid?'

At last. 'That's correct.'

'Murdered, you say?'

'Last night.'

'Means I'll have to let the room again, I s'pose.' The economic repercussions of Monica Purvis's death clearly overcame any feelings of grief that her landlord may have been harbouring. 'Better come in, then.' He turned and then paused. 'Got any ID?'

With a flourish perfected by years of practice, I produced my warrant card. 'And who are you?'

'George Washington's the name.'

'Really? Any relation?'

'Do what?'

'Never mind.' We moved into a dismal hallway and, coincidentally, into an overpowering stench of boiled cabbage. On reflection this was probably an advantage in that it undoubtedly disguised even more obnoxious odours. There was a cracked mirror on one wall and worn and holed coconut-matting stretched across the floor and up the stairs. 'D'you know what Monica Purvis did for a living?' I knew what she did, of course I knew, but I was interested to know what Washington thought she did, or at least what tale he would tell. I wasn't disappointed.

'Yeah, air hostess.'

I've heard prostitution called some things, but rarely that, even though I've met some air hostesses who had all the qualifications. 'Really? That's interesting.' Interesting in that he probably knew what she did, but wasn't quite sure where that placed him with the law.

'Yeah. Worked nights mostly.'

Well, Washington had certainly got that bit right. He led the way up the rickety staircase. The banister rail looked a bit dodgy so I relied on my sense of balance.

Surprisingly, Monica's room was reasonably clean and tidy. When compared with the rest of the house, that is. The single bed was covered with a worn candlewick bedspread that had once been blue but had since faded in places so that it now had white patches. There was an armchair and a television set with a twelve-inch screen. A corner washbasin had a dripping tap that had stained the cracked porcelain a rusty brown.

On the wall opposite the door was a mahogany chest of drawers. There were two small drawers at the top and three full-width ones beneath them. On top of the chest, in an untidy array, stood a hairbrush, a lipstick and an old pot of vanishing cream – the contents of which had largely vanished – in front of a mirror that was brown around the edges. It hadn't been designed that way.

'Go to it then, Dave. And mind where you're putting your dabs.'

Dave Poole grinned, produced a pair of latex gloves from his pocket and wrenched open the left-hand top drawer. 'There's corres in this one, guv,' he said.

'Corres' is policemen's shorthand for any form of paperwork. I walked across and peered over Dave's shoulder.

'Seems to be letters mainly, and bills,' said Dave, poking tentatively at the little pile of paper with his forefinger. 'And a rent book.'

'Let's have it then.' There were about ten letters altogether, a few receipts, mainly from clothes shops, and a letter, dated ten days previously, from a credit-card company informing Mrs Purvis – *Mrs* Purvis, eh? So, where is Mr Purvis? – that credit facilities were being withdrawn until the outstanding amount of £2,327.17 had been settled. It further ominously advised that if that sum was not forthcoming within twenty-eight days, steps would be taken to recover it. I was going to enjoy giving them the good news. I too have jousted with credit card companies.

As if in answer to my unspoken question about Monica's marital status, Dave produced a photograph from the back of the drawer. 'This looks interesting, guv.'

The dog-eared print portrayed a young couple standing on the steps of what was obviously a register office. A pretty blonde, holding a bouquet, clutched the arm of a grinning youth in a tight-fitting suit with a large carnation in his button-hole. And an earring penetrating the lobe of his left ear. I'm not bad at spotting villains and I'd just spotted one. 'I'll put money on that being Monica,' I said, pointing at the blonde, 'and that, with any luck is *Mister* Purvis. I wonder where he is.'

'Yeah, I wonder.' There was a desperate tone in Dave's voice. He knew that it would fall to him to find the missing bridegroom.

The landlord, apparently fascinated by this high-tech police approach to murder, was still standing in the doorway. 'Ever see this bloke here?' I held the photograph by its edges and pushed it near his face. 'And don't touch it.'

'I think so. Must have been about a month ago. He come here one morning, asking for Monica.'

'And?'

'And nothing. She wasn't here, so he pushed off. Course,

on the other hand' – Washington peered more closely at the photograph – 'it might not have been him at all.'

'Thanks a lot.'

Dave pulled open the next drawer down and the bottom fell out. 'Just clothing in this one, guv,' he said, staring gloomily at the pile of dirty underwear, sweaters and tights that was now on the floor. He kicked it aside with his foot and opened the other two drawers. They were empty.

'I hope you're going to pay for that,' said Washington, peering at the broken drawer.

'Don't upset me, squire, I'm in a bad mood this morning,' said Dave. I imagine Madeleine had given him a hard time when eventually he'd got in earlier today.

We turned our attention to the wardrobe, by which I meant the curtained recess alongside the fireplace. A couple of dresses – quite modest in design for a tom; I suppose they were her day gear – hung on hangers together with a black skirt in plastic wrapping that looked as though it was fresh from the cleaners. Next to it was a raincoat made of black PVC. 'Where's one supposed to bath in this place?' It was pure interest; I wasn't thinking of taking advantage of the facilities fearing that I'd come out dirtier than I went in.

'There's a bathroom down the hall,' said Washington. 'But it's fifty p.'

'Really? Tell me, George,' I asked conversationally, 'what rent did you charge her?'

Washington pursed his lips, but he knew I'd just found the rent book. 'Two hundred,' he said quietly.

'A month?' I was winding him up now.

'A week,' said Washington, even more softly.

'How many other people live here?'

'Seven.'

'Any other prostitutes?'

Washington did some self-righteous puffing up. 'Now look here—'

'Monica Purvis was on the game which is why you were charging her two hundred notes a week, my friend. And if there's just one more under your roof you stand in great danger of getting done for keeping a brothel.' I didn't see why I should

15

offer this Rachmanesque shark any comfort. 'Even living on immoral earnings.'

'I told you, she was an air hostess.' Washington began whining now.

'Which airline?'

'I dunno, guv'nor.'

'This character who called here . . .' I jabbed a finger at the wedding photograph now shrouded in one of Dave's little plastic bags. 'Give a name, did he?'

'No, he never said.'

'Leave a message, then? Like tell Monica I'll be back. Anything like that?'

'No, he never said.'

'Did he ask where she worked, then?'

'No, he never said.'

In the face of Washington's repetitive denials, I gave up.

'Er, guv . . .' Dave was kneeling in front of a small suitcase that he had found at the bottom of the makeshift wardrobe, dragging out some more clothing.

'What, Dave?'

'This was inside this suitcase.' He was holding up an air hostess's uniform: skirt, jacket and jaunty little hat. 'I must say the skirt's a bit short, even for an air hostess.'

'I take it you're an expert on the length of air hostesses' skirts, then, Dave.'

Dave grinned. 'Been known to take an interest in the past, guv. Before I was married, of course,' he added hurriedly.

'Of course,' I murmured. 'Anyway, from your extensive knowledge of such things, do you recognise which airline it belongs to? The badge mean anything?'

'No,' said Dave and as I was about to speak again, he added, 'Yeah, I know. Find out.'

'Better take it with us.' I waved at the pile of letters. 'And bag that lot up, Dave. We'll take those too. In the meantime, we'll get a team up to give this place the once-over.'

Washington appeared distressed at this instruction. 'Team?' he echoed.

'Don't worry, it's a forensic science team, not from the

environmental health.' I paused, quite deliberately. 'Oh, I don't know though,' I added, gazing around.

It was the same team that had scoured Monica's West End 'office' for clues. As before, fingerprint expertise was deployed and the E-vac, a small vacuum cleaner that can be relied upon to suck up the finest of particles, was put to good use. By the time the on-site scientists had finished the room was cleaner than it had been for years.

We returned to the office.

'The cufflink, guv.'

'What about it, Dave?'

'I've had one of the lads out and about this morning . . .'

'And?'

'Needle in a haystack job.'

When Dave said that, I knew it was true. Despite his appearance and his overtly casual approach to the business of crime investigation, he was a good detective. The DI at Putney had been foolish enough to tell me about this young skipper of his who had worked day and night to get a persistent robber convicted. I liked what I'd heard and poached him as soon as a vacancy had cropped up on the Serious Crime Group. But the DI had also said that Dave had 'wife trouble'. I still didn't know whether it was true, but it was the sort of thing that senior CID officers tell you if they think you're about to have one of their best thief-takers away. But it didn't work in my case. After all, I'd got wife trouble of my own, and told myself that I knew how to handle it. *Like hell I did!*

'What d'you reckon then, Dave?' I asked.

'The press?'

'D'you think anyone's likely to own up to leaving their cufflink on the floor of a murdered tom's flop, Dave?'

'Well, guv'nor, look at it this way. The villain's not going to anyway, but if some other bloke, terrified that he might get scurfed up in a murder inquiry, sees it, he might just give himself up. To eliminate himself like. Would help a bit, wouldn't it?'

'How so?' I queried.

'Well, someone might have had their cufflinks nicked, or lent them to someone.'

'True, Dave, true.' I didn't think so at all, but it would placate Dave, so I reached for the phone and dialled the Head of News at Scotland Yard. 'Bob, it's DCI Harry Brock, SO1 West. I've got a problem,' I began, and explained what I had in mind.

The detective sergeant from the laboratory came swanning into the office that afternoon. His name was Wright. 'We got some decent prints from her room, guv,' he began.

'Whose were they, hers?' I'd been let down before.

'We got some of hers too,' said Wright. 'But we've lifted a few others.'

'Any identifiable?'

'Two.' Wright slid a thin docket across my desk and withdrew his hand quickly. Like it may get bitten off. 'Most of those we found have got no record, but these two have got form. Mind you, sir,' he went on, assuming the usual lofty air of the expert, 'given the number of clients she must have had, they probably won't mean anything.'

What he said was true, but I was about to be stricken by the clutching-at-straws syndrome. 'We'll have to see, won't we,' I said. 'And the print of the shoe?'

'Trainer, guv.' From his briefcase Wright extracted a large colour photograph of the imprint that had been found in the blood alongside Monica's bed. 'Manufactured in Taiwan for the British company that markets them. I've spoken to them and they reckon that this one's between twelve and fifteen years old, but it obviously hasn't been worn much. These ridges, in five groups of seven' – he took out a ballpoint pen and waved it gently over the print – 'are pretty rare now, as are these diamond shapes around the edge of the sole. They've changed the design apparently.' The pen came to rest on a mark. 'But there's a cut here, shaped like a seven. That's not part of the design, so whoever owns a trainer with that mark on it, was at the scene at the time of the murder, or immediately afterwards.' He leaned back and grinned triumphantly. 'Of course, finding it could be a bit difficult.'

'I'd worked that out for myself, *Sergeant*.' I have to admit that I spoke a trifle sharply. I don't like being treated like an idiot by some desk-bound policeman masquerading as a scientist. 'And of course the owner may have lost it, thrown it away or had it nicked. Never jump to conclusions.'

'Yes, well . . .' Wright sat up, thought and then stood up. 'If there's anything else I can help with, sir, just give me a bell.'

I waited until Wright had reached the door. 'What size shoe is it?' I asked mildly.

That threw him. 'Ah, yes, size.' He rummaged in his fat briefcase and found another piece of paper. 'Forgot to give you the report, sir. It's a size nine. Fairly common size, of course.'

'Of course,' I said.

The man at the credit-card company who had sent Monica Purvis the threatening letter was not at all pleased to be told of her untimely death.

'But what about our money?' he whined. 'It was nearly two and half thousand pounds. Well, more now with the interest.'

I don't know much about civil law, but I did my best to help him. 'I suppose someone will be dealing with the probate of her estate,' I said, sensing that Dave was doing his best to suppress a laugh. 'But I shouldn't think it's worth as much as two and half p, so I shouldn't hold your breath.'

But that presumption was to prove wildly inaccurate.

Three

My office is in an eight-storey building called Curtis Green which, it seems, only policemen have ever heard of. It used to be called New Scotland Yard North. But that was before a cunning government – which needed the space – persuaded the Commissioner of Police to move his headquarters half a mile to a glass and concrete pile in Victoria Street, which, by a happy coincidence, it was decided would also be called New Scotland Yard.

Talleyrand Street, close by Shepherd Market, where Monica Purvis met her Maker, is one mile exactly – as the crow flies – from my office at Curtis Green. If I looked out of the window I could have seen it, except that my window is on the other side of the building. Not that I have much time for looking out of windows, not when you consider that my colleagues and I are responsible for investigating all the serious crimes from there to Hillingdon. And that's one hell of a lot of crimes, believe me.

It was a nice day. I decided to walk to the West End. A mistake. In July the centre of London is thick with tourists of all shapes, sizes, colours and financial stability. To walk up Whitehall and across Trafalgar Square in a policeman's uniform is a nightmare. I know. I did it, years ago. Cannon Row police station is where I started, twenty-one years ago. Working the shift, morning, noon and night. Literally. And a ball-aching job it was too. Several times I nearly packed the job in.

Mind you, it did have its moments. One Christmas I arrested a photographer in Trafalgar Square. But that wasn't all. I also nicked the stooge dressed up as Father Christmas – kids could stand beside him to have their picture taken. But we knew the photographer of old, and knew that he rarely, if ever, had film in his camera. He certainly hadn't this time, not that it mattered: there was a warrant out for his arrest. But the station van was picking up a knock-off outside Buckingham Palace, so while another PC took the photographer, I frogmarched the struggling Father Christmas all the way up Whitehall to the nick, passing several horrified children in the process. I reckon that put police public relations back a few years.

And despite three years of street duty, I still don't know how high Nelson's Column is. I used to make it up. No one seemed to mind. But now that policemen are thin on the ground *anyone* who looks like he's a native Londoner gets stopped and asked damn-fool questions. I got no further than the tinned soldiers sitting on nags at Horse Guards.

'Pardon me, sir, are you English?' An essential question this one, posed in a strong Brooklyn accent. And the first of many questions I was to be asked before I reached the West End.

'Yes.'

'Would you happen to know how high is the Nelson monument on Traffle-gar Square?'

'One hundred and four feet, nine and a half inches, plus Nelson himself at seventeen feet. It's life-sized, you see,' I said with a straight face.

'Gee!' The man from Brooklyn fed this inaccurate statistic into a hand-held computer, imparted the information to his wife and concentrated on filming the tinned soldiers with a video camera. A pigeon sat on his baseball cap and took a great interest.

I eventually got to Shepherd Market. But not before I'd popped into my favourite shirt shop in Sackville Street and bought a tie. Good quality silk at ten quid in their sale. Not bad.

Prostitutes comprise a fascinating sorority. Although they hire their bodies to the carnally hungry for money – and often have an inflated conception of their own value – they are generous folk in many other ways. And are frequently homespun philosophers.

In days gone by it was not uncommon, when an otherwise respectable married punter succumbed to a heart attack while doing the business, for the voluptuous tart who had seen him off the planet to call a policeman, and with his help and connivance drag the said punter outside to the public highway. The PC would then calmly call an ambulance and report a collapse in the street, thus shielding the deceased's widow from the embarrassment of learning that her husband's final moments had been spent in having it off with a tom. But that was before terrifyingly honest policemen and political correctness ravaged the ranks of the police force. And to think they now call it a *service*.

The whores' early shift comes on duty at about half past two in the afternoon. They form little groups in and around Shepherd Market and discuss experiences, the going rate for screwing, and exchange intelligence about any particularly nasty bastard who, in the interest of self-preservation, should be avoided like the plague. Or the pox. Or Aids.

These working girls also have an innate ability to spot a copper. I have never worn a trench coat or a trilby hat, but I do wear a suit and a collar and tie. I've always fancied myself as a pretty trendy dresser. When I was on the Flying Squad I came across a good German tailor down the East End and he's made my suits ever since. Speaking his language helps, I suppose. Which reminds me, I must introduce Dave to him, see if I can get him looking half decent.

Maybe it's the way I walk that alarms the populace, or a confidence born of dealing with the unrighteous for so many years. Whatever, the moment I appeared, the little groups of working girls split up and moved about, metaphorically whistling.

I homed in on the nearest one. 'I'm Detective Chief Inspector Brock.'

'Looking for a freebie, love?'

'Don't take the piss.'

'Ooh, nice!'

'Monica Purvis. Name mean anything?'

'Nope. Should it?' She wore tight scarlet shorts and fishnets. Fishnets again! A close-fitting, knitted white crop top that bulged promisingly, started six inches above where the shorts stopped. For some reason best known to herself she had a ring through her navel which matched the three in each of her ears and, in case you missed the other adornments, an imitation diamond embedded in her nose.

'She was murdered last night, just around the corner from here.'

'I know.'

'Well, what are you poncing about for? You *do* know her.'

'Yeah, well.'

'Well what?'

'What d'you want to know?'

'Who she went with. What's your name, by the way?'

'Sadie Thompson.'

'Very funny. Who was she with? Any idea?'

'Nah! Never see her going. She was here about seven thirty. Then I picked up a john. Never saw her again.' She glanced across at her curious colleagues. 'S'all right,' she said. 'He's a copper. Asking about Monica, poor little cow.'

The others looked relieved. They could deal with a policeman investigating a murder. It was the vice lot from West End Central nick they really hated. If *they* started asking questions, like who's your pimp, or is that place a brothel, they'd get blanked.

'I saw her.' A black girl sashayed across and teetered to a standstill on her high heels. Long black legs and a clinging, cerise dress so short that she dare not bend over. 'She went with a trick about tennish. Now piss off. If he sees me talking to the Old Bill, he'll bloody crucify me,' she said out of the corner of her mouth as she turned abruptly and walked away. A long way away, I guessed.

The sharp-looking black man who had put the fear of Christ up the black girl had walked in from Curzon Street. He took one look at me and scarpered. It must have been something about me.

'Sadie.'

'What now?'

'Who's the black girl?'

'Dunno.'

'Look, I need to talk to her, but not here. One of your mates has been topped, and there might be others unless he's stopped. This killer is a raving nutcase.'

'She's called Sherry Higginbottom, but for Christ's sake don't tell her I told you her last name.'

Once everything settles down in the Metropolitan Police there is a great urgency to move it all again. This week the Vice Squad at West End Central police station was on the second floor. God knows where it'll be next week.

'Help you?' A tired-looking youth in jeans and a rugby shirt dragged his eyes away from a file – it was an effort – and stared at me.

'You in the Job?' One had to make certain. These days there are more civvies than coppers hanging around in police stations.

'Who wants to know?'

'DCI Brock, SO1 West.'

He rose smoothly to his feet, but leaned on the desk with one hand. I stared at the hand. He removed it. 'I'm PC Gomez, the Intelligence Officer, sir.'

One gets surprises every day. That's what's so rewarding about police work. 'Sherry Higginbottom, a tom who works Shepherd Market. What d'you know about her?'

Gomez took refuge in a filing cabinet, eventually unearthing a dog-eared folder. 'Aged twenty-seven, lives in Battersea. Only does it in cheap hotels, usually down Pimlico way, but apparently she's worth it.'

'How do you know she's worth it?'

'Information received, sir.' Gomez risked a grin.

'Previous?'

'Cautioned the usual statutory twice, declined to speak to a woman officer at the station, declined to be put in touch with a welfare organisation, and since then been busted seven times.'

'By busted I take it you mean arrested and charged.' I don't like Americanisms: it's the television that does it.

'Er, yes, sir.'

'Good. Well, she's about to be arrested again.'

'What for, sir?' Gomez picked up a government-issue ball-point pen, tested it on an old copy of *The Job* and drew Sherry

Higginbottom's file towards him again, expectantly.

'I want to talk to her.'

'Oh!'

I descended to the front office of the police station and tracked down the duty inspector. 'I want Sherry Higginbottom nicked.'

'May I ask what for, sir?' The inspector stood up and tugged at his woolly-pully.

'I want to talk to her about the murder of Monica Purvis, and I don't want to do it in Shepherd Market where her ponce may take objection to her talking to the law. So I'd be grateful if you would despatch a PC to bring her in. Toms get arrested all the time, so it won't look suspicious. *Comprenez?*'

'What?'

'Understood?'

The duty inspector was amenable, which makes a change. 'Yes, sir.'

I only waited eighteen minutes. I timed it. A young woman officer – about to be disappointed because she thought she'd got a real arrest – escorted Sherry to the custody suite.

The sergeant sniffed and said put her in the interview room. Well, I imagine that's what he said. I wasn't in the custody suite.

Sherry sat sideways on, extending her very long black legs so that I had a good view of them, and of her red G-string.

'Sorry to drag you in like this, but I thought it would be better if we had a chat here.'

'That's OK, love. Makes a break to get off me feet without getting on me back.' The accent was pure Hoxton, always supposing there is a pure Hoxton nowadays.

'So tell me about this trick you saw Monica going off with.'

'Early thirties, I s'pose. Seen him before, once or twice.'

'Any idea of his name?'

'No, but Monica seemed to know him. But it was the first time she'd gone off with him. As far as I know.'

'Can you describe him?'

'Now you're asking.' Sherry ferreted in her handbag and pulled out a packet of Marlboro. 'All right to smoke?'

'Sure.' I pushed a tin lid across the table.

'Want one?'

'No, thanks. I've given up.'

'Won't last. Never does.'

'Thanks. A description?'

'Oh yeah.' She crossed her legs and started to flick the back of her shoe off and on her heel. 'About your height, I s'pose. What's that, six feet?'

'Yes. About.'

'Yeah, well, about six feet. Big guy. Broad shoulders. Looked like he might have been a brickie, or worked out doing weights an' that. Oh, he had a number three, too.'

'A what?'

'A number three. You know, a crew cut.'

'Beard, moustache?' A little prompting may help, I thought.

'No, nothing like that. Wore a T-shirt and jeans last time I saw him.'

'What, last night?'

'Yeah.'

'Carrying anything, was he? A sports-bag, perhaps? Holdall, duffel-bag, rucksack, bum-bag?'

'Cuddly toy.'

'Leave it out, Sherry. This is serious.'

'Yeah, sorry. No, nothing that I saw. Oh, there was one other thing. He had a ring in his . . .' She paused to think about that. 'Yeah, in his left ear. Big, it was. Bigger than usual.' She laughed. 'Looked like a bleedin' curtain ring.'

Aha! I took the plastic-covered wedding photograph from my pocket. 'Could this have been him?'

Sherry looked carefully at the photograph of the happy couple. 'Well, that's Monica for sure, but I should think it was taken about four years ago. And that could have been the trick she went off with.' She looked up. 'Is that her old man, then?'

'I presume so. Unless they're into having wedding photographs taken just for the hell of it.'

'Yeah, well, it might have been him.'

'Any idea where they went? This was in Shepherd Market, was it, where he picked her up?'

26

'Yeah, it was. No, they just pushed off.'

'Did you hear anything? Like a price, or where they were going?'

'No. He come in the Market and went straight up to Monica. They had a chat. I couldn't hear nothing what they said. But Monica never looked too happy about it.'

'D'you think he was bent, then?'

Sherry gave an expressive shrug of her shoulders. 'Search me.'

I resisted the temptation, pleasurable though it would undoubtedly have been. 'Was she straight?'

'Yeah, I think so. In fact, I know so. I'm the one who does the whips.' She opened her small handbag and extracted a coil of thin and very nasty-looking plaited leather. She laughed and put it back. 'She had one or two punters who wanted it, so she sent 'em over to me. I sorted them out, poor darlings. If their mothers had given 'em a good hiding once in a while, they wouldn't be bothering me.' She considered that for a moment or two. 'Or p'raps that's why they want some more.' She shrugged again. 'Funny things, men.'

Like I said, there are a lot of philosophers among prostitutes. Nevertheless, I remembered that we'd found a whip and two sets of handcuffs in Monica's room, and I told Sherry that we had.

She shrugged. 'Perhaps the last tenant left them there,' she said.

'Did she ever go in for bondage?'

'Not that I know of. Why?'

I explained that we had found the body tied up.

'She'd never have fallen for that. No girl on her own would let a punter tie her up. We're all worried about being attacked, but it goes with the territory. In fact Monica used to keep a knife handy, just in case.'

'Did you ever see it?'

'Yeah, she showed it to me once.'

'Would you recognise it again, Sherry?'

'Yeah, probably.'

I made a note to get someone to show her what we now knew to be the murder weapon. 'You said you'd seen this bloke before,' I said, returning to the trick Sherry had seen Monica going off with. 'Recently?'

'About a month ago, I s'pose, but she never went off with him that time. There was a bit of a ding-dong and just then a copper walked through and this bloke done a runner.'

'Did this policeman talk to Monica?'

'I think he did. Dunno what about, though. He pushed off then, the copper I mean, and Monica picked up a trick.'

'Is this policeman a regular round the Market?' This was really pushing my luck. If Sherry could tell me who he was it would save me hours – or, to be accurate, my trusty Detective Sergeant Poole – of searching through duty states in an attempt to find out who was on the beat that day. Always supposing, of course, that the idle bastard wasn't off his own beat and poaching on someone else's.

'Seen him a few times.'

'Don't happen to know his number, do you?'

'Oh, sure. And his inside leg measurement.'

Pure sarcasm. But then I have known some policemen whose inside leg measurement was more familiar to certain street women than his divisional number. But that was all in the past. It is now a sea-green incorruptible police force. Service.

'If you see him again, clock his number and give me a ring, will you?'

'OK, love. Is there a reward? Gone missing, has he?'

We were getting sidetracked. I posed the standard police question. 'This bloke that Monica went off with last night, know him again, would you, Sherry?'

'Too bloody right, I would. D'you reckon it's down to him?'

It was my turn to shrug. 'Maybe, maybe not.'

The average prostitute, working the West End of London, may pick up as many as twenty tricks on a good day, and the risk factor is pretty high. There are some very nasty bastards about. If the crew-cut gorilla who still had half his price ticket stuck in his ear was the front-runner for the murder of Monica Purvis we would be lucky indeed. Very lucky.

But police work rarely pans out that way.

Four

'Rope' can mean many things. It can be a pearl necklace or a knotted string of onions or a lineal distance of twenty feet. Alfred Hitchcock even coined it for a film title. And it was once used to hang murderers.

But Monica Purvis had not been tied to her bed with a pearl necklace, a string of onions, or even an old celluloid film, neither were her bonds twenty feet long. She had been tied up with less than four feet of rope; rope as in a twist of fibre, which could be hemp, jute, sisal or manila. Or nylon or polypropylene. And sure as hell her killer, if I ever found him, wouldn't be topped.

'What d'you make of the rope, Doctor?'

Dr Sarah Dawson was the rope expert at the Metropolitan Forensic Science Laboratory in Lambeth. She had long black hair, long legs, an hour-glass figure – currently concealed beneath a severe white coat – a brain, and horn-rimmed specs. I somehow doubted that she had an eyesight problem; she probably thought that these heavy black frames would deter libidinous detectives who, justifiably, fancied her. Maybe she hadn't heard of spectacle fetishists.

'Technically speaking, Harry, to be a rope it should be one inch round or more. This' – Sarah pointed at the length of cord with a pair of forceps; don't ask me why forceps – 'has a diameter of three millimetres exactly. That makes its circumference somewhere about seven-point-oh-six-nine millimetres. Roughly. Or in English about five-sixteenths of an inch.' She smiled archly.

'You never cease to amaze me with your expertise, Doctor. So it's not a rope, it's a cord. Yes?'

'Call it what you like, Harry, but you've got one hell of a job on your hands.'

'I knew that before I came. Go on then, make it worse.'

'These' – again the forceps pointed accusingly at the lengths of cord – 'are manufactured by the polymerisation of a single monomer to form a polyamide before being spun into its present form.'

'That should make it easy to track down.' I smiled confidently at this helpful young lady.

'Not really. It's another way of saying it's nylon cord.' That's the trouble with forensic scientists: they always want to be so bloody smart. 'This particular brand,' she continued, determined to depress me further, 'is probably the most common. I think you could expect to find it in Homebase, B&Q, Payless, Woolworth's or any outlet that supplies curtains. And practically any hardware shop you care to name.'

'What you're saying is that I have no hope of finding out who bought it . . .'

Sarah tipped her glasses forward, her eyes twinkling over the top of them, and smiled sweetly. Very sweetly. Sickly sweet. 'I don't know, Harry. You're the detective.'

'D'you fancy having dinner with me tonight?' I asked.

Sarah smiled sweetly again. 'You're much too busy,' she said. 'And if you're not, your wife wouldn't like it,' she added.

That, I thought, was unnecessarily cruel. All right, so my wife and I are on the point of divorce, but I'm forty and time is valuable. 'We're separated,' I said. 'Well, not separated, more estranged.'

Sarah gave me one of those I-can't-say-I'm-surprised looks. But I wasn't going to enlarge on the reasons. They were none of her damned business and, anyway, it was all still too painful. Even after all these years, I still couldn't forgive Helga. We rarely mentioned it now, but the poison had spread to other things, things that before the tragedy would have been laughed off. Now, however, the slightest tiff rapidly developed into a full-scale row. Like this morning over breakfast. Sure, we slept in separate rooms, but there was only one kitchen and that was the place where Helga always seemed to pick an argument. I suppose she regarded it as her domain. Anyway, it was the only place we ever met these days.

I was driven from Lambeth back to Curtis Green. Well, very nearly. Traffic was at a standstill on Westminster Bridge. Two taxis had collided and the drivers were in the centre of the road engaging in what was clearly a battle of wits between two unarmed opponents. I walked the rest of the way.

'I've found the PC, guv.' Detective Sergeant Poole looked pleased with himself.

'Didn't know we'd lost one, Dave.' I knew which PC he was talking about and didn't enquire too deeply how he'd tracked him down; Dave Poole in his threatening mode is not a pleasant sight.

But Dave was accustomed to my sense of humour. 'The one who went through Shepherd Market when Monica was having a set-to with the bloke Sherry Higginbottom claimed she went off with the night of the murder.'

'Ah! Where is he?'

'Late turn. On at two. I've left a message for him to come over.'

At twenty past two a constable appeared in my office. And saluted. I assumed that he had not long been released from the brain-washing concentration camp they call the Hendon Training School. 'PC Webster, sir. I understand you wanted to see me.'

'Perhaps,' I said cautiously. 'Take your pointed hat off your head and the weight off your feet. And smoke if you want to.'

Such amiability from a detective chief inspector clearly unnerved PC Webster, but he did as I asked. Except that he didn't smoke. Probably didn't drink either.

'About a month ago, you were walking through Shepherd Market . . .'

Webster's brow furrowed and he had the worried look of someone who was wondering whether the time was yet ripe to send for his Federation representative to begin formulating his defence. 'Possibly, sir.'

'Look, son, I'm investigating a murder. I don't give a toss

if you were off your beat, lost, shopping or just idling and gossiping.' I assumed that idling and gossiping was still a disciplinary offence. If so, I could think of a few senior officers who deserved to get done for it. Without venturing forth from New Scotland Yard. 'All I'm interested in is a tom called Monica Purvis who was murdered the night before last. My informant' – Sherry Higginbottom would love to have known that she now enjoyed such elevated status – 'suggests that the man Monica went with that night was the same man she had an argument with and which was witnessed by you.'

'Ah!' said Webster.

Progress at last, perhaps. 'Well?'

'Yes, sir. I seem to remember something like that.'

'Now don't go trying to oblige me.' I'd run across PCs before who desperately wanted to be detectives. But creating non-existent evidence was not the way to go about it. Not any more. That's all changed. 'Just tell me what you saw. If you saw anything.'

'It was about seven o'clock, sir—'

'When was this?'

'Must have been a month ago, sir. About the end of June, I should think.'

'Go on.'

'Well, I'd just come out from grub and took a turn through Shepherd Market. Just to wind 'em up a bit.' Constable Webster afforded himself a brief grin. 'There was this bloke talking to the Purvis girl and wagging his finger, threatening like, but as soon as he saw me he took off.'

'Talking, you say?'

'Well, it seemed more like a bit of an argument. Like they were trying to settle on a price that he thought was too much and she thought was too little. Anyway, like I said, he wagged his finger at her and then cleared off. Happens all the time.'

I admired such worldliness in one so young. 'Did you hear anything that was said?'

The Webster brow furrowed again. 'I think he said something like, "I'll be back."'

Oh joy! This was getting me nowhere. 'Can you describe him?'

'About six feet tall, probably fifteen stones. Earring in his left ear. Muscular sort of bloke. Wearing a T-shirt and jeans.'

'Age?'

'About thirty-one, maybe thirty-two, sir. Early thirties, anyway. Oh, and he had a tattoo on his left forearm. A dagger, I think it was.'

'My informant said that you spoke to Monica Purvis.'

'Only briefly. I asked her if she was all right.'

'And what did she say?'

My helpful constable ran his tongue round his lips. 'She said, "It all depends what you fancy, copper," and then . . . then she . . . she . . .'

'Spit it out, lad.'

'She, er, pulled open her blouse, sir, and exposed herself. She wasn't wearing a bra.'

Lucky young Webster. 'Disgraceful,' I said. 'Know this character again, would you?'

'I think so, sir.' Webster looked guilty as a sudden thought occurred to him. 'But I didn't apprehend a breach of the peace,' he added, culling a bit of common law from the recesses of his memory, 'so I didn't put anything in my pocketbook. I didn't think it was a reportable incident.'

'It wasn't. Did he look the sort of layabout who'd wear cufflinks?'

'What, on a T-shirt, sir?'

God preserve me from tunnel vision. Even so, Webster's addition to my pitifully small pile of evidence wasn't bad. The best I could hope for, I suppose. But there was this awful nagging feeling that the knucklehead who'd chatted up Monica and then went off with her the night she was killed probably had nothing to do with her death anyway. It was possible though that the description Webster had given matched the errant bridegroom in the photograph we'd found at Charleston Terrace. 'Have a look at this.' I held out a hand and Dave gave me the photograph. 'Could that have been him?'

Webster studied the bridegroom closely. 'It's possible, sir, but the guy I saw was a bit older than this.'

'Would be,' I said. It was obviously time to talk to the bridegroom. To say nothing of the previously convicted owners of the fingers that had left impressions in Monica's West End room.

'What do we know about the two who were careless enough to leave their fingerprints at Talleyrand Street, Dave?' I asked as PC Webster hurried from my office, doubtless to do a bit of canteen boasting that he had suddenly become a vital witness in a murder inquiry. After all, reputations have been founded on less.

'The addresses for them are one and two years old respectively, sir.' Dave, his back to me, was ferreting about in a stack of files on his desk.

'Could we have chapter and verse on that, Dave? Be nice to know who we're talking about.'

'Ah, yes, right, guv.' He laid two files in front of me. 'They're the printouts of the CRO microfiches,' he said, by which he meant that he was giving me the pair's criminal records.

'So, we have a Michael Cozens and a Paul Simister. Or should that be Sinister?'

'No, it's an M, guv'nor.' Dave greeted this silly remark of mine with a perfectly straight face.

Michael Cozens was thirty-five and had one previous conviction for fraud. Three years ago he had attempted to pass off a cheque his employers had received from an insurance company but which he'd altered to read £900 instead of the original £90.

Working as an accounts clerk in a motor dealer's, Cozens had made the mistake of assuming that a big company wouldn't notice the enhanced amount when their statement came through. But it didn't get that far. Unfortunately for Cozens the bank noticed it and queried it with one of Cozens' directors. The director, his suspicions aroused, did a bit of investigating and found that Cozens had been milking the funds fairly regularly. The police were informed and Cozens copped eighteen months. Where he lived now was something that we – that is to say Dave Poole – would have to find out.

As for Paul Simister, he was also in his thirties. And, according to his antecedent history, was a bricklayer working on the 'lump' at the time of his conviction five years previously. Well, bless my soul, a bricklayer. Sherry Higginbottom had described the bloke that Monica was seen with on the night of her death as looking like a brickie. It couldn't be that easy, surely? The next line proved that it wasn't.

The immortal prose of the CID showed that he had been found guilty of buggery, attempted buggery and falsely representing himself to be a leading seaman in the Royal Navy. And for that unhappy trio of counts, doubtless related in some way, he had received two years. So what the hell was a homosexual doing in a prostitute's place of work? Perhaps he'd lived there before Monica did, or maybe he was a workman who'd done some decorating, although by the look of the place that would have been a hell of a long time ago.

I looked up in time to see Dave grinning at me. He'd obviously worked out that I'd just reached the details of the convictions in Simister's file.

'What about the bridegroom, Dave?' I wasn't about to let him have it all his own way.

'Got a lad up at St Catherine's doing the business, guv.'

St Catherine's House in Kingsway is the General Register Office and, apart from births and deaths, contains details of all marriages solemnised in England and Wales. But knowing my luck, the Purvises had probably got spliced in Scotland or Northern Ireland. Or even bloody Torremolinos.

This time, however, the gods smiled. Whether it was a cynical smile remained to be seen. Whatever, at five that afternoon a fresh-faced Detective Constable John Appleby appeared in the office. 'Found him, sir.'

'In the records as opposed to in the flesh,' I remarked.

'Yes, sir.' Undaunted by this cynicism Appleby produced a sheaf of papers from his inside pocket and sorted through it rapidly. 'Monica Purvis married Charlie Purvis at Islington Registry—'

'Register,' I murmured. 'It's a *register* office, Appleby, not a *registry* office.'

'Really, sir?' Appleby looked at me as though that crumb of information was of earth-shattering irrelevance. Come to think of it, it was. 'Anyway, they were married at Islington *Register* Office five years ago, sir. So then I did birth searches based on the ages given at the time of the marriage . . .' He looked up, expecting plaudits.

'Go on, then.'

'Charlie Purvis—'

'Is his name Charlie or Charles?'

'Charlie, sir. That's what's on his birth certificate anyhow. He's now thirty-two and she's twenty-seven.'

'Was,' I said gloomily. 'So, what addresses were shown on the marriage certificate?'

'Both lived at 35 Pagoda Road, Islington, N1, sir.'

While all this was going on, Dave's fingers had been dancing about on the keyboard of the PNC, an acronym for the Police National Computer, a source of useful information bearing in mind the anorak's maxim WYSIWYG: what you see is what you get. What we got was a criminal record for Charlie Purvis. Two years ago, he'd been sentenced to three years for his part in an armed robbery at a building site. According to the arresting officer's comments, Purvis had claimed that he was only walking past at the time, and that it was all a case of mistaken identity. But they all say that, don't they? Theoretically he was still in the nick but, knowing that we have such a merciful government, I caused Dave to make a phone call. Purvis had been released six months previously.

'Is there any mention of a dagger tattooed on his right arm, Dave?'

'No, guv.'

Hooray! Either the sloppy bastard who did the corres when Purvis was nicked hadn't noticed a tattoo, or he'd had it done since. Or it was someone entirely different who'd chatted up Monica.

The chances of Purvis having returned to the salubrious address shown at the time of his arrest – believe it or not, the same 35 Pagoda Road, Islington – were remote, but we had to try. And there was no time like the present.

It was a blow-out. We struggled to Pagoda Road through the rush-hour traffic, only to discover that Charlie Purvis had not returned there. The present occupants had lived there for two years and had never heard of Charlie Purvis. They'd heard of Monica Purvis though. They'd read all about her untimely end in the *Daily Mirror*.

We struggled all the way back through the rush-hour traffic.

Dave Poole addressed himself to the PNC once more and put a marker against Purvis's name informing a nationwide constabulary that the said Purvis may be able to assist DCI Brock – of SO1 (2) New Scotland Yard – in his inquiries. At the same time Dave entered the names of Michael Cozens and Paul Simister with a similar caveat, although the chances of a raving iron like Simister having had anything to do with Monica's death was unlikely. But you never knew. Stranger things have happened.

I looked at my watch. Eight o'clock. 'We shall pay a visit to the two addresses we have for Messrs Cozens and Simister, Dave.'

'What, now, guv?' Dave managed to conjure up an expression that said he was appalled at having to work on but was, at the same time, quite relieved at not having to go home to Kennington. And Madeleine.

'Yeah, now. Why? Is Madeleine going to give you a hard time?'

'She's out.' It was an unusually terse reply, even for Dave.

It looked very much as though what the DI at Putney had told me was true: Dave *had* got wife trouble. I wondered who she was out with.

Five

It is in the nature of things that when a detective sets out from central London to visit two addresses, they will be on diametrically opposed sides of the great metropolis. Nothing changes. According to their criminal records Michael Cozens, fraudster, had lived in Needle Road, Bromley. And Paul Simister had resided at Unsworth Road, Hounslow.

On the basis that Simister was overtly one of the gay community, and thus was possibly out of the running anyway, we went first to Bromley in the hope of finding Michael Cozens still there. Miracle of miracles, he still was.

It was a twee three-up-two-down semi in an area where net curtain salesmen must make a packet, not only from supplying nets.in the first place, but from replacing those worn out by constant twitching.

'Mr Cozens?'

'Yes?' Cozens looked older than his thirty-five years, was slender and on the short side, maybe five-eight, with a ferret-like face and slicked-back hair. He peered round his front door with a hunted look.

'We're police officers.'

The hunted look intensified. 'Is it about the burglary across the road?' Cozens knew damned well it wasn't. Don't ask me how I knew he knew. I just knew.

'No, Mr Cozens, we're making inquiries about an incident that took place in Mayfair.' I wasn't going to give too much away at this stage.

'What is it, love?'

I glanced over Cozens' shoulder. A bare-footed, nubile, frizzy-haired redhead had appeared in the hall behind him. I guessed she was about twenty-five. She was wearing a pair of ragged-ended, tight-fitting shorts, high on the thigh, and a well-filled, dark blue T-shirt bearing the crest of Oxford University. The sight of her caused me, briefly, to wonder why Mr Cozens should find it necessary to consort with prostitutes.

'It's nothing,' said Cozens. 'I won't be a moment.'

Optimist, I thought. The woman nodded and went upstairs, her curiosity easily satisfied it seemed.

'I think it may be better if you came to the station to discuss this matter.'

'Why, what am I supposed to have done?' An element of panic became evident now, combined with defensive innocence, but not too much.

'I didn't say you'd done anything, but you may find it less inhibiting if we talk about this without your wife being present, *if you take my meaning*.' That was the polite way of putting it; he knew that if he didn't cooperate, he'd be nicked.

'Oh, I see.' At last Cozens got the drift and perhaps sensed that my inquiry was something to do with prostitutes. Which probably meant that he consorted with them quite often; I'm not a detective for nothing, just next to nothing. 'She's not actually my wife.'

I should worry. They don't even call it living in sin any more.

Cozens walked back down the hall and called up the stairs. 'I've got to go out for a while, honey. Shouldn't be too long.'

'OK!' said the woman's disembodied voice. I assumed that he went off with strangers quite often.

Bromley police station is not one of my favourite nicks, but Widmore Road, from whence the local Old Bill occasionally sallied forth, was only about half a mile from Needle Road.

The custody sergeant looked up expectantly as we entered his little domain and drew a stack of official forms towards him. Dave whispered in his ear, the custody sergeant looked miserable and we adjourned to the interview room.

Michael Cozens now took it upon himself to protest. I wondered why he had waited until he was in the nick, rather than doing it on his own doorstep. A bit of a mystery that: it's usually the other way round. Except for drunks that is; they only start to struggle violently when they catch a glimpse of the old blue lamp.

'I suppose just because I fell foul of the law once, you're going to carry on hounding me,' was Cozens' opening gambit. 'I've paid my debt to society and, what's more, my wife left me and took the kids. I don't even know where they are now,' he added in a whine.

I've never quite understood what paying one's debt to society is supposed to mean. 'You tried to swindle an insurance company out of eight hundred and ten quid by means of a forged cheque,' I said, 'to say nothing of the few thousand pounds you stole from your erstwhile employers, for which you got a well-deserved eighteen months. Bit lenient, I thought, particularly considering they let you out after nine.'

'So, what d'you want with me now?' sneered Cozens. 'Someone nicked the Crown jewels, have they?'

I could see that mixing with villains in stir had done this lippy petty fraudsman no good at all. It was clearly time to bring him down to earth. 'I am investigating the murder of a prostitute called Monica Purvis in a room on Talleyrand Street near Shepherd Market,' I began portentously. It's always good to make these pronouncements portentously.

That did it. Cozens' mouth fell open, he paled and started to shake, quite visibly. 'I didn't have anything to do with that.' It came out with a sort of strangled breathlessness.

'I see you've read about it.'

'Of course I have, but what makes you think—?'

'What makes me think that you may know something about it is that your fingerprints were found in the murdered woman's room.' I sat back and waited. It was a ploy I'd used in the past, something I'd heard that the Commissioner did. He would sit back in his chair and wait. And even quite senior officers would eventually feel impelled to say something. Usually something quite stupid.

'I think I ought to send for a lawyer.'

Like that, for instance. 'Why?'

Cozens blinked. 'Well, if you think that I murdered this girl—'

'Did you?'

'No!' The response was anguished this time. But I've had anguished responses to my questions before. It means one of two things: either the suspect is innocent, or he's a damned good actor.

'So how come your fingerprints were in the room where we found her body?'

Cozens sagged, like someone had let the air out of him. 'Does this have to go any further? I mean, does Sylvia have to know about this?'

I presumed he was talking about the redhead he lived with. 'Who is Sylvia?'

'Sylvia Moorhouse. She's the girl I live with.'

I shrugged and assumed a sympathetic expression. It was a pretence. 'Depends on what you have to say next.'

'All right, so I've been with a pro once or twice.'

By 'pro' I presumed he meant prostitute rather than professional. Oh, I don't know though. 'How often?'

'Not lately.'

I sensed rather than saw Dave smother a laugh. 'And was one of these prostitutes Monica Purvis?'

'I don't know. I never asked their names.'

I believed him. Even if he had asked them, I doubt that he would have been told their real names. Despite their trade, toms tended not to give anything away. And I do mean anything. 'As I said just now, this took place in a room on Talleyrand Street in Soho. You obviously know where that is.'

'Yes, of course.'

'When was the last time you went with a prostitute, then?'

'About three weeks ago.'

How very convenient. 'And where were you Monday evening?'

'Is that when it happened?'

'Just answer the question.'

'I was at home. With Sylvia.'

'Doing what?'

'Watching television.'

I wasn't about to go through the routine of asking him

41

what he'd been watching. That was old hat. Now that video-recorders are widely available, it is simplicity itself to record a whole evening's programmes and watch them the next day or whenever. 'I'm going to have to verify that.'

Cozens had recovered his colour since the first revelations about Monica's murder, but now he went white again, presumably appalled at the implications. 'You're not going to actually *ask* Sylvia, are you?'

'How else d'you suppose I can verify your story?'

He ran his hand through his hair. 'What are you going to tell her?'

'Nothing I don't have to.' Why this wave of sympathy overtook me I don't know. It was most out of character. 'In the meantime, you'll stay here.'

Cozens didn't like the sound of that very much and I thought for a moment that he was going to demand either to be charged or released. As is his right. I blame the television, of course: people know too damned much about their rights these days. It makes the job a bloody sight more difficult than it used to be.

But he seemed resigned to me doing the job my way. 'Will it take long?' he asked.

Dave and I returned to Needle Road. Sylvia opened the door and then peered over our shoulders, beyond us, searching. 'Where's Mike? And who *are* you, anyway?'

'We're police officers, Miss Moorhouse.'

'I prefer *Mizz* Moorhouse, but what's this all about? Mike hasn't been on the fiddle again, has he?' She remained standing in the doorway, clearly unwilling to admit us.

'You know about that, do you?'

'Mike tells me everything.'

Does he indeed? I wouldn't put money on it, lady. 'D'you mind if we come in? Or would you rather discuss this on the doorstep?' I had a feeling that the old net curtains were starting to twitch.

And so, belatedly, had Ms Moorhouse. 'Yes, yes, come in,' she said hurriedly, and almost dragged us into the sitting room. Laura Ashley had been at work here. The curtains and the loose covers on the three-piece suite were of an attractive floral design and they all matched. The obligatory twenty-eight-inch widescreen TV set stood in the corner, video-recorder beneath it. A hi-fi from the lower end of the price scale was contained in a custom-built stand, its laminate trying to pretend it was real wood. 'You'd better sit down.' She waved a hand towards the sofa and Dave and I perched on it like Tweedledum and Tweedledee. Cozens' common-law bunched herself up in an armchair, hugging her knees. She caressed her top lip with her tongue and smiled. She probably thought it was seductive.

'Are you a graduate of Oxford University, Ms Moorhouse?' I nodded at her T-shirt.

The redhead put her legs back on the floor and pulled the T-shirt away from her breasts, staring down at the logo, as though surprised to see it there. 'No! I bought it in a charity shop. So, what's this all about?' The T-shirt was released to mould itself, once more, to her bosom. I was pretty sure she wasn't wearing a bra, but Dave would undoubtedly tell me later on.

'Your, er . . . Mr Cozens is assisting us with our inquiries—'

That was as far as I got. 'Oh my God, I knew it.' Ms Moorhouse pushed her hands through her unruly hair.

'Knew what?'

'I knew he'd get into trouble again. We're short of money, you see. Mike got made redundant recently and I don't make all that much from hairdressing.'

A hairdresser, eh? She could have fooled me, the state her own hair was in. Mind you, that's not unusual: people who sell shoes always seem to be down at heel. 'I didn't say he'd done anything. I said he was assisting us with our inquiries.'

'Yes, but that's what it means, isn't it? You see it on the telly, all the time. A man is assisting police with their inquiries, they say, and the next thing he's in court.'

That indeed was the problem. The police *have* to say 'a man is assisting us with our inquiries'. If we don't, and say instead that we've arrested someone for the murder of John Smith or whoever, some smart-arse lawyer will get up on his hind legs and say 'Ah, you'd already made up your minds that he was guilty, so you weren't allowed to ask any more questions, and if you did I'm going to make damned sure I get them ruled inadmissible.'

'As far as Mr Cozens is concerned, it's a process of elimination, Ms Moorhouse. Are you able to tell me where he was Monday evening?'

'Here, of course.' There was no hesitation about that.

'And what were the pair of you doing?' That was open to a very dusty answer.

'Watching the telly. We saw *The Bill*, as a matter of fact. Then a film, then the late news.'

Of course you did. 'And he was here with you all evening?'

'Yes. He got in about four—'

'From where?' Had she fallen into the trap? Just now she'd told me he was out of work.

'He'd been out looking for a job. I told you he'd been made redundant.'

'So you did.' Mind you, all this malarkey could have been pre-arranged. If Cozens had topped Monica Purvis, he would have been well advised to concoct an alibi with his live-in lover long before the police arrived on his doorstep. But for the time being, we had to make do with Sylvia's confirmation of his whereabouts.

'Would you mind if we took a look around?' I asked. This was the crunch question, always. But I got a surprise.

'Go ahead. Take the place apart if it'll help Mike.'

'Where does Mr Cozens keep his cufflinks?' asked Dave, coming to life for the first time since the interview began.

'Cufflinks?' Then it dawned. Ms Moorhouse's carefully pencilled eyebrows knitted together. 'Is this something to do with that photograph that was in last night's paper? Something to do with you wanting to trace a cufflink that had been found at the scene of a murder?'

I shot a murderous glance at Dave. 'Oh no,' I said blithely. 'That's nothing to do with this.'

Anyway, we looked around, but none too seriously. When someone says go ahead, search the place, you know instinctively that they've nothing to hide. Well, most of the time. There weren't any trainers and there wasn't a cufflink called YES, partner of ours called NO.

We let Michael Cozens go home, having first admitted him to police bail. Well, be reasonable. What the hell else could we do?

It was now gone ten o'clock.

'Tell you what, Dave, I'll buy you a beer and we'll call it a night. We'll go searching for Simister in the morning. What d'you say?'

'I'd rather you dropped me off in Kennington, guv, if it's all the same to you. Madeleine'll be doing her pieces.'

I've never been an advocate of physical violence. Always thought, like Churchill, that jaw-jaw was better than war-war. And the last thing I wanted to be was a party to putting Dave in the position where Madeleine would beat him up again. 'Yeah, righto, Dave.'

I stopped the car in Dave's road but out of maximum missile range, just in case. I'd never met Madeleine, but from what I'd heard she was no respecter of rank. 'See you tomorrow, Dave.' I hope, I added under my breath.

I popped into the office. There was a sheaf of messages on my desk and the incident room sergeant was still hovering. 'Anything important in that lot, Colin?'

Detective Sergeant Colin Wilberforce, a wizard at administrative organisation, just smiled. 'Nothing that won't keep, sir. Apart from twenty-seven messages about a bloody cufflink.'

Depressed, I descended to the Red Lion public house on the corner of Derby Gate. It was closed.

Six

As I walked into the office, Colin Wilberforce glanced at me with the sort of look that says nine o'clock is the middle of the morning. 'Only four more, sir.'

'Only four more what?'

'Messages about the cufflink.' Colin waved at a pile of paper that I presumed to be the results of the great cufflink hunt.

'Oh, that. Anything valuable among them?'

'Most of them are from shops that sell them, telling us what we knew already.'

'Which is?'

'That you can buy them practically anywhere. There's one from a bloke who lost one on a cruise of the Caribbean and which is of sentimental value.'

'Terrific.'

'And another from some guy who lost one in Kew Gardens three years ago.' Colin paused before delivering the punchline. 'But apparently his had a pair of compasses and a try-square on it. Mean anything to you, sir?' It's a feature of the Metropolitan Police that everyone probes to see if you're a freemason.

'No.' I could see we were not going to get far by appealing to cufflink owners among the general public. 'File them,' I said. 'No, on second thoughts, give them to Dave to read and tell him to file them. It was his idea.'

Dave appeared with three cups of coffee on a tray and kicked the door shut. 'Morning, guv. Seen the messages?'

'Yes. So, what d'you suggest now?'

Dave shrugged. 'Put them on the back burner,' he said phlegmatically. 'Something'll turn up.'

That's what I liked about Dave: he was a supreme optimist,

but he'll be cured, eventually. When he's got my service and my rank.

Wilberforce pulled a statement across his desk. 'The murder weapon was shown to Sherry Higginbottom, sir. She's one hundred per cent certain that it's the one Monica kept for protection.'

'Didn't do her much good,' I said.

'By the way, sir, Holmes is arriving this morning,' said Wilberforce, testing me. Why do detective sergeants think that all DCIs are dinosaurs?

I bit back the obvious retort; I knew that HOLMES was the Home Office Large Major Enquiry System. It was typical of the Bramshill boffins at the Yard to devise an acronym and then come up with a name that would fit it. If it was a major inquiry then of course it was going to be large. I wasn't greatly interested anyway: in my experience this electronic gismo usually broke down at precisely the moment you needed it. Give me a pen and a piece of paper any day.

'Whose idea was that?'

'The commander's, sir,' said Wilberforce.

The commander was a uniform wallie and wouldn't know a major inquiry if one came up and bit him. And if it did, he'd delegate. 'Well, they won't have much to put on it,' I said. 'Got a database for cufflinks, has it?' I shot a glance at Dave but he chose to ignore me. 'Time we visited that bugger Simister, Dave.'

'If he's still there, guv,' said Dave gloomily.

'I'm still wondering what a gay was doing in a tom's drum,' I mused.

Dave looked up from his cufflink messages. 'You have *read* his file, have you, sir?' he asked.

Dave was about to play a trump card. I knew the signs. He'd done it before. 'No. Why?'

'He got done for buggery, attempted buggery—'

'I got that far,' I said.

'Yeah, well, he got done for buggery on a woman.' Dave smiled that sort of self-satisfied smile that indicates that he'd got one over on the governor.

'*Now* you tell me.' I stood up. 'We'd better go and find the bastard, then.' Had I been a fictional detective, I would have reached for my hat. But I don't wear a hat.

Unsworth Road, Hounslow, the last known address of Paul Simister, comprised a street of seedy, rundown terraced dwellings. Number 34 was seedier and more rundown than most of them.

A face, roughly similar in appearance to the photograph on Simister's criminal record, peered round the door. 'Yeah?'

'Paul Simister?'

'Who wants to know?'

He knew perfectly well who wanted to know, but he obviously wanted to go through the routine. That's what too much television does for you. 'Police.'

'So?' Simister made no attempt to open the door further. Perhaps it was stuck.

I helped him and pushed it wide, him with it. 'We'd like a chat.'

'You can't come barging in here without a warrant.' Simister stood defiantly in the centre of the tiny hall, hands on hips, muscle-bound arms akimbo.

'I just did.' I was in no mood to traipse through the requirements of the Police and Criminal Evidence Act. I put a finger on his chest, indicating that he should sit on the stairs. He did, thus giving me some moral and physical ascendancy.

'Don't hit him, guv,' said Dave, leaning against the wall. It was part of our softening-up routine. Sorely tempted though I had been down the years, I'd never struck a suspect.

'Monica Purvis,' I said.

'Who?'

I guessed that if Simister read a newspaper at all, he would instinctively turn to the back page, but although murder is hardly worth reporting these days, the tabloids had made a front-page story of the brutal killing of Monica Purvis. The barbaric slaying of a prostitute in Soho will still get Fleet Street editors salivating.

'Don't sod about,' I said. 'You know who I'm talking about. We found your dabs all over her room in Talleyrand Street.'

'Oh!'

'Oh indeed.' In Simister's position I don't think I'd've said any more than that. 'When were you last with her?'

Simister seemed to give that some thought: a difficult process for him, I should imagine. 'About a fortnight ago, I suppose,' he said eventually.

'And two nights ago? Where were you then?'

'Out and about.'

'I hope you can do better than that,' I said.

'Don't really remember. Down the pub, I s'pose.'

'Which pub?'

'The Faggot. That's where I usually go.'

'How fascinating,' I said, 'but were you there two nights ago?'

'I reckon so.'

'Who were you with?'

'What?'

I put my face closer to his. 'Who were you with?' I asked again, enunciating each word slowly and loudly.

'Don't remember.'

'Not one of those sad, lone drinkers, are you?'

'Don't know what you mean.'

I glanced at Dave; he had one of those what-the-hell-are-you-buggering-about-for looks on his face. 'Right, down the nick,' I said.

'What for?'

'On suspicion of having murdered Monica Purvis. What did you think it was for, fiddling your DSS benefit?' I could have added 'and for being about six feet tall, weighing some fifteen stones, having an earring in your left ear and a dagger tattooed on your left forearm'. He fitted exactly the description of the man PC Webster had seen talking to Monica Purvis in Shepherd Market about a month ago, during the course of which conversation threats were uttered, as we say in the trade. At least, that's how I preferred to interpret what Webster had described.

'I never had nothing to do with that,' said Simister, but he stood up. He knew the drill.

'Anyone live here with you?'

'My bird, but she's out at work.'

I forbore to ask what she did for a living; anyway it was the morning. 'Name?'

Simister looked as though he was about to argue but then he shrugged. 'Tracey.'

'Tracey what?'

'Tracey Milner. Why?'

'I have an unquenchable thirst for knowledge.'

Hounslow police station is in Montague Road, a few yards up from Bell Junction, and I like it even less than I like Bromley nick. Nevertheless the rule book says that suspects have to be taken to the nearest police station, and Hounslow was it.

Hardly breaking step, Dave explained to the custody sergeant that Mr Paul Simister of 34 Unsworth Road, Hounslow, had 'volunteered' to come to the station to assist me in my inquiries. The custody sergeant looked sceptical and wrote the details on his pad.

Simister looked around the interview room and yawned. 'So, what's it all about?' he asked.

'About a month ago, you were seen by police talking to Monica Purvis in Shepherd Market. You were also seen to make a threatening gesture and were heard to say "I'll be back".'

'So what?'

Good. Simister didn't deny it; so it was him. Progress at last. 'What was that all about?'

'Business.'

'What sort of business?'

'Oh, come on,' sneered Simister. 'She was on the game. That sort of business.'

'So why were you wagging your finger at her?'

'Because I was pissed off at the price she wanted to charge.'

'Which was?'

'Two Cs.'

'Two hundred pounds. For what?'

Simister paused. 'I like tying my birds up and she said if that's what I wanted it'd cost me two hundred sovs.'

Oh joy! It was no oversight that I had not released the exact details of Monica's death to the press. On the other hand,

50

Sherry Higginbottom had said that Monica never indulged in perversities of that sort. There again, people do tell lies, particularly prostitutes. 'And did you ever do that to her?'

'No, like I said, she wouldn't wear it unless I forked out, and I haven't got that sort of money.'

'How was it, then, that your fingerprints were found in her room above the antique shop in Talleyrand Street where she plied her trade?'

Simister shifted uncomfortably in his seat. 'I'd had it off with her before, straight like, but now I felt like something a bit different.'

You'll have to better than that, old son. 'So why did you tell her that you'd be back?'

'I was going to see if I could raise the cash. She was a good performer and I fancied having a bit of a variation, see.'

'And how were you going to raise the cash? Do a quick blagging somewhere?'

'Course not.' Simister looked hurt and started picking at the edge of the table with a nicotine-stained forefinger.

I glanced at Dave who raised his eyebrows. I stood up. 'OK, you can go.'

Simister seemed surprised by my generosity. 'Can I get a lift home?' he asked. 'It's about three miles.'

'Don't push your luck,' I said.

'Was that wise, guv, letting him go?' asked Dave, just as surprised as the departed Simister had been.

'He's a bit suss, Dave, but there's not enough to hold him. Once I nick him official, the clock starts running. We'll save him for another day. In the meantime, he'll be getting cocky. Probably be down the boozer tonight, shooting his mouth off about how he outwitted the Old Bill. Ah, that reminds me . . .'

'I know, guv.' Dave was ahead of me. 'You want me to make discreet inquiries at the Faggot to see if he was in there two nights ago.'

'Who said anything about discreet,' I said. 'Got any cigarettes?'

'I thought you'd given up,' said Dave.

*   *   *

51

After consuming a pie and a pint in a Hounslow hostelry of dubious reputation, we returned to Curtis Green and considered our options. Cozens and Simister were our only two front-runners so far, but we still had to trace Monica Purvis's husband Charlie, the errant convicted robber. But life being what it is I had this nagging suspicion that none of the three was the man we were looking for. Nevertheless, Charlie would have to be found.

'How about putting out an appeal for him in the press, guv,' ventured Dave. 'You know, to eliminate him from our inquiries.' He looked hopeful, but then young coppers are like that: they'll do anything except get off their backsides and go out and look. It was an unkind thought; Dave was a good copper.

'In my vast experience, Dave,' I said loftily, 'the phrase "to eliminate him from our inquiries" is an indication to any villain that we are desperately keen to feel his collar. No, my son, we'll do it the hard way.'

'I thought we would,' said Dave, well knowing that I meant that *he'd* do it the hard way.

'Start at the prison from whence he was released. See if they've got a record of any address he might have said he was going to.'

I could see from Dave's face that he didn't have too much faith in this old-fashioned detective work, but he reached for that invaluable document, the Metropolitan Police internal telephone directory which, in addition to listing police stations together with the names of its senior officers who have long since been transferred elsewhere, also contains a list of prisons.

After the usual bit of stonewalling that is a characteristic of those who staff Her Majesty's Prisons, Dave replaced the receiver. 'Thirty-five Pagoda Road, Islington, sir,' he said in that tone of voice that implied that I should have expected nothing else.

'Have a go at whoever owns that place, Dave—' I began.

'But we've been there, guv, and we spoke to—'

'Yes, I know,' I said patiently. 'I'm not completely senile. But we don't know whether the present occupants own it, or are renting it. In the former case an estate agent will have been involved; in the latter a letting agency. Go to it. Oh, and by the way, are you taking a run out to the Faggot tonight, to check Simister's alibi?' I mentioned it again, just in case Dave had forgotten.

Dave's shoulders drooped. 'If I must,' he said.

That was unusual. Dave was a keen detective, never averse to putting in a few extra hours when the job demanded it. 'You got something spoiling for tonight?' I asked.

'Yeah, sort of, guv.' He hesitated, strangely reticent.

Aha! A bit on the side, maybe. Not that I'd blame him, from what I'd gathered about Madeleine. 'Something important?'

'I was going to the ballet.' Dave looked definitely embarrassed by this admission.

I burst out laughing, which didn't help matters. 'I never saw you as a balletomane, Dave,' I said.

Dave raised his eyebrows, probably surprised that I knew such a word. 'It's Madeleine, you see, guv.'

'Oh, I see!' I said, not seeing at all. 'Madeleine's the ballet enthusiast, is she?'

'In a manner of speaking.'

It was obvious that the usually loquacious Dave was not very willing to talk about any of this. But I pulled rank. 'What manner of speaking?'

'She's a ballet dancer.'

'Bloody hell, I never knew that.' I was genuinely amazed. Dave had kept his wife's profession a dark secret. Most coppers seem to marry nurses, teachers or policewomen. But it explained a lot about the fights that were rumoured to take place between Dave and Madeleine: ballet dancers are extraordinarily fit and from my limited knowledge of the profession, some of their artistic gymnastics are but a short step from an Irish whip. 'How long's she being doing that, then?'

Dave gave me a sorrowful look as if I'd thought that she might have taken it up until something better came along, a bit like the reason I'd become a copper twenty-odd years ago. 'Since she was ten, guv.'

'*Ten?*'

'Yeah, well, they have to start early. She went to ballet school, see.'

'Yes, of course.' I nodded sagely, affecting a deep knowledge of ballet, but it was not something I'd ever been interested in or, for that matter, had time to be interested in. 'Well, you'd better trot off to the ballet, Dave. Don't want you upsetting Madeleine.'

Dave opened a file, gazed unseeing at it, and closed it again before looking up. 'Er, I've got a couple of spare tickets if you and the missus are interested, guv. Madeleine always gets a few freebies.'

Much as I wanted to take a look at Madeleine – from a safe distance – the thought of my team of CID officers relishing the story that the governor had been to the ballet was something I could do without. I could also do without ringing up my estranged wife to propose an evening watching a load of poofs prancing about the stage. Were I to suggest the wife-swapping festival in Hamburg that the Germans call *Fasching*, she'd be there like a shot. Very much into sex is my wife. But not with me. I delayed the decision. 'How did you meet her?'

'Someone had been screwing the staff lockers at the theatre where she was performing that week,' said Dave, now on safer ground. 'Had to interview everyone. Well, one thing led to another. I took her out to lunch a few times—'

'Lunch? Couldn't you afford dinner?'

'Most of the time she's dancing when other people are having dinner, sir,' said Dave crushingly. 'But we did have one or two late suppers. Anyway, are you and the lady-wife interested?'

'Me and the lady-wife are not on speaking terms,' I said without elaborating. Then I had an idea, but not wishing my sergeant to witness a rebuff I went into my own office and made a phone call.

'How d'you fancy an evening at the ballet?' I asked, once I'd been put through to Dr Sarah Dawson, the rope expert at the laboratory.

There was a pause before she replied. 'I never took you for a cultured policeman, Harry,' she said. 'Yes, I'd love it. Which ballet is it?'

'I haven't a clue,' I said.

'I was talking about the ballet, not the Purvis murder.' Sarah knew how to crush pushy coppers.

I returned to my office. 'You're on, Dave,' I said. Then I noticed the commander standing in a corner, peering closely at the computer screen where the 'actions' were recorded: that list of things to do that keeps tabs on a murder inquiry. He was the Special Operations commander of the area – whose only bright idea had been to install HOLMES – and, as befitted an officer of his exalted rank, wore a suit and half-moon spectacles.

'Ah, Mr Brock, how's it going?' He turned and peered at me over his glasses.

He was always formal in his dealings with lesser mortals and wouldn't use my first name in case I used his in reply. He wouldn't know how to deal with that. 'We are applying ourselves assiduously, sir,' I said.

'Good, good.' And having delivered that little pat on the back, the commander went home.

Seven

The ballet had been Stravinsky's *The Firebird* and the 'freebies' that Madeleine had arranged were good seats in the stalls. Dave upset some nearby aficionados by explaining loudly to Sarah Dawson and me that Madeleine was one of the principal dancers and then aggravated the offence by excitedly pointing her out when first she appeared.

After the ballet was over, Dave took us backstage to meet her. She was petite, perhaps no more than five feet two, had short, blonde hair and the sort of shapely legs that a tutu showed off to great effect.

'I'm very pleased to meet you, Mr Brock.' Madeleine raised herself on to her toes, her blue eyes twinkling, and took my hand in a firm grip. 'Dave has told me a lot about you.' I could quite see why Dave had fallen for her – she absolutely exuded sex appeal – but somehow I couldn't visualise her beating him up, especially as Dave was about ten inches taller than she was and heavy with it. But you never knew. What I did know was that detectives are the very worst for repeating rumours that have no foundation in fact; strange that, considering that their job is supposed to be the collection of hard, provable evidence.

But the next morning we were back to the intensive graft of attempting to find out who had killed Monica Purvis.

'Enjoy the ballet, guv?' Dave appeared with the usual tray of coffee.

'Yes, very good, Dave,' I said. 'I liked your wife, too. Very attractive.'

'Good dancer, isn't she?' said Dave, deflecting my comment. Policemen are always concerned that their wives or girlfriends are going to be seduced by other officers, no matter what their rank. It has happened in the past. Many times. 'Did Dr Dawson enjoy it?' he asked.

'Very much,' I said. What I didn't tell Dave was that taking Sarah Dawson to the ballet had probably enhanced my chances of cultivating her. But then I hadn't told her that the tickets were free – it doesn't do to boast of such things in these days of political correctness – or that Dave was my sergeant, although she probably knew that. Nevertheless, it's amazing the impression a bit of culture makes on a woman. And I had a feeling about this girl. My own marriage was up the pictures, of that there was no doubt, and we'd've divorced ages ago, but we couldn't afford to split up. Consequently we'd remained in an uneasy alliance under the same roof.

But my reverie was interrupted by the telephone, and the inquiry suddenly went pear-shaped. Colin Wilberforce, the incident-room sergeant, answered it. I saw him stand up and heard him say 'Yes, sir' three times before replacing the receiver and sitting down again.

'Someone important, Colin?' I was disconcerted by the usually phlegmatic Wilberforce's reaction to the call.

'Yes, sir, the Commissioner's staff officer. The Commissioner wants to see you immediately.'

'Did he say what it was about?' I asked airily. It's not every day that a detective chief inspector is sent for by the top man, even to be promoted. And that was not even remotely in the offing. Not by a long chalk. Even if some blabbermouth had told Sir Charles Austen that I had been the beneficiary of free tickets for the ballet and had been socialising with a junior rank, it would have been a heavy from the Internal Investigations Command demanding an interview with me.

'No, sir, he didn't say. He did say it was urgent though.'

'Probably wants to tell me what a good detective I am,' I said, well knowing this to be unlikely in the extreme. 'See if you can rustle up a car for me, Colin.'

A few years ago a canopy had been added to the façade of New Scotland Yard since when it had taken on the appearance of a third-world airport, but the marbled, front-entrance lobby – perversely called Back Hall – was, as ever, a hive of activity. Visitors sat staring at the eternal flame while waiting for some policeman to stir himself sufficiently to descend to the ground floor. Uniformed senior officers peered fretfully out of the windows waiting for a staff car to appear, and the security guards cast suspicious glances at anyone having the temerity to seek admission, even if he had held a warrant card for twenty years.

I took the lift to the eighth floor of the Tower Block and walked down the long corridor until finally I trod carpet. Very few corridors at the Yard are carpeted, but this was one of them. Perhaps the only one; I'd never been important enough to find out.

'Good morning, sir. DCI Brock, SO One Two. I understand the Commissioner wants to see me.'

'Take a seat, Mr Brock,' said the Commissioner's staff officer, a pale-faced youth. Having graduated from Bramshill Police College by way of the Special Course, he had risen rapidly until he had reached the rank of chief superintendent. And he knew the theory, oh yes; there wasn't a regulation he wasn't familiar with. He had benefited from every command course, carousel course and specialist course the Police College had to offer. In between those sojourns, he had carefully avoided the sharp edge of coppering by occupying one staff appointment after another, including a tour on the directing staff at the very same police college and a spell as an instructor at Hendon. So one shouldn't criticise really: he hadn't had the time to fit in any real police work, had he? Well, be fair.

After the customary period spent signing unimportant pieces of paper – a ploy designed to bolster his importance in the eyes of inferiors such as me – this administrative genius rose and tapped lightly on the Commissioner's door, entering without awaiting the great man's bidding. I presumed that this familiarity with the high and mighty was meant to impress me.

Seconds later, he emerged. 'The Commissioner will see you now, Mr Brock,' he said.

Sir Charles Austen was fifty-nine years old and in his earlier days in the Metropolitan Police, he had skipped lightly from one appointment to another thereby acquiring what is known in the Job as a seagull reputation: staying only long enough to crap on everyone before flying on. Now, having passed through several provincial forces in chief officer posts, he had reached what is arguably the top job in British policing.

'Ah, Mr Black, come in and sit down.' Austen smiled.

'The name's Brock, sir,' I said.

'Yes, of course.' Austen moved a paperweight – there was nothing beneath it – and afforded me the sort of pained smile that indicated I might have changed my name just to annoy him. 'You're investigating the murder of . . .' He paused and glanced briefly at the single sheet of paper on his otherwise naked desktop. 'Monica Purvis.'

'Yes, sir.'

'We have a problem.' The Commissioner took a delicate hold of the sheet of paper between finger and thumb and transferred it to his out-tray.

'We *have*, sir?' I pretended to look concerned. Whenever a senior officer told me that *we* had a problem it usually meant that *I* had a problem.

'Geoffrey Halstead.' The Commissioner brushed his moustache with the back of his hand and moved his telephone an inch.

The name was vaguely familiar to me but it did cross my mind that Austen may be engaging in word games. I played safe and repeated the name.

'Minister of State at the Home Office, Mr Brock.'

'Yes, of course, sir.'

'He came to see me yesterday afternoon in somewhat of a panic.' There was a long pause during which I imagined the Commissioner expected me to say something, but I'd heard about this game and remained silent. 'It seems he knew this woman.'

'Really, sir?'

'Yes, really, Mr Brock.'

'But why should he come to see you?' I was not happy about this business. When politicians called on the Commissioner it was usually because they'd something to hide and wanted either preferential treatment or some sort of immunity from nosey, gauche policemen. Like me.

There was another long pause before Austen replied, but eventually he said, 'He was afraid that the police may be regarding him as a suspect for the woman's murder.' There was yet another pause and then, 'Are we so regarding him, by any chance, Mr Brock?'

'Not until now, sir,' I said, somewhat bemused. Sir Charles Austen had reached the top of the tree without ever having been a CID officer and although in the past he had been very good at instituting new traffic schemes and reasonably proficient at controlling vast legions of football hooligans, the cunning of the average villain – from whatever strata of society – was something of which he had no first-hand experience. Perhaps unwisely, I asked, 'Did you caution him, sir?' This was tantamount to asking the Commissioner if he knew his job. If I was in the running for promotion I reckoned that would have put the kibosh on it, but some things have to be asked. Even so, it was probably an unfair question; I wasn't at all sure that the Commissioner knew the caution, and as he wasn't a member of the Police Federation probably wouldn't have been given one of their little plastic cards that explained it all.

'Of course not,' said Austen brusquely. 'Mr Halstead came here to complain of a crime, not to admit to one.'

'But I thought you said that he—'

The Commissioner held up a hand; it was a magisterial, staying gesture. 'I know what I said, Mr Brock, but Mr Halstead was being blackmailed.'

'Do we have any proof of that, sir?'

'We have the Minister's word, Mr Brock.' The Commissioner frowned; he did not much care to be interrogated by a junior rank on professional matters.

'I see, sir.' *Oh, the naivety of the man.* 'Did he say why he was being blackmailed?' I was beginning to put two and two together but I was interested to see how far Sir Charles had gone in playing the amateur detective.

'He confessed to having had a sexual liaison with this Monica Purvis woman. He's a married man, of course.' Austen spoke slowly and clearly, as though treating with an idiot.

Jesus! One of the previous Commissioners would have said that he was screwing her, but that particular Commissioner *had* been a detective for most of his service.

60

'So what do you want me to do, sir?' I was becoming increasingly mystified as to why Austen had sent for me to tell me all this. All he needed to have done was to get his super-efficient staff officer to ring me and tell me the tale: that this Halstead guy had been blackmailed about an affair with the late Monica Purvis. But my nasty suspicious mind told me that if you can't remove the blackmailer, the next best thing was to remove the cause of the blackmail. Furthermore, in my experience of illicit sexual relationships it was often the woman herself who was the blackmailer. Even to the dimmest detective that was a Grade A motive for murder.

'Am I to understand that Mr Halstead does not wish us to investigate the blackmail, sir?' I wanted to get this absolutely right.

'Now that she is dead, the blackmail will cease, obviously, Mr Brock. There is no reason, therefore, that Mr Halstead should be seen at all. I merely thought that you should be aware of what he had told me. Far be it from me to interfere with your investigation, but it may perhaps be politic to tread carefully if you should feel the need to interview Mr Halstead. He is an MP and a minister, after all.'

The implication was that I shouldn't go anywhere near Halstead. He'd been cunning enough to come to us before we went to him.

Suddenly it all became clear. As Halstead was Number Two at the Home Office there were obvious reasons why Sir Charles would rather have him as a friend than an enemy. Don't ask me why, but some Commissioners aspire to adding a second honour to the knighthood they receive automatically on appointment, and it is Home Office ministers who sanction such recommendations. And Austen was within six months of retirement.

'I will put my trust in your discretion, Mr Brock,' said the Commissioner, rising to his feet. It sounded awfully like a threat. 'You will, of course, keep this to yourself.'

'Of course, sir.'

Twenty minutes later, back in the office at Curtis Green, I told Dave all about it. There is no way an investigating officer can keep things like that from his bag-carrier.

'Blimey, guv'nor, what do we do now?'

'We interview the bugger, Dave,' I said, 'but not yet. We'll let him sweat a while. I don't want him thinking that just because he's been to see the Commissioner we'll go rushing round to the Home Office in a lather.'

'So what do we do now?' Dave asked again.

'We shall proceed with our inquiries, Dave.' The truth was that I wanted time to think about the best way of tackling this Mr Halstead. So far, we only had Halstead's word, second-hand at that, that he had been blackmailed by Monica Purvis. I wasn't too worried about the Commissioner's caveat, but I was a little concerned at the prospect of jousting with the sort of smart lawyers with whom such people surround themselves at the first whiff of grapeshot. 'What have you done about the air hostess's uniform we found at Charleston Terrace?'

'I'm seeing a mate of mine in Special Branch at Heathrow, guv. This afternoon. He reckons he can identify every airline uniform in the business.' Dave cackled lasciviously. 'I didn't ask him how.'

I glanced at my watch. 'I'll chaperone you,' I said. 'There are a lot of nubile young women at Heathrow and I don't want you getting into trouble. Madeleine would never forgive me.' I forbore from suggesting that she may beat him up; I was beginning to doubt that story.

We partook of a pie and a pint in the Red Lion in Derby Gate and then drove out to the airport.

Dave's Special Branch mate was a detective constable called Bob Winston who had spent at least half his service at Heathrow and we found him propping up the bar in Terminal Three.

Dave introduced me. Winston took out a handkerchief, dabbed at his lips with it and muttered something about having met an informant. As if I cared. Then he took us to one of the claustrophobic SB offices tucked away in some corner.

Dave opened the evidence bag and spread the uniform on a desk. 'Recognise it, Bob?'

Winston picked up the cap and stared briefly at the insignia.

'Indeed!' There was no hesitation. 'I suppose you want to see their chief security officer?'

Dave glanced at me and I nodded.

Winston led us along corridors, moving walkways, round corners, across a concourse and up an escalator. Finally we reached the offices of the airline whose badge was on the late Monica Purvis's cap.

The chief security officer had a cupboard-sized room, its walls covered with airline posters and the obligatory model of a Boeing 747 on his desk. There was also a languid young blonde perched on the edge of the desk, but on our arrival she stood up and sauntered out of the office without a word.

'This is Sid Marley.' Bob Winston indicated a middle-aged man who had ex-copper written all over him, and introduced us.

'Af'noon, gents. I'm ex-Job meself,' said Marley, confirming my assessment. 'What can I do for you?' He had this irritating habit of speaking with a cigarette in the corner of his mouth.

Dave handed him the cap, jacket and skirt. 'One of yours, so Bob tells me.'

Marley picked up the cap and turned the lining inside out to reveal a label bearing Monica Purvis's name in black ink. 'Yes, I remember this girl,' he said. 'Got made redundant about eighteen months ago.'

'Redundant from what?' I asked.

Marley looked up and gave me a crooked grin. 'As a matter of fact, she got the big E,' he said. 'She was on one of the check-in desks but got the chop for bad timekeeping. We tried to get this back from her . . .' He coughed, cigarette still in mouth, and blew ash all over the skirt. 'Blimey, what's she done to it?' he asked, picking it up and shaking it. 'It can't be more than fourteen inches long.' He glanced at the inside. 'She's taken that up herself,' he said. 'Supposed to be just above the knee, not halfway up her arse.'

'She was on the game when she was murdered,' said Dave. 'I reckon she probably had the odd punter who liked her dressing up in this gear. Makes a change from a schoolgirl outfit, I suppose.'

'Takes all sorts,' said Marley. 'Anyway, like I said, we tried to get it back, but we couldn't contact her, so we gave up. Not worth bothering about really. Solicitors and all that. Cost more to recover it than to buy a new one.' He shrugged, probably at what he perceived to be the gross unfairness of the world. Personally I thought he was a lazy sod; I'd met a few like him in the Job over the years. 'On the game, you say?' He glanced at Dave, an enquiring expression on his face.

'It was in all the papers,' said Dave. 'Got stabbed to death in a room in Talleyrand Street, off Shepherd Market.'

'I never saw that,' said Marley. He coughed again and lit a fresh cigarette from the end of the old one. He looked around briefly before spotting an ashtray bearing the logo of British Airways and the slogan 'The world's favourite airline'. 'So, how can I help you, gents?'

'Was there anyone she was particularly friendly with here at work? Any rumours? Anything that might help us?' I sounded desperate, and I was.

Somewhat belatedly, Marley waved his hand at a few chairs. 'Have a pew, gents,' he said before sitting down behind his cluttered desk. For a moment or two, he gazed at the mess. 'Got so much going here, you know. Someone's nicking cash, I'm bloody sure of it. The guv'nor expects miracles. Just like the Job really.'

'Anyone she was particularly friendly with?' I prompted.

'Ah, yes. Now, let me see.' Marley pondered my question for a while, gazing upwards through a haze of smoke. 'It's a problem, you know, all these women. Always getting chatted up, taken out.' He laughed, humourlessly. 'Getting laid.'

'She certainly did,' said Dave. 'Made a career out of it.'

'Lot of them do.' Marley nodded sagely, not to be outdone in the matter of worldly cynicism. He turned and took a clipboard off the wall. 'I've got a name in the back of my mind,' he mused, thumbing through the sheaf of papers under the clip. 'Just can't recall it.' Suddenly the papers detached themselves and cascaded to the floor. He swore, put his cigarette in the ashtray and leaned down to recover them, coughing as he did so. I hoped he wasn't going to have a heart attack. Spreading the photocopied sheets on his desk, he shuffled through them, humming as he did so. 'Got it,' he said at last. 'There was this girl who works here that she was friendly with. The Purvis girl and her husband used to go out a lot with a Sylvia Moorhouse and her bloke.' He tapped the side of his nose. 'You have to keep your ear to the ground in this job, gents,' he added, and smiled knowingly.

Well, well. So Michael Cozens' live-in lover was friendly with the dead woman, a woman whom Cozens had paid for sex. 'Does she still work here, this Sylvia Moorhouse?' I posed the question casually. I didn't want this half-baked idiot buggering up my inquiry by telling the Moorhouse girl of police interest in her.

'Yes, as a check-in girl, but she's on the night shift tonight,' said Marley.

'Surprise, surprise,' said Dave.

'Talking of surprises,' I said, as we drove away from the airport, 'why should Sylvia Moorhouse have told us she was a hairdresser, I wonder?'

Eight

Yesterday's revelations that Geoffrey Halstead, a Minister of State at the Home Office, had been involved with Monica Purvis and that Sylvia Moorhouse, Michael Cozens' live-in paramour, had been a close friend of the dead woman came as something of a diversion. Until now I had been coasting along quite happily in the belief that our victim's murderer had to be either Cozens or Paul Simister or even Monica's husband Charlie. But now, like the inner convolutions of a kaleidoscope, the whole picture had changed. But that's criminal investigation for you: every day in every way things get a bloody sight more complicated.

'So what do we do now, guv?' asked Dave. It seemed to be one of his favourite expressions.

'Put yourself in my place, Dave,' I said, 'because one day you will be. What would you do?'

'Go and talk to Sylvia Moorhouse again, guv, I suppose.' Dave was peeling an orange, the odour of which did not please me.

'Do you have to eat oranges in the office?' I demanded, somewhat testily. I've never liked oranges.

'Madeleine says they're good for me,' said Dave, oblivious to my implied criticism. 'It's the vitamin C apparently.'

'Oh, I see.' I found myself being dragged into this business of worrying about what the enchanting Madeleine said. 'Yes, I think we shall.'

'Shall what?' Dave quartered the orange and put a piece in his mouth.

'Go and see Sylvia Moorhouse.'

'She's night duty, guv, according to Sid Marley.'

'So what?' There used to be a time when a night-duty

constable was likely to be roused from his bed mid-morning to answer some footling question from an inspector, regardless of the said constable's welfare. It's all changed now, of course: a PC would probably sue the Commissioner for discrimination or victimisation or some damned thing. 'We'll wake her up.' After all, a murder inquiry was important stuff.

'Might upset her.' Dave finished his orange and deposited the peel in the wastepaper basket. He looked helplessly around his desk, pulled out a pocket handkerchief and wiped his hands on it. 'We don't want a complaint.'

'Like Aids, you mean?' I asked sarcastically. Young policemen today seem terrified to do anything in case they're complained against.

Dave shrugged and stood up. 'Right then,' he said.

We drove once more to Needle Road, Bromley, and beat on the door of the Cozens–Moorhouse ménage. Several times. And often enough to cause a few nearby net curtains to twitch.

Eventually the door was opened by a dishevelled Sylvia Moorhouse. Clearly roused from her bed, she was attired in a silk peignoir and, I suspect, nothing else. Her red hair, unruly at the best of times, had now taken on the appearance of an explosion in a wire-wool factory but she had made the time to apply a little make-up. 'What on earth do you want?' she demanded. 'I was in bed.'

'We'd like to talk to you, Ms Moorhouse,' I said. 'And I'm so sorry if we have disturbed you,' I added smoothly.

'Oh, it's you again,' said Sylvia, recognition dawning at last. 'I'm off nights, you know.'

'Know the feeling,' I murmured, although in all honesty I hadn't known the feeling for some years.

'You'd better come in.' Leaving Dave to close the front door, I followed the woman into the living room.

'Mr Cozens not here today?'

'No, he's got a job, at last.'

'Splendid,' I said. 'Doing what?'

'He's working for an engineering firm, in the office. Doing their profit and loss accounts mainly.' Sylvia waved a hand at a sofa. 'Sit down.' It was almost a command.

67

'Profit and loss, eh?' I said. That boded ill for Michael Cozens' new employers, of that I was convinced. If history repeated itself, albeit with greater efficiency than previously, it would be his profit and their loss.

'I'm just going to make a cup of tea. Would you like one?'

'Yes, thank you.'

We waited while Sylvia busied herself in the kitchen. After ten minutes of cup-rattling and snatches of an unrecognisable song, she returned and put the tea tray on an occasional table. With a flash of suntanned thigh which she only belatedly covered again, she sat down in the armchair opposite us, so that we were separated by the table. 'Is this the same business you came to see Mike about the other day?' she asked, pouring tea. 'Sugar and milk?'

'Please,' I said.

'No sugar for me, thanks,' said Dave. Presumably Madeleine had been at him again; he always used to take sugar.

'Yes,' I said, 'it is connected with that.'

'Oh!' Sylvia handed us cups of tea across the table.

'When we saw you last, Ms Moorhouse, you said you were a hairdresser.'

'What about it?'

'Well, you're not, are you? You actually work at Heathrow Airport as a check-in girl.'

'Passenger services supervisor.' Her job description came out automatically, as though she had had to explain the difference many times.

'Why did you tell me you were a hairdresser?'

'I am. By trade, that is. It was what I was trained for.' She seemed completely unfazed that I had caught her out in a lie. 'But there's not as much money in it. That's why I got the job at the airport. I'm hoping to fly soon. That'll mean a big increase in pay.'

'Long way from Bromley,' said Dave. 'Go round the M25, do you?'

'Good Lord, no. It's nearly sixty miles going M25. No, I claw my way straight across the bottom of London. It takes for ever, but it's only twenty-five miles. I have to think of the petrol, you know.' Sylvia took a sip of tea. 'Anyway, why are you so interested in me? I thought it was Michael you'd come to see again.'

'I thought it rather strange that when we came to see you the other day, you didn't mention that you knew Monica Purvis.'

Sylvia inclined her head and gave me a quizzical glance. 'Why should I have done? *You* didn't mention her.'

'D'you mean to say that you didn't realise we were investigating her murder?'

Sylvia was in the act of leaning forward to place her cup and saucer on the occasional table as I spoke. But she never made it. The cup and saucer fell from her hand, hitting the floor but not breaking. A few splashes of tea spread across the carpet but she seemed not to notice. She put both hands to her cheeks. 'Murdered? My God, that's terrible. I never knew that.'

'You mean you didn't read about it in the papers?'

'I don't read newspapers,' she said. 'It's all far too depressing. So what happened?' She appeared quite overwrought at the news I had just broken to her. The blood had drained from her face and she was shaking quite noticeably. I suppose being told that a friend has met a violent end is enough to do that to people. On the other hand it may have been that she had just made the connection between the death of Monica and our interviewing Michael Cozens. But I dismissed those propositions immediately. She'd read about the cufflink in the paper – had told us she had – so she must have known about Monica's murder. And in any event someone at the airport would have told her. Great places for gossip are airports.

'She was stabbed to death in a room in Talleyrand Street, Soho. She'd been working as a prostitute.'

Sylvia didn't so much lean back in her chair as collapse against the cushions. 'I don't believe it,' she said. 'Why should she have done a thing like that?' This latest piece of shattering information clearly added to her distress. Or demonstrated her skill as an actress.

'One story I've heard is that she was made redundant by the airline for which you both worked.'

'Yes, that's true. It was for bad timekeeping, but you

can't help that when you work at Heathrow. Like I said, the traffic's awful. And if you get behind an accident, well, there's nothing you can do about it.' Sylvia shook her head. 'But prostitution . . . there was no need for her to do that, I shouldn't have thought. She was quite well educated, you know. Went to a convent school, so I heard. She told me once that she could have gone to university.' She shook her head again. But then the revelation came. 'Oh my God!' she said, her hands going to her face once more. 'You don't think Michael had anything to do with it, do you? Is that why you came? What makes you think he might know anything? Is it because he was in trouble with the police before?' The words came tumbling out, breathlessly.

I was in a difficult position here. If I told Sylvia that Cozens' fingerprints had been found in a tom's pad, she'd probably hit the roof and then hit Cozens. And that could well have ended a beautiful relationship. That didn't worry me, but I really wanted these two to stay together, at least until the murder was cleared up. After that they could do what they liked.

So I ignored the question. 'I'm told that you and Mr Cozens socialised with Mr and Mrs Purvis quite a lot.' I was going out on a limb here on the basis of what Sid Marley, the airline security officer, had told me. Personally I had no great faith in him. Not only was he a chain-smoker but, I suspected, a soak as well. Certainly his breath smelled of alcohol when we had seen him in the early afternoon and I imagined that his idea of lunch was several large Scotches interspersed with pints of bitter.

Sylvia now appeared to notice the cup and saucer on the carpet and leaned forward to pick them up. 'We had a few meals out together, yes,' she said, without looking directly at me. 'But that's what people who work together do, isn't it?'

I could have said that they even go to the ballet. 'I suppose so. Very often was it?'

Sylvia gave that some thought, or seemed to. Pursing her lips and furrowing her brow, she eventually admitted that they had gone out as a foursome on perhaps five or six occasions.

'Where were the Purvises living at the time?' I asked.

'Islington, I think. Yes, it was.'

'So I suppose you met somewhere central?'

'Sometimes. We did go to their place on one occasion. Grotty little house.' Sylvia spoke with all the condescension of someone who lived in Bromley, and wrinkled her nose. 'But most of the time it was a pizza or a curry in central London.'

'But I suppose you stopped seeing each other when Monica was sacked.'

'No, it was before that. Charlie got sent to prison, you know.' Sylvia looked up.

'Really?' I murmured.

'He was arrested for something to do with a robbery. He didn't do it, of course. It was all a terrible mistake, but he got three years.' She stared accusingly at me as though I'd been personally responsible. 'Monica really cracked up after that.'

'I imagine so,' I said, straight-faced. *So cracked up that she promptly went on the game.*

'She went all to pieces. I think that's what really started her bad timekeeping. She didn't seem to care any more.'

I decided to take a chance. 'Did Monica ever mention anyone called Geoffrey?'

'Geoffrey? Geoffrey?' Sylvia savoured the name. 'I seem to remember there was one chap called Geoffrey. Bit of a snooty type, but he always asked for Monica, or asked after her, when he came through.'

'What was that about, then?' Dave obviously decided it was time he took an interest.

'I don't know really.' Sylvia sounded defensive.

'Oh, come on,' Dave continued. 'I know that my wife shares what she calls "girlie" secrets with her mates.'

'D'you mean was she seeing him?' Sylvia was either thick or playing difficult or acting again.

'I mean was this Geoffrey bloke screwing her?' Once he got going, Dave tended to reject euphemisms.

'I really don't know.' Sylvia tossed her head, whether at the suggestion or the manner in which it was put was not apparent. But it didn't matter anyway; Halstead had already admitted to the Commissioner that he and Monica had had an affair.

Sylvia glanced at the clock on the mantelpiece. It was one of those clocks with four balls that rotate first one way and

71

then the other so that you become hypnotised if you watch it for too long. Or get seasick. 'Well, if there's nothing else, I'm due at my judo class in half an hour.'

'No, I don't think so,' I said, standing up. There was more, a lot more, but I sensed that we were not going to get very much out of Sylvia Moorhouse. Not yet.

It proved to be a bad day. When Dave and I eventually got back to Curtis Green, a summons awaited me. To see the Commissioner again. Immediately. On a Saturday? Ye gods, this had to be important. The only other time I remember the Commissioner being in on a Saturday was to claim his free place at Trooping the Colour.

This time the Commissioner's staff officer – clearly unhappy at being dragged in on his day off – did not hesitate. This time there was none of the paper-shuffling performances to which I was treated on my last visit. I was ushered straight in. Either I was getting important or I was in dead trouble.

'Good afternoon, sir.'

'Ah, Mr Brock, sit down. Geoffrey Halstead came to see me again this morning.' Sir Charles Austen looked distinctly unhappy. 'Well, actually, he asked me to go across to the Home Office. He had a very busy schedule apparently.'

'I imagine so, sir,' I murmured, amused that the Commissioner should be making an excuse for rushing across to Queen Anne's Gate, and on a Saturday, too. But he wasn't fooling me: the ribbon of a Knight Grand Cross of the British Empire would look rather nice in front of the others he'd acquired.

'The Minister has been the subject of another blackmail demand.' The Commissioner sighed deeply.

'Oh dear!' I said, and received a sharp look from Austen. I decided that this was not the time to remind him that he had been convinced that such attempts at extortion would end with Monica Purvis's death. 'What form did this demand take, sir?'

'I have it here.' Austen spoke wearily, and I got the impression that his interview with the Minister of State had been an uncomfortable one. 'It seems to have been done on a computer,' he added, pushing a single sheet of paper across the desk.

'I doubt that we'll be able to get much in the way of fingerprints off that,' I said, an implied criticism that the man in charge of the Metropolitan Police had not practised even the basic essentials of preservation of evidence.

'It had already been handled by the Minister and his private secretary,' said the Commissioner. 'There didn't seem much point in wrapping it in a plastic bag.'

I skimmed through the note. It read: *Just because she's dead doesn't mean your safe. Two K into the usual keeps it quiet. Have a nice day.* It had been produced in a typescript that my computer calls Kidnap. A resourceful blackmailer obviously; it saved wasting time cutting letters out of newspapers. But then I suppose that's regarded as a bit old hat these days.

'You'll notice, Mr Brock, that he has written "your" when he should have written "you are", or even the accepted contraction thereof.' Austen pointed a finger at the document and looked pleased with himself.

'I noticed that, sir,' I said, trying not to sound too irritated; I hate being patronised. 'Did Mr Halstead explain what was meant by the phrase "Two K into the usual"?'

'Ah, yes.' Austen leaned forward and linked his hands on the desk. 'When this all started, the blackmailer instructed Halstead to pay sums of money into a particular account at a leading high street bank. I imagine that the man then withdrew the money from various cash machines.'

I looked suitably aghast and was about to speak when the Commissioner held up a hand. 'I know what you're going to say, Mr Brock, but yesterday, when the Minister came to see me, was the first the police knew that he was being blackmailed.'

'D'you mean he paid up, sir?'

'I'm afraid so,' said Austen. 'You see he was frightened of what might happen to his career and his marriage if it all got out.'

'So what's he propose doing, sir? Keep on paying?'

'I advised him strongly that he should let the police deal with it, but he's very reluctant to do so.'

'I take it you explained to him how police preserve the anonymity of victims, sir.'

'Of course.'

'Well, I'm afraid that I'm going to have to investigate it now. It could very well be germane to my inquiry into the death of Monica Purvis.'

The Commissioner nodded slowly. 'Try to be a little discreet, Mr Brock,' he said.

'I shall be discretion itself, sir,' I said, 'which is more than can be said for Geoffrey Halstead.'

'What d'you mean by that?'

'When Monica Purvis was working at Heathrow as a passenger services agent – or whatever they call themselves – Geoffrey Halstead used to ask for her, or enquire after her, every time he went through the airport. That doesn't seem too discreet to me.'

Austen appeared shocked. 'He never said anything about that to me. He didn't mention that she used to work there. I presumed that he had met her when she was, er . . .'

'Soliciting,' I said. 'I don't suppose he mentioned that Monica Purvis's husband was banged up for three years for armed robbery, either, sir.'

'Good grief.' Sir Charles Austen seemed quite appalled by this latest revelation, probably because he belatedly realised that he should have armed himself with the facts of the case before rushing across to the Home Office that morning. He was probably thinking now that he had made a bit of a fool of himself, and who was I to argue? 'I'm beginning to suspect that there's quite a lot that Mr Halstead has not told us,' he said.

'I think that may well be the case, sir.'

Nine

I decided that today was the day I would have to tackle Halstead about his sordid affair with the late Monica Purvis and his willingness to cough up every time his blackmailer told him to.

But first there was the morning conference, the time when the officer in the case – that's me – found out what the slaves had been doing.

Television viewers of fictional crime are frequently misled into believing that murders are solved by a DCI – who never seems to know whether he's called a chief inspector or an inspector – and his assistant. And no one else. It's not true. The fact is that murder inquiries, in the Met anyway, have a team of at least fifteen officers. The guv'nor usually avoids getting his hands dirty, but is available to make the arrest, thus covering himself in glory.

When I was a detective inspector I spent a fruitless three months at the Police College. Some provincial theorist on the directing staff suggested that the officer leading the hunt for a killer could be likened to a conductor conjuring the best from a vast orchestra of junior detectives, scientists, pathologists, scenes-of-crime officers, fingerprint experts and photographers.

I gazed around the assembled company. It resembled a ragged band of street musicians rather than the CID equivalent of the Royal Philharmonic Orchestra; most of them were wearing mix-an'-match suits, those who were wearing jackets at all, that is.

I outlined what had been learned so far about the Monica Purvis murder, but I wanted to know a lot more.

I addressed Frank Mead, the DI in charge of the 'leg-work'

officers: 'Anything in the corres we found at Monica's place at Charleston Terrace?'

'No, nothing that gives us anything.'

Frank was good at his job and if he said that there was nothing in it, then there was nothing in it. I went on. 'I want to know everything there is to know about Monica's background, Frank. So far it's been suggested that she went on the game after getting the chop from the airline she worked for, and that she was well-educated, could have gone to university in fact. Get the lads digging—' I was interrupted by a polite cough from one of the women detectives. 'And lasses,' I continued, 'digging into her past life. I'm particularly interested in the current whereabouts of her husband, Charlie Purvis, who's got a three-stretch behind him for blagging. Dave will give you his last known address and young Appleby did a search at St Catherine's House, so you can get personal details about them from the statement file. Anything on the trainer found at the scene?'

'No, guv,' said Mead. 'We've tried sports shops, suppliers, even a few sports clubs, but we've come up blank.'

That didn't surprise me. Given that DS Wright, the laboratory liaison officer, had said that the trainer was at least twelve years old, I hadn't thought we'd much chance of finding out who owned it anyway. 'And the rope?'

'Same, sir,' said Mead. 'No joy at all. Obtainable just about everywhere.'

Which was exactly what Dr Sarah Dawson had said. I could see that this was going to be one of those long-drawn-out inquiries. 'I also want to know as much as there is to know about one Sylvia Moorhouse and her partner, a guy called Michael Cozens. He's done time as well for a bit of white-collar crime, but in my view he's definitely sussy for this one. Right, get to it.'

'You didn't mention Halstead, guv,' said Dave, when the team started to go about its business.

'You're not supposed to know anything about that, Dave,' I said, 'and I'm certainly not telling that lot in there.' I cocked a thumb at the door of the room we'd just left. 'At least, not yet.'

'Does that mean you're going to interview him on your

own?' asked Dave, a distinct note of concern in his voice.

'Not bloody likely,' I said. 'Commissioner or no Commissioner.' It was pure bravado, but you mustn't let the junior ranks think that you haven't got a bit of bottle. 'Get the telephone number of the Home Office.'

I was eventually put through to Geoffrey Halstead's private secretary and explained that I needed to see the Minister urgently.

'May I ask what it's about?' There was an offhand note of disdain in the secretary's well-bred voice, probably engendered by the horror of having to deal with a policeman other than through an intermediary.

'I think you'd better ask the Minister,' I said, and gave Dave an owlish grin.

There was a pause during which I could hear snatches of muttered conversation in the background. The private office staff were definitely not liking this.

'I'm afraid the Minister's in a meeting this morning,' said the secretary, deigning to speak to me again, 'and he's in the House this afternoon. Perhaps if you could explain why you want to see him . . .' He wasn't going to give up.

'I'll tell you what,' I said, 'when you've fixed up an appointment perhaps you'd ring me back.' I was not impressed by civil servants who thought that their master's bells tolled for them.

It took five minutes. 'The Minister can see you at half past ten,' said the now more conciliatory voice of the secretary. He was probably wondering what this lowly policeman had that he could ask for an appointment with a Minister of State, and get it.

According to *Who's Who*, Geoffrey Halstead was forty-seven years of age and had been a Member of Parliament for the last seventeen of them. His slightly greying hair was smoothed back from a widow's peak and he wore a suit that must have cost at least eight hundred quid. He glided across the office with all the urbanity of a politician with years of experience of dealing with the common herd.

'My dear chief inspector,' he said, shaking hands. It wasn't a very firm grip. 'Do take a seat.' He glanced at Dave. 'You too, er . . .'

'This is Detective Sergeant Poole, sir,' I said. 'He's assisting me in my inquiries.'

'I see.' Halstead didn't seem too pleased at that, but I knew of policemen who had conducted a one-to-one interview, had heard a confession and then found that they had no corroboration. Certainly if, by some miracle, this guy gave himself up this morning, I knew damn well that he would deny it later, on the advice of counsel, of course. Consequently there was no way I was going to talk to him without a witness who was on my side.

'I'm aware of your two discussions with the Commissioner,' I began.

'It's a very distressing business, Mr Brock.' Halstead shot his crisp, white cuffs before linking his hands on the desk. I noticed his cufflinks: pure gold, and no trace of YES and NO, ABC and XYZ, or any of the other combinations that were currently of interest to me. He leaned forward slightly and looked apologetic, and I had the feeling that he now expected the police to get him out the mess he had got himself into. He glanced nervously at Dave, head already bowed over the record-of-interview book, making notes.

'I understand that you have paid sums of money to a person who has been making demands with menaces from you. Perhaps you'd care to tell me the background.'

'This is all very embarrassing, Mr Brock, but I was foolish enough to get embroiled with this young woman when she was working at Heathrow Airport.'

'Embroiled in what way?' I wasn't going to let him off too lightly.

Halstead paused, as though reluctant to put into words details of his sexual fling with a prostitute. 'Eventually it became an affair. But it wasn't like that to start with. Whenever I had occasion to travel through the airport, she always took care of me . . .'

Dave looked up for long enough to cast a cynical glance at the Minister before carrying on writing.

'She was a very personable young woman,' Halstead

continued, as if attempting to excuse his conduct, 'and I asked her out for a drink one evening, just as a way of thanking her for all her assistance.' He played with his signet ring for a moment or two. 'And I'm afraid that one thing led to another. It's all too easy what with Heathrow being surrounded by hotels.'

I was amazed at the stupidity of the man. The hotels at Heathrow are full of well-known faces, which in turn attract journalists on the look-out for them. If Halstead's blackmailer hadn't cottoned on to it there, it was a racing certainty that some muck-raking reporter would have found out sooner or later, given the largesse they are known to distribute to hotel staff. 'We are talking about Monica Purvis, aren't we, sir?' I asked. It crossed my mind briefly that there might have been others, but Dave needed the victim's name for the record.

'Yes. The poor young woman who was murdered.'

'You do appreciate that she was a prostitute, don't you?'

'I only discovered that when I read the report of her murder, Mr Brock.'

A likely story. She'd put herself on offer and he couldn't resist it. 'Did you use an airport hotel often?'

'Just the once. It was a bit risky, I must admit, but we were very discreet. After that we went to hotels well away from London.'

'Perhaps you'd care to give my sergeant a list of those hotels, sir,' I said.

'Is that necessary, Chief Inspector?' Halstead was obviously not very happy about that. 'I mean, why do you want to know?'

'You were being blackmailed,' I said, 'and it's quite possible that the blackmailer was, or still is, employed at one of those hotels.'

'Oh, good Lord, I never thought of that.'

Nevertheless, Halstead scribbled down a few names on a sheet of paper and handed it to me. For a Minister at the Home Office it was clear that he had a lot to learn about policing. Real life, even. 'We shall be very discreet, sir, I assure you,' I lied.

'Yes, good, good. By the way, I never paid the bill. Monica always did that. On her credit card.'

Well, if that didn't beat cock-fighting. Not only was he screwing Monica at every opportunity but the poor little cow finished up paying for the privilege. But I was wrong.

'I always reimbursed her, handsomely,' Halstead continued hurriedly, 'in cash, of course. You see I didn't want my wife to find a credit-card bill for a hotel in the wilds of Essex on a date when I was supposed to be visiting a prison on the Isle of Wight, if you see what I mean.' He smiled, but it lacked any warmth.

'Very wise,' I murmured. 'And that reimbursement included her fee, did it?'

Halstead obviously didn't like the implications of that. 'I gave her a present from time to time, if that's what you mean, Mr Brock,' he said grimly.

'That was in cash, too, was it?'

'In cash,' Halstead reluctantly agreed.

It amounted to paying a prostitute for her services. I knew it and Halstead knew it. 'And how often did you and Mrs Purvis spend a night in a hotel?'

'*Mrs* Purvis, did you say?' Halstead sat up sharply.

'Oh yes, she was married.'

'Good grief!' Halstead sank back again. 'I didn't know that,' he murmured.

I do like that in married philanderers: he obviously thought it was all right for him to have it off, but it seemed he was none too happy about *her* going over the side. Presumably because it could produce complications over which he had no control. Like husbands.

Time to put the knife in. 'And her husband was serving a three-year sentence for armed robbery at the time.'

'Oh my God!' Halstead blanched. 'I had no idea.'

No, I thought, I don't think you did, and I doubt that it would have made much difference anyway; perhaps it would have added a little excitement to your squalid affair. In fact, vague promises about being able to do something for her husband may even have reduced the cost of his sexual encounters. Perhaps to zero.

'How remiss of me,' Halstead said suddenly, 'I haven't offered you gentlemen any coffee.' Instead of using his intercom, he stood up and walked to the door of his office to issue instructions to an unseen secretary. I assumed it to be a device to give himself time to think about the implications of shafting a prisoner's wife.

'I asked how many times you used a hotel,' I said, as he returned to his refuge behind the large desk.

'Six.' Halstead didn't hesitate.

'There are only three hotels on this list.' I waved the piece of paper he had given me.

'We used each one twice, Mr Brock.' Halstead spoke confidently, as though there was nothing foolish in that.

'And you continued to see her even after the blackmail started?'

'Yes.'

Well, that reckoned. There's no man quite as stupid as one tempted by illicit sex. 'I should point out, Minister,' I said, intent on keeping up the pressure, 'that your being blackmailed makes you a suspect for the woman's murder.'

'But that's ridiculous,' Halstead blurted out, 'and I resent the implication. Would I have spoken to your Commissioner about it had I been guilty of such a heinous crime?'

Halstead obviously wanted to remind me that he had direct access to Sir Charles Austen. Dave stopped writing and looked up, probably wondering if his chief inspector would be replaced before the day was out.

What the hell? I'd committed myself now. 'I hope you're recording this conversation verbatim, Sergeant,' I said, glancing briefly at Dave, before turning to face Halstead again. 'The job of an investigating officer in a murder inquiry is to explore every avenue, Minister, no matter how unlikely or how tenuous.' Not that I thought my line of inquiry was either unlikely or tenuous. But it did sound pompous.

'I appreciate that you have a job of work to do, Chief Inspector,' said Halstead at his smooth ministerial best, 'but I am a member of the government and members of the government are not likely to commit murder, whatever the provocation.'

'Then why, as a matter of interest, did you not report the

blackmail when you received the first demand?' I raised an eyebrow and waited.

'I was afraid that it would get into the press,' said Halstead unconvincingly.

'I'm sure you, of all people, know that the police deal with such matters discreetly and sympathetically, Mr Halstead,' I said. Now was the time either to blow it or bow out. 'And I'm afraid I don't believe a word of what you've told me so far.' I wasn't looking at Dave, but I could sense that he winced. 'You were being blackmailed because you were having an extramarital affair with a prostitute who was married to a man serving a prison sentence. On your own admission, you took her to hotels, firstly at Heathrow and later outside London. As you saw fit not to report the blackmail to police, I suggest that you took matters into your own hands and murdered her, thus removing the cause.' I paused to add weight to my next statement. 'Or did you discover that Monica Purvis was herself the blackmailer?'

'Now just look here—'

A middle-aged woman entered the office with a tray of coffee, but shrewdly sensing the strained atmosphere – as secretaries are wont to do – she put it down on a table and left. Halstead ignored her and the coffee.

I produced my little plastic card, without which I never could remember the caution. 'You do not have to say anything,' I began, 'but it may harm your defence if you do not mention when questioned something which you later rely on in court. Anything you do say may be given in evidence.' That, I thought, will either bring on the pains or get me the sack. Or both.

'How dare you,' blustered Halstead, his face suffusing with controlled anger. Whether that rage was real or devised didn't matter too much, but I had undoubtedly produced a reaction of sorts. 'I shall take this matter up with the Commissioner immediately, Chief Inspector. Furthermore, in the unlikely event of your interviewing me again it will be in the presence of my solicitor. In the meantime, I have nothing further to say.' He drew a file from his in-tray and opened it. The coffee remained untouched.

Oh joy! I thought, and wondered how many minutes would elapse after my return to Curtis Green before Sir Charles Austen sent for me.

'I think you've upset him, guv'nor,' said Dave mournfully, as we stepped out into the sunshine of Queen Anne's Gate. 'I've never had a cup of coffee in the Home Office,' he added, as though that was the gravest outcome of my abortive interview.

'And your chances are reducing by the second, Dave,' I said.

It was in fact an hour before I received the summons. But to see the *acting* Commissioner at two o'clock.

If there was an acting Commissioner, where had Austen gone? I rang his staff officer, affecting innocence.

'I've been told to see the *acting* Commissioner at two o'clock, sir. Is that right?'

'I imagine so, Mr Brock,' said the staff officer. 'Sir Charles is on leave. For a month. He left for Cyprus last night. Mr Leonard, the Deputy, is acting in his absence.'

Well, well! What a cunning old Commissioner.

Jack Leonard, as Deputy Commissioner, was the disciplinary head of the Force and that did not bode well. His office was only slightly less ornate than the Commissioner's, but I was not too bothered about furnishings right now.

'Detective Chief Inspector Brock, sir. I understand you wanted to see me.'

'So I do, Mr Brock. Come in and take a seat.'

That sounded hopeful. I sat down.

'I had a telephone call from Geoffrey Halstead this morning. It seems that he was upset at your accusing him of murdering Monica Purvis. He said that you administered the caution to him.'

'Yes, sir, that's correct.'

Jack Leonard was a big man in every way. Having spent much of his service in the CID, he looked uncomfortable in uniform and more often than not wore plain clothes. He had a bull neck and a red face and bore the reputation of not suffering fools, gladly or otherwise. There was a rumour circulating at the Yard that he had refused the knighthood that was normally given to a Deputy Commissioner when it was perceived that he was going no further. 'And do you think he committed this murder?' The Deputy stroked his moustache and smiled.

'It's possible, sir,' I said, and outlined what was known of the case so far, laying particular emphasis on the fact that Halstead had had an affair with the girl and had been blackmailed because of it, but had failed to report the matter to the police. I also mentioned that Monica Purvis's husband had been in prison at some stage during the affair.

Leonard smiled bleakly at that last piece of information. 'I see,' he said. 'Well, tread carefully, Mr Brock. That's all.'

I stood up. I'd come in expecting to be torn off a strip or even suspended from duty, but was merely told to tread carefully. 'Did he make an official complaint, sir?' I asked. This I had to know.

'I think that's what he was trying to do, Mr Brock, but I told him that, as the officer responsible for discipline, I was unable to accept a complaint directly. I gave him the telephone number of the Internal Investigations Command. And I told him that if he wished to discuss a case under investigation, his solicitor should consult with the Solicitor to the Metropolitan Police, or the Crown Prosecution Service.'

What a refreshing change. I left the Deputy's office hoping that Sir Charles Austen would stay on leave for a very long time.

Curiously, Halstead never lodged an official complaint.

Ten

It was three o'clock by the time I got back to Curtis Green. Dave Poole looked up expectantly as I entered the incident room and indicated, with a jerk of my head, that he should follow me into my office.

'You can relax, Dave,' I said. 'The Commissioner went on leave last night so the Deputy took the call. Halstead made noises about our interview but didn't get anywhere. Reading between the lines, I got the impression that he finished up with a flea in his ear.'

Dave chuckled, probably more from relief than anything else; he didn't get on with the DCI who would have taken my place had I been suspended.

'Mr Mead's found Charlie Purvis, guv,' he said.

'Where?'

'In a pad in Kentish Town, I think he said.'

'That was quick.'

'Yeah, but Mr Mead's got some good snouts, guv.' Dave had obviously taken my comment as a criticism. 'Comes of having been on the Squad, I suppose.' My sergeant had always hankered after a posting to the Flying Squad, but I don't think that their macho image would appeal to him somehow. He was a good copper without throwing his weight about.

'By the way, Dave, what about Simister's alibi? When we interviewed him at Hounslow nick he claimed he was with Tracey Milner in the Faggot pub the night of the murder.'

'It looks as though he was, guv. I spoke to the licensee on the phone and he said that he'd had to call the police that night. Apparently someone made an obscene suggestion to Simister's bird and a few punches were thrown.'

'Any knock-offs?'

'Apparently not.' Dave pulled a sour face; he had difficulty in contemplating a disturbance that didn't result in any arrests.

'Did they take any names and addresses?'

'No. It was marked up as all quiet on arrival.'

'So there's no evidence that Simister was actually there other than the word of the licensee?'

'Not really, guv, no.'

'Slap-happy bastards.' I wasn't at all convinced about Simister's claim to have been drinking all night. It could have been a set-up, even one involving the licensee. Perhaps a word with Tracey Milner – when Simister was out of the way – would produce a different story. But right now I was going to begin at the beginning. 'Get hold of whoever was involved in dealing with that call and get him over here.'

'It was a half serial of the TSG, guv. There was a skipper in charge. A woman,' he added disdainfully.

I had no great faith in the Territorial Support Group, in fact regarded them as a load of cowboys who went in mob-handed – in this case, a sergeant and ten constables – to deal with a punch-up that, in the old days, one PC would have handled. 'OK, get the sergeant to ring me, pronto.'

'Very good, sir.' Dave reached for the telephone.

I always knew when Dave thought I was making a fuss: he called me 'sir' instead of the usual 'guv'.

'In the years to come, Dave,' I said loftily, 'you will find that the most unlikely questions are asked when a case gets to court, and if the police witness doesn't have the answer he can be made to look an incompetent fool by some smart-arse barrister who's read all the statements ten times over and decides to nit-pick.'

'I think I've found that out already, sir,' said Dave, clearly wishing to indicate that he was not entirely without experience as a CID officer.

'Oh, good,' I said with a smile.

Surprisingly the phone call from the TSG came only twenty minutes later. 'PS 21, sir,' said a female voice. 'I understand you want to speak to me.'

I reminded her of the incident to which she and her half serial had been called at the Faggot public house in Hounslow.

'Oh, yes, sir, I remember it.'

'And?'

'All quiet on arrival, sir.'

'That much I gleaned from the message, Sergeant,' I said. We still called them 'messages' even though they were computerised entries on the CAD, yet another acronym, this one meaning computer-aided despatch. I think. Although by now the boffins at the Yard have probably changed it into something else equally unintelligible. I got very tired of all these abbreviations. In fact I firmly believed that office-bound policemen invented them and then used them in everyday conversation to convey the impression that they were terribly clever. 'So what really happened?'

'We were called at 2103 hours to a disturbance – men fighting – but when we arrived it was all over.'

'Who called you?' I asked.

There was a pause and I could hear the rustling of pages being turned. 'The licensee, sir,' said the sergeant eventually.

'And you took no names and addresses.'

'No, sir, I didn't see the need.' The sergeant spoke defiantly rather than defensively, an implied criticism of those who – she thought – sit in offices and don't get involved in the muck and bullets of day-to-day policing.

'From your local knowledge, Sergeant,' I said unkindly, 'can you tell me if an individual called Paul Simister was there with a woman called Tracey Milner.'

'I'm afraid I don't know either of them, sir.'

'*Really?* I'm surprised. He's got form for sexual offences.' But I was wasting my breath: the days when women police officers regarded such matters as their personal preserve were long gone. 'Well, thank you for your assistance, Sergeant,' I said acidly. 'Perhaps you'd be so good as to come up to Curtis Green as soon as possible. There are some photographs I want you to look at.'

'I am rather tucked up, sir . . .' the sergeant began.

'So am I, Sergeant,' I said, 'investigating the murder of a prostitute for which Paul Simister is, at this moment, a suspect. If there's a problem I'll speak to your chief superintendent.'

Half an hour later, the sergeant arrived and positively identified Simister as one of the men involved in the incident at the Faggot PH. I sighed, deeply. Another suspect written off. Maybe.

By one of those curious coincidences that occasionally occur in the investigation of a crime, Charlie Purvis's 'flop' turned out to be in an old semi-detached house in Hilldrop Crescent, which is in Camden Town rather than Kentish Town, for what difference that made.

According to DI Frank Mead, Purvis lived within spitting distance of Number 39 which, before it was bombed to destruction in the war and replaced by a block of council flats, had been the one-time residence of Dr Hawley Harvey Crippen. It was where Crippen, an American doctor of sorts, had murdered his wife, the nagging Belle Elmore, back in 1910 and buried her in the basement. The case became a cause célèbre when one of my predecessors, Detective Chief Inspector Walter Dew, arrested Crippen and his girlfriend, Ethel Le Neve, after pursuing them across the Atlantic in response to a radio message. I suppose I should have inferred something from all that symbolism.

Charlie Purvis wasn't there, but the landlord was. I introduced myself and Dave.

'Ephraim Murphy, sir. How can I assist?' The tall West Indian beamed at us and gently 'washed' his hands. Somehow, I doubted that he had heard of Dr Crippen.

'I'm looking for Charlie Purvis,' I said. 'Is he in?'

'Not at this precise moment, sir.'

'I see. Any idea when he'll be back?'

'Not long, I should think. He's gone down the road for fags.'

'Splendid. Perhaps you'd let us into his room, Mr Murphy.'

'Er, is this entirely legal?' asked Mr Murphy nervously. He was in the difficult position of wishing to offend neither me nor Purvis.

'Probably not, but we have some sad news to impart to him.' Although I was a hundred per cent certain that Purvis knew of his wife's death – may even have been responsible for it – I wanted to have a poke about in his belongings before he got back. 'Better to break it to him upstairs rather than on the doorstep.' The really sad news I was about to impart was that I was probably going to nick him for murder. Maybe.

'Oh dear. Yes, yes. Come with me.'

The landlord led us up two flights of rickety stairs to a room on the top floor, a room that in years past had undoubtedly been servants' accommodation, and unlocked the door.

'On a clear day you can see the Crystal Palace television mast from here,' said Mr Murphy proudly.

'Not unless you clean the bloody windows, you can't,' muttered Dave.

The room was a tip and the odour usual to such places pervaded: unwashed flesh, dirty clothing and stale tobacco smoke.

'Charming place he's got here, Dave,' I said.

'Yeah, smashing, guv. P'raps *Hello!* magazine'd like to do a spread on it.'

There was nothing to see: nothing of importance, anyway. The bed was unmade, and a portable TV set in the corner seemed to be the most valuable item in the room. In front of the window stood a plain, wooden table, its edges scarred with cigarette burns, upon which there was nothing more exciting than an old copy of the *Sun* newspaper. A wardrobe, its mahogany-veneered doors peeling and its mirror cracked, yielded a pile of soiled underwear, a pair of jeans and a pair of heavy boots of the sort that are worn on building sites. The chest of drawers was empty.

It appeared to be very much a temporary abode and I wondered where most of Purvis's possessions were. Assuming he had any more, that is.

'Who the bloody hell are you?' Ten minutes later a shaven-headed Purvis stood in the doorway, legs apart, biceps bulging under a filthy tee-shirt, a picture of truculent aggression. There was no sign of either a tattoo or an earring.

'Are you Charlie Purvis?'

'What if I am? What are you doing in my bloody room?' He took a pace towards us.

'Police.'

'So? Got a warrant, have you?'

'You got something to hide, then?' Dave spoke quietly, almost conversationally, but I knew that that was when he was at his most dangerous.

'You ain't got nothing on me,' claimed Purvis. 'I done me time, *and* I was nicked for something what I never done.'

'It's about Monica,' I said.

'What about her? If you've come here to tell me she's dead, I know. Read it in the paper, didn't I?'

'You don't seem too upset,' I said.

'Why should I be? Dirty little cow, hawking her mutton all round Soho. Good riddance I say.'

'How long ago did that start?'

'How long ago did what start?' It was fairly obvious that Purvis was going to as obstructive as possible.

'When she went on the game?'

'While I was in the nick.' Purvis took out a packet of cigarettes and lit one.

'You were sent down three years ago,' I said, 'and were released twelve months ago.' Although Purvis had been sentenced to three years, he hadn't done his full whack, but then no one ever does. Prison sentences these days are a bit of a joke. 'So it was during that time, was it?'

'That's what I said. She got made redundant from the airport about eighteen months ago. Wrote to me in the nick to tell me, but I never heard from her again. She never visited, selfish bitch.'

'When did you last see her?'

'About a year ago, just after I come out. I saw Syl and—'

'Would that be Sylvia Moorhouse?' Dave asked.

'Yeah. I give Syl a bell and she told me that Monica was at it.'

'Sylvia actually told you that Monica had become a prostitute?' When we last interviewed Sylvia Moorhouse she had expressed surprise that her friend had taken to the streets.

'Yeah. Anyway, what's all this got to do with me?'

'You were married to her, remember?' said Dave drily.

'So what? I never had nothing to do with her after I come out.'

'You just said that you last saw her about a year ago.' Dave put his hands in his pockets, leaned against the wardrobe and then, thinking better of it, levered himself upright again.

'Yeah, well, apart from that.' Purvis looked decidedly shifty.

'And where was that? Where did you meet her?' I asked.

'Syl told me what Monica was up to and that she was living down Paddington. So I went down there one morning, took her for a cappuccino and tried to talk her out of it, to come home, like, but she said as how she never wanted nothing more to do with me. She reckoned she was making plenty of money doing what she was doing and she weren't going to share it with no ex-con.'

'And that was it?'

'Well, I give her a bit of a slap, like, and, yeah, that was it. I ain't never seen her since.'

'Are you in employment at the moment?'

'No, I'm between jobs, as you might say.'

'Sylvia Moorhouse told me that the four of you socialised a lot. You, Monica, Sylvia and Michael Cozens. Is that correct?'

Purvis scoffed. He walked across to the window, opened it and stubbed out his cigarette on the sill. Then he sat down on the bed. 'If having it off and swapping partners at half time is what you call socialising, then yeah.' He looked disapproving, but I suspected it was a pretence.

'So what was the arrangement?' Dave's salaciousness was beginning to get the better of him.

'Not many perms when there's only four of you, is there?' said Purvis, sarcastically curling his lip. He lit another cigarette. 'Monica fancied Cozens rotten – that was bleedin' obvious – and he fancied her, so while they was at it me and Syl had it off. So's we wouldn't be left out, like. Anyway, Syl turned out to be quite a good screw.'

'And this went on until you were nicked, did it?'

'No. I packed it in when Monica suggested three in a bed.'

'What, you, Monica and Sylvia?' Dave was clearly taking a great interest in this ménage à trois.

'I wish.' Purvis manoeuvred a shred of tobacco on to the tip of his tongue and spat it out. 'No, Monica, me and bloody Cozens. Well, I didn't go for that. I wouldn't have trusted that Cozens. A bit AC/DC if you ask me.'

Dave laughed. 'So that was the end of it, was it?'

'No.' Purvis shook his head. 'I let Monica get on with it. She was welcome to Cozens, slimy bastard. And me and Syl started seeing each other regular, but separate, like. You know, not as a foursome.'

'Where?' asked Dave.

'What d'you mean, where?'

'Where did you and Sylvia have it off?'

Purvis paused for a moment or two. Either he couldn't remember or he was about to make it up. 'Down Bromley, where she lived.'

'And where was Cozens while you were screwing his bird?'

'Up Islington screwing Monica, I s'pose,' said Purvis, and then he laughed. 'But sometimes he was downstairs watching football on the telly. He never give a toss.'

'So it wasn't all over, was it?' Dave clearly had trouble grasping the intricacies of this bizarre arrangement. 'You were still swapping partners.'

Purvis appeared slightly baffled by the question. 'Yeah, but like I said, at first we used to do it in a group, in the lounge at Bromley, sometimes in the bedroom, and once in the garden,' he said. 'Cozens liked to watch me and Syl at it. Got some sort of kick out of it, sick bastard.'

'Where did you and Monica meet?' I asked suddenly.

Purvis seemed disconcerted by that. 'What?'

'It's a simple enough question,' I continued. 'Where did you first meet her?'

'Heathrow.'

'How?'

'There'd been a fire or something in the terminal building where she was working and I was on the contract. I was brickying then. I saw her on the desk one day and chatted her up. They like a bit of rough, some of these classy birds, and she certainly went for it. I took her out for a Chinese and had it off with her in her flat in Hounslow the same night.'

'And *was* she a classy bird?'

'Oh yeah. Spoke very educated. Matter o' fact she'd been to a convent school, so she reckoned. She said that her old man wanted her to go to university, but she never fancied it. Wanted to work for an airline, she said. She didn't much like the job she'd got and wanted to go flying. You know, as an air hostess.'

That at least tallied with what Sylvia Moorhouse had said about Monica.

'Catholic, was she?' asked Dave, picking at a piece of loose paint on the window ledge.

'Dunno, never asked,' said Purvis, 'but I s'pose having been at one of them convents, yeah, she probably was.'

'Did she ever mention anyone else she was seeing on a regular basis?' I had no intention of mentioning Geoffrey Halstead MP by name. 'Apart from Cozens, that is.'

'No, she never said.' Purvis didn't hesitate. 'But then she wouldn't, would she?'

'Where was she born?' I knew the answer to that from the search that young Appleby had done at St Catherine's House – it was Cheltenham in Gloucestershire – but I wanted to know what she had told Purvis.

'Haven't a clue.'

'You never saw her birth certificate?'

'Why bother when you've got the real thing?' said Purvis. 'Anyhow, what's with all the questions?'

'I'm trying to discover who killed her, Mr Purvis,' I said, 'which brings me to my next question. Where were you on the night she was murdered?'

Purvis's face broke into a broad grin. 'Screwing Syl down Bromley,' he said. 'Ask her if you like.'

'Oh, I shall,' I said. 'Rest assured of that.'

Eleven

S ylvia Moorhouse had lied about being a hairdresser, which
she might or might not have been in the past, but she
certainly wasn't one now. And, it would appear, she was
having an affair with Charlie Purvis – so he claimed – even
though she was still living with Michael Cozens, thereby
giving the impression of being in a relationship with him. It
was clearly time to visit the devious Sylvia again.

Furthermore, I needed to have another word with Cozens
who had denied knowing Monica's surname but, according to
Charlie Purvis, actually knew her more intimately than on just
a client–prostitute basis.

Dave summed up Sylvia Moorhouse in his usual succinct
way: 'I reckon she's a bit sussy, guv,' he said.

Not wishing to embark on a fruitless journey, I got Dave
to telephone Sylvia at her home. Having established that she
was there, we made an appointment to see her and journeyed,
yet again, to Bromley.

She was attired in the Oxford University T-shirt and ragged
shorts that she had been wearing the first time we saw her –
perhaps it was her only off-duty outfit – but she had at least
done something with her hair: it was straightened and plaited
into a single pigtail that almost reached her shoulder blades.
It was an improvement, but then anything would have been.

'So, it's you again,' she said.

'Yes, it's me again, Ms Moorhouse.'

'Well, if it's Michael you want to see, he's left.'

'For work?'

'No, for good.'

'When did this happen?'

'Yesterday.'

94

'Did he say why?'

'No, he just upped and left.'

A likely story. I fancied that at last he had tired of Sylvia unashamedly having it off with Charlie Purvis. 'Where did he go? Any idea?'

'No, and I couldn't care less.'

By now we had moved into the sitting room and Sylvia lit a cigarette, puffing at it nervously.

Time to try a different line of questioning, I thought, and to hell with the consequences. 'Were you aware that Monica was seeing an MP on a regular basis?' I asked.

'Really?' Sylvia affected surprise. 'Good for her. Who was he?' She plonked herself down on the sofa opposite us and looked from me to Dave and back again.

'I don't know. It was just a rumour I picked up during the course of my investigation.' I wasn't going to give her the name; people like Halstead have a nasty habit of suing for libel, particularly when it's the truth that's been told. And Sylvia Moorhouse may be just the sort to telephone a newspaper the moment Dave and I left the house. So long as the newspaper was prepared to pay her a substantial sum of money, of course. I could almost visualise the tabloid headlines: MINISTER IN LOVE-NEST WITH MURDERED PROSTITUTE.

She shrugged. 'We get to meet a lot of important people at the airport,' she said.

'When I saw Michael Cozens last, he denied knowing Monica Purvis.'

Sylvia scoffed. 'D'you blame him?' she asked. 'You take him down to the police station and practically accuse him of murdering Monica and you expect him to say he knew her?'

'In fact, my information is that he was having an affair with her.' I paused and stared straight at the woman. 'At the same time that you were having an affair with Charlie Purvis.'

'What a load of bollocks!' said Sylvia angrily, her voice rising to something near a screech. It was a masterful performance of outrage. 'Who told you that?'

I smiled. It was time to break up a beautiful and fulfilling friendship. 'Would you believe, Charlie Purvis?'

'The bastard.' She stubbed out her half-smoked cigarette in

an ashtray that bore the legend 'Grand Hotel'. 'In his dreams,' she added.

'He said that your socialising, as you called it – you, Mr Cozens, Charlie and Monica – took the form of sexual orgies, here in this room, in the bedroom and once in the garden.' I glanced at Dave. 'Those were Mr Purvis's words, Sergeant, weren't they?'

Dave made a big thing of thumbing through his pocketbook and then nodding. 'Yes, guv,' he said.

'OK, the four of us used to get together from time to time. I admit that, but as I told you last time, it was up West for a curry or a pizza. There was nothing else on the menu.'

'According to Charlie, on one occasion Monica suggested three in a bed with him and Cozens. But Charlie said he turned that down and, thereafter, went solo with you. There were times, he said, when Cozens was down here watching football on the television while you and Charlie were at it upstairs.'

Sylvia burst out laughing. 'Well, I'll say this for Charlie: he's got a vivid imagination.'

'He also said,' I continued, 'that on the night Monica was murdered, he was in bed with you. Here.'

'I told you before,' said Sylvia, adopting an air of restrained patience, 'that I was here with Michael that night, alone. We watched TV. We saw *The Bill*, a film and the late news. Charlie wasn't here. And,' she added defiantly, 'he's never been to bed with me.'

'Why should he make up this story, then?' I asked.

'You'd better ask him that,' said Sylvia. 'Probably turn out to be wishful thinking. But I'll tell you this much: I can't stand the creep. He's a rough brickie for God's sake. I don't know what Monica saw in him, but he's definitely not my type.'

And there we left it. For the moment.

On the journey back from Bromley, it crossed my mind to ring Sarah Dawson and suggest dinner, but by the time we got back to Curtis Green, someone had shaken the kaleido-scope again.

'There's been a development, sir,' said DS Colin Wilberforce as I strode into the incident room.

'Which is?'

'Michael Cozens has been found.'

'Oh good. Where?'

'Chiswick, guv. He was floating in the river, face down. Very dead. And his car was found abandoned at Strand-on-the-Green.'

'What bad luck,' I said. But I was thinking less of Cozens' demise than my frustration at being denied the opportunity of questioning him further. 'Where's the car now?'

'Chiswick nick, sir.' Wilberforce paused and turned the pages of the book in which he kept notes. Then he looked up with an expression of puzzlement on his face. 'Apart from the usual trivia one finds in cars, it contained a copy of *Hansard*.'

'Too good to be true,' I muttered. 'Where is it now, Colin?'

'At the lab, sir.'

'Pathologist said anything yet?'

'Death by drowning, guv,' said Colin. 'Dr Mortlock's initial opinion is that Cozens may have been pushed in.'

'When does Mortlock reckon this happened?'

'Yesterday evening, probably about ten o'clock, but he'll be more certain once he's completed the post-mortem.'

'Any fingerprints in the vehicle?'

'So far the only identifiable dabs are Cozens'. There's another set but they'll probably turn out to be Sylvia Moorhouse's. We'll need to have hers for elimination.'

'If I remember correctly, Cozens said that he didn't know where his wife – his lawful wife, that is – had gone, so we can't inform her.'

'I've tried, sir, but got nowhere.'

'And the copy of *Hansard*, Colin?' The implication was that Geoffrey Halstead had had a hand in Cozens' death, but I found that a little too obvious. Nevertheless, I would need to check.

'There's some blurred marks on it, sir, but nothing that the fingerprint lads can make anything out of.'

'Just my luck,' I said. 'Has anyone told Sylvia Moorhouse?'

'No, guv,' said Colin. 'I told Chiswick to keep the lid on

it. I thought you may want to see her reaction when the news was broken to her.'

'Too bloody right I do,' I said.

And so, two hours later, Dave and I were back at Bromley.

'Not again! What now?' Sylvia seemed reluctant to ask us in a second time. She had changed into a shapeless kaftan from beneath which her bare feet peeped. I noticed that the varnish on her toenails was chipped.

'I'm afraid we have some bad news for you, Ms Moorhouse,' I said.

'Oh?' She glanced over her shoulder. 'I suppose you'd better come in, then.' She didn't seem surprised.

But we got no further than the hall. 'It's about Michael Cozens,' I began.

'What about him?'

'I'm afraid he's dead.'

Sylvia Moorhouse collapsed at our feet.

'She's fainted, guv,' said Dave; an unnecessary observation, I thought. He bent down and picked up the woman with effortless ease. I opened the door to the sitting room and Dave placed her on the sofa.

I turned off the television and searched the drinks cabinet for a bottle of brandy. Pouring a stiff measure I handed it to Sylvia who, by now, was beginning to regain consciousness.

She took a mouthful and half sat up. 'What happened?' she asked.

'You fainted,' I said.

'No, I mean what happened to Michael?'

'He fell in the river and drowned. At Chiswick.'

'What on earth was he doing in Chiswick?' she asked, and then answered her own question. 'Of course, it's where he works.'

'Where exactly did he work?'

'I don't know. He never told me; I just know it was an engineering firm in Chiswick. But how did it happen?'

'Could be that he had too much to drink last night and went for a walk by the river, perhaps to clear his head, and fell in. We don't really know as yet. His car was found parked at Strand-on-the-Green. I suppose it was just an unfortunate accident.' I was by no means convinced that it was an accident, but then I am, by nature, suspicious.

'How awful. Poor Michael.'

'When police searched his car, they found a copy of *Hansard*.'

'What's that?' asked Sylvia.

'It's the official record of proceedings in Parliament,' I said. 'Any idea what he might have been doing with it?'

'Good Lord, no. As far as I know, Michael took no interest in politics, apart from voting in elections.' Sylvia finished the brandy and leaned forward to place the empty glass on the coffee table. 'D'you think he might have committed suicide?' she asked.

I shrugged. 'I don't know. We shall probably never know.'

'Are you going to be all right on your own, Ms Moorhouse?' asked Dave. 'Or would you like us to call someone, a neighbour perhaps?'

She shook her head. 'No, I'll be OK.'

There was something nagging me in all this. I had the feeling that I was being jigged around on the end of a piece of string, and led towards places I didn't want to go. 'D'you know if Mr Cozens had any relatives, Ms Moorhouse?' I asked. 'They will need to be informed.'

'I know that both his parents are dead, but I believe he had a brother in Manchester. I know they exchanged Christmas cards, but I don't think he'd seen him for years.' She stood up and crossed the room to a drum table. 'His address book is here somewhere . . .' she said, opening a small drawer. 'Ah, here we are.'

'May I keep it for the time being?' I asked, holding out a hand.

'Why?'

'I'm investigating a suspicious death, Ms Moorhouse—'

'I thought you said it was suicide.' Sylvia's tone was reproachful.

'No, it was you who suggested that. But his address book could be useful to us. I'll return it as soon as we've finished with it.'

Somewhat reluctantly she handed over the small, plastic-bound book.

Back at Curtis Green, I studied Cozens' address book. Apart from Monica's telephone number, which came as no surprise, there was a George Cozens with an address in Manchester, but nothing else of significance.

'Get the Old Bill up there to call on brother George and break the sad news, Dave. Oh, and ask them to check where he was last night. Just to tie up the loose ends.'

'D'you think he might have thrown his brother in the river, then, sir?'

He was calling me 'sir' again. 'No, do you?' I asked. 'But if we don't ask, someone else will.' I was thinking of the commander when I said that; a born nit-picker was the commander. 'And get Mr Mead's team to check out the other names and addresses in the book' – I tossed it across the desk – 'just in case.'

I arrived early the next morning. There was much to do.

'The pathologist's report has just been faxed through, sir,' said Wilberforce, handing me several sheets of paper.

I sat down at a spare desk and lit a cigarette. Despite attempting to give up smoking, the strain was beginning to get to me.

Mortlock's report was as dry as his sense of humour. Cozens had had a lot to drink apparently: well over the odds for driving. There were no marks on his body to indicate that he had been assaulted, but it was the next sentence that jolted me.

Cozens' lungs contained no water, the medical explanation for which is that he did not drown.

I reached for the phone and by some miracle managed to get straight through to Dr Mortlock.

'Henry, it's Harry Brock. I've got your report in front of me. Why hadn't Cozens got any water in his lungs?'

I listened patiently to Mortlock's technical explanation and then attempted to repeat it to Dave.

'It's called vagal inhibition, Dave. Apparently when someone gets pushed into water when they're not expecting it, the shock kills them.'

'Bloody hell,' said Dave, and lit a cigarette. He too had given up giving up. 'So we've got a second murder inquiry on our hands.'

'Unless the commander lets us give it to Chiswick, Dave,' I said.

'Yeah, like I said, guv, we've got a second murder on our hands.' Dave can be very cutting at times.

I glanced around the incident room. The blank screens of HOLMES, the murder inquiry computer, stared at me. The huge noticeboard was covered with photographs of the dead woman, of Charlie Purvis, Simister, Sylvia Moorhouse and Michael Cozens.

Sylvia's had been taken by DI Mead's team, unbeknown to her; the others extracted from their respective criminal records and enlarged. The photograph of Monica was blown up from the wedding photo we'd found at Paddington and was alongside the photograph of her that had been taken at the mortuary. Very soon, Cozens' post-mortem photograph would be there too.

Beneath this imposing picture gallery was a list of addresses and telephone numbers.

I often wondered why we plastered the walls with all this stuff, why we had clever charts and computers, and why we had piles of statements that were meaningless and which we knew were meaningless when we took the damned things. The problem is that detectives get paranoid, worried that someone – a judge, counsel, a senior officer, or worse the Police Complaints Authority – will ask a question that they cannot answer. So they write it all down, *just in case*. It's called the JIC syndrome. Sometimes it's called the CYA syndrome: cover your arse.

But at the end of it all, it's a human being – the detective – who solves the crime. And usually it's a result of an error on the part of the person who committed that crime. The irony of it is that often such persons are arrested for something entirely unconnected with their original crime.

Like driving too fast and being stopped by a nosey copper who doesn't know when to stop asking questions.

'What's wrong with HOLMES, Colin?' I asked Wilberforce.

'It's gone down, sir.'

'Gone down where?' I hate this technological jargon and have an inherent distrust of all the gadgetry that goes with it.

'It's broken down, sir,' said Colin patiently.

'D'you know,' I began, adopting my reflective mode, 'when I started in the Department we used to have a whiteboard and a marker pen. They never broke down.'

'No, sir,' said Wilberforce, bending over a file.

I glanced at my watch. 'Any coffee on the go, Dave?' I asked.

I went to see the commander and told him about the finding of Cozens' body. I explained what I knew about vagal inhibition, which wasn't much, and mentioned the copy of *Hansard* that had been found.

'The implication is that Geoffrey Halstead, the Minister of State at the Home Office, was involved, sir,' I said.

'What on earth makes you think that?' It was obvious that the commander didn't like the sound of that. Such things worried senior police officers, probably because at his level any promotion he may be hoping for had to be sanctioned by the Home Secretary.

I explained that Halstead had been having an affair with the dead woman and had been blackmailed because of it.

'Good God! I didn't know that. Why wasn't I informed?'

'He's seen the Commissioner twice about it apparently, sir, and when I saw the Commissioner he directed me to tell no one.'

'But that's outrageous.' But then the commander realised that his comments might have been interpreted as a criticism of Sir Charles Austen to a junior officer. 'I mean it's outrageous that a man in Mr Halstead's position should have . . .' He paused. 'Well, you know what I mean, Mr Brock.'

'Yes, sir, I know what you mean,' I said. 'He telephoned the Deputy as well to complain that I'd cautioned him and suggested that he was responsible for the murder.'

'You did *what*?' It was obvious that the commander thought that I'd gone mad.

'I shall have to interview him again, sir,' I ventured, 'and I suppose the Deputy should know in advance.'

'Yes, well, you can leave that to me, Mr Brock. I'll tell him. But do nothing until you hear from me again.'

'Er, time is of the essence, sir. In a murder inquiry, delay can be extremely damaging to a clear-up.'

'I'm well aware of that,' the commander said testily. He didn't like being lectured by detectives. 'I'll let you know as soon as I can.'

As I left the office, he was already on the intercom telling his secretary to order up his car; he obviously had no intention of trusting such delicate information to the telephone.

It didn't take long. Half an hour later, I was sent for again.

'The Acting Commissioner said that you're to go ahead and interview Mr Halstead, Mr Brock.' The commander was clearly put out by the whole business. 'But he said that you're to tread carefully. Mr Leonard thinks it most unlikely that Mr Halstead was involved in this latest murder. And that's my view too.'

'As it is mine, sir,' I said.

Back in my own office, I telephoned Halstead's private secretary.

'The Minister will see you at four o'clock this afternoon, Chief Inspector,' he said.

Just time to summon one of his army of solicitors, I thought.

Twelve

It was a pleasantly warm day and I decided that Dave and I would walk to the Home Office from Curtis Green, whether Dave liked the idea or not. We went down King Charles Street and cut across the corner of St James's Park – as ever, full of milling tourists and dirty pigeons – and up Cockpit Steps to Queen Anne's Gate.

There was some sort of demonstration outside the Home Office. Half a dozen scruffily clad men and women, holding banners aloft demanding justice for Fred King, whoever he may have been, were standing silently to one side of the entrance. A solitary policeman leaned against the wall and looked bored.

'Seen any of them before, Dave?' I asked.

Dave searched the faces of the demonstrators afresh. 'No, guv. Should I know them?'

'Thought you might have seen them at your tailors,' I said.

Dave muttered something inaudible, and doubtless insubordinate.

One of the few remaining advantages of holding a police warrant card these days is that one does not have to go through the performance of filling in a Home Office pass, waiting for telephone calls to be made and an escort to be provided.

As I'd anticipated, Geoffrey Halstead's solicitor was indeed closeted with him when we were ushered into the Minister's office. The lawyer was a thin, balding individual of about fifty, wearing an expensive suit, gold-rimmed spectacles and a scowl. Sitting at a side table, he had a legal pad already open in front of him. To one side of this pad was a thick file, tied with pink ribbon, which I couldn't imagine had anything to do with my interview. Such theatricals were, I assumed, intended to intimidate me.

Halstead needn't have bothered. I'd already convinced myself that he would have had nothing to do with the death of Michael Cozens, but I was duty-bound to make the usual inquiries, particularly as I had a theory about Michael Cozens. This time, however, I would have to rely on the Minister's unspoken reaction to my questions; the solicitor would make damned sure he didn't say anything incriminating.

'Does the name Michael Cozens mean anything to you, sir?' I asked.

Halstead was sitting sideways on to his desk, his legs crossed. 'Nothing at all, Chief Inspector.' His reply was immediate, bland, and delivered with a sardonic smile. The solicitor took out a gold pen and wrote down both question and answer. So did Dave. 'Why do you ask?'

'His body was found in the river at Chiswick early this morning. It would appear that he had been murdered.'

'Really? How unfortunate. Are you suggesting that I may have had something to do with it?'

The solicitor looked up, a frown on his face. 'Geoffrey!' he said, a cautionary note in his voice.

'Well, I had to ask,' said Halstead. 'Last time Mr Brock called on me he more or less accused me of murdering this Monica Purvis woman.'

'I'm not suggesting that you had anything to do with it at all, sir,' I said soothingly, 'but a copy of *Hansard* was found in his car.'

'Perhaps he was a political lobbyist,' said Halstead, smiling. 'If he wasn't he must have been hard up for reading material.'

'I understand that he was an accountant, of sorts. He had a previous conviction for fraud.'

The solicitor emitted a dry cough and then spoke, the light from the large, picture windows glinting on his spectacles as he turned to face me. 'May I ask what the point of this is, Chief Inspector?'

'I merely wished to establish whether Mr Halstead knew the deceased man,' I said. 'You see, he had been intimate with Monica Purvis. My information is that Cozens and his common-law wife, one Sylvia Moorhouse – who, incidentally used to work at Heathrow with Monica Purvis – were on friendly terms with the dead woman and her husband Charlie Purvis. Given that Cozens was a petty criminal and that he had also had sexual relations with Monica Purvis' – I couldn't resist rubbing that in – 'it crossed my mind that he may have been the person who was blackmailing the Minister.'

That obviously came as a shock to the solicitor. Taking off his glasses, he turned to Halstead. 'Blackmail?' he said, an alarmed tone in his voice. 'What's this about blackmail, Geoffrey? You never mentioned anything about blackmail to me.'

Halstead dismissed his lawyer's question with a deprecating wave of the hand. 'It's not important,' he said, 'and it's all over now, anyway. I'll tell you about it later.'

So Halstead hadn't told his legal adviser about being black-mailed. Interesting. I chuckled at that. Inwardly. And anyway it wasn't all over: Halstead had received at least one demand after the death of Monica Purvis. But if he now received another that would destroy my theory.

The Minister faced me once again. 'If I'd known this man *and* if I'd known he was the blackmailer, Chief Inspector, I'd've informed the Commissioner, naturally,' he said smoothly.

'Naturally, sir,' I said. 'I suppose he wasn't a constituent of yours, was he, this Cozens?'

'I don't know all my constituents personally, Mr Brock,' said Halstead sarcastically. 'Where did he live?'

'Bromley.'

'Then the answer's no. Incidentally, you say that this man's body was discovered this morning . . .'

'That's correct,' I said. 'But the pathologist is of the view that he went into the river on Monday evening, probably at about ten o'clock.'

A broad smile crossed Halstead's face. 'The precise time at which I was going through the division lobby, Mr Brock,' he said. 'I'm sorry about that.'

'You don't have to justify yourself, Geoffrey,' said the

solicitor, annoyance at his client's flippancy only just controlled. I guessed he was piqued at not having been given the opportunity to snipe at me.

'I was merely saving the chief inspector the inconvenience of having to come and see me again,' said Halstead. I got the impression that he was treating the whole business as a joke. I suppose now that Monica Purvis was dead, he thought his troubles were over.

'Thank you, sir,' I said, as Dave and I rose to our feet. 'I'll not need to bother you further.' I made a point of ignoring the solicitor.

The demonstrators were still outside the Home Office. Presumably believing that I was someone important, one of them thrust a photocopied leaflet at me. I handed it to the PC who was still leaning against the wall. 'Give it to Special Branch,' I said, 'they collect things like that.'

'Well, that was a blow-out,' said Dave when we arrived back at Curtis Green.

'I knew it would be,' I said, 'but I don't think Halstead's entirely off the hook.'

'D'you fancy him for Monica Purvis's murder, then?' Dave seemed genuinely surprised that I should still be regarding Halstead as a suspect. 'I thought you'd more or less written him off.'

'Not a bit of it, Dave. Look at the facts. First of all he was in a rush to establish an alibi for the time when Cozens was pushed into the river, an alibi I didn't ask for. Why should he do that? And secondly, on his own admission, he'd had it off with Monica on at least seven occasions: once at a hotel at the airport and six times at three other hotels. And he was being blackmailed. What better motive is there than that? Which reminds me, I must have a word with Mr Mead about those hotels. See what luck he's had with the staff.'

'But Halstead's an MP . . . and a minister,' said Dave.

Oh, the naivety of youth. 'MPs have been sent to prison before, Dave,' I said.

'Yeah, I suppose so.' Dave lit another cigarette.

'There's no suppose about it, Dave,' I said, and listed the few I knew of.

'But someone as well known as Halstead wouldn't have risked attacking Monica Purvis in her pad in Soho, surely. After all, his picture's in the papers quite often. Anyone might have recognised him.'

'Politicians have been known to do stupid things, Dave. In fact, they're more prone to stupidity than most other people. It's the job, I suppose: it makes them arrogant.'

As if drawn by some sixth sense, DI Frank Mead appeared in the office. 'A word, guv'nor?'

'I was just coming to see you about the hotels that Halstead and Monica Purvis used, Frank. Any joy?'

Mead sat down and opened a Book 40, the book used in the Metropolitan Police for just about anything. 'I've been to the three hotels that Halstead gave you and they check out. I've got the dates here if you're interested, but the couple booked in under the name of Mr and Mrs Purvis—' He broke off to glance up, his face twisting into a grin. 'And, as Halstead said, Monica settled the bill on each occasion using her credit card.'

'Anyone on the staff who might have put the squeeze on Halstead, Frank?' I asked. 'It's a long shot, I know.'

Mead shrugged. 'They're all chain hotels, guv, and the staff changes are so rapid that it's almost impossible to check. Well, you know how it is.' I nodded in agreement. 'Short of going through hundreds of staff records, which wouldn't actually prove anything, I think we're on a loser.'

I had to agree with him there. If Halstead's blackmailer had worked at any one of the hotels he'd used, including the one at Heathrow, there would be very little chance of discovering him now. But it may be something that we would have to do if all else failed. Something else nagged me too: given that a lot of foreign labour was employed in such places, the blackmailer could, by now, have returned to his – or even her – own country. Which led me to think that with the international drawing facilities called Maestro and Cirrus there would have been nothing to stop our extortionist getting money out of a cash machine almost anywhere in the world.

Frank gave me another of his wry grins. 'There was something else though, Harry. One of the floor waiters I spoke to at the hotel they used in Chelmsford took a bottle of champagne up to the room occupied by Halstead and Monica, knocked and barged in without waiting for an answer. He said there was a girl kneeling on the bed wearing nothing but fishnet stockings and an air hostess's hat. The man he knew as Mr Purvis went into a towering rage and shouted at him to "get the hell out of here".'

'Well, well,' I said with a laugh, 'what a naughty minister.'

'I wondered if he might have something to do with the blackmail,' Frank continued, 'but after we'd had a chat it was obvious that to him they were just another couple. He had no reason to suspect that they were not Mr and Mrs Purvis. And when he told me about some of the bizarre goings-on he *had* witnessed over the years, a girl in just fishnet stockings and an air hostess's hat pales into insignificance.'

'If you're satisfied, then so am I, Frank,' I said.

'I think Halstead probably was, Harry,' said Frank with a chuckle. 'Oh, and by the way, I've followed up the account details you got from Halstead – the one into which he paid the money, by posting a cheque incidentally – and they relate to a high-street bank in Kilburn. I had to get a judge's warrant before the manager would discuss it, but the account was opened some six months ago.'

'What name was it opened in, Frank?'

'A woman called Mary Woods. Address in Kilburn. I'm told that she would have had to produce evidence of identity, a passport usually, to open the account, but the manager can't remember anything about her, nor can his staff. I called at the address they had for her – it was a house with about ten bedsits – but no one there remembered anyone named Mary Woods. It's a shifting population up there, and the chances are that she was there for only for a few days, if at all.'

'Wonderful,' I said. 'Were the cheques made payable to this Mary Woods?'

'Yes, they were.'

'Funny that Halstead never mentioned the name,' I mused. 'I think he knows more than he's telling.'

'The bank records show that the account was opened with a grand in cash,' Mead continued. 'The only other deposits were those made by Halstead and they amounted to ten thousand pounds. All the money has now been withdrawn, save for a monkey, by using cash machines, each one of which was in a different part of London, on different days of the week and at different times of the day.'

Well, at least that ruled out my theory about the money being drawn from abroad. 'And if she draws out the five hundred quid that's left, she'll probably do it from yet another machine,' I said gloomily.

'I reckon so.' Mead closed his book with a gesture of finality.

'Any way in which we can put a stop on that withdrawal, Frank?'

'Only with a great deal of difficulty,' said Mead, tapping his teeth with his ballpoint pen. 'I put it to the manager and he said that it's her money and they can't freeze the account without a court order.'

I guessed that would be the answer. 'What about the background inquiries on Monica, Frank, and more particularly have we been able to track down her next of kin yet?' I'd been concerned that there was nothing to indicate the existence of relatives in any of the woman's possessions and Sylvia Moorhouse and Charlie Purvis claimed not to know of any. Consequently we had been unable to inform her family, assuming there was one, of her death. However, the publicity surrounding the murder should have brought forth some response, I'd've thought. 'Any results?'

'I lumbered young Appleby with those inquiries,' said Frank. 'D'you want to see him?'

'Yes, send him in.'

Detective Constable John Appleby entered the office armed with a bulging document wallet, the sort that takes loose papers. He was still so new to the Department that he was desperate to please. His tie was done up to the neck and he wore a jacket, and his black leather shoes were actually clean and polished. I hoped it would never change, but it probably would. I wondered if any of his sartorial enthusiasm would rub off on Dave.

'Sit down, John, and tell me what you know.'

'Monica Purvis, sir.' Appleby flicked open the wallet. 'Aged twenty-seven, a daughter of the late Lionel and Alexandra Jackson, aged sixty and fifty-three respectively when they died. She has one brother, Peter, aged thirty.'

'So much for the paperwork at the General Register Office,' I said. 'What's next? You say her parents are dead?'

'They were killed in a car accident on the M1 while travelling north to see their son and his family, sir.'

'When did this happen?'

'Nine months ago, sir.'

'And the son?'

'Peter Jackson lives in Edinburgh, sir. He's an architect and runs his own practice up there. He's married to' – Appleby glanced down at his papers – 'Sonia, née McDonald, and they have two children who are called—'

'Yeah, fine, John.' I held up a hand. 'How long have we known of the existence of the brother? What d'you say his name was?'

'Peter Jackson, sir. Only found out yesterday morning.'

'And has he been informed of Monica's death?'

'Sergeant Wilberforce sent a message to the Lothian and Borders Police straightaway, sir.'

'Good. Any response?'

'Of a sort, sir,' said Appleby, still perching on the edge of his chair. 'They could get no reply apparently. Inquiries of the neighbours suggest that they're on holiday. The local police say they'll keep trying.'

'I should hope so,' I said. 'Ask Sergeant Wilberforce to keep on at Lothian and Borders and let me know the minute he's got a positive reply. Anything else?'

'Yes, sir. I've been making some inquiries about Mrs Purvis's background. She was born in Cheltenham and went to a boarding convent school in Berkshire. I saw the mother superior there and she said that Monica was a very bright girl. They had high hopes that she would go to university apparently.'

'Yes, I heard that from Sylvia Moorhouse,' I said.

'Anyway, she decided against it and left school at the age of eighteen. She was always keen to get into the airline business, so the mother superior said. The last she heard of her, Monica that is, she was working for a small airline at—'

'Heathrow,' I put in.

'No, sir. Gatwick.'

'Oh? That I didn't know. How long was she there?'

'Only a month or two, sir. Then she left and went to Heathrow. The story is that she got to know one of the bosses of the airline she went to work for and . . .' Appleby paused. 'Well, sir, rumour is that she got the job in exchange for sexual favours.'

'Why am I not surprised?' I mused. 'What have you found out about her late parents, John, anything?'

Appleby opened his document wallet again and fingered out a single sheet of paper. 'Lionel Jackson was a property developer, sir, but was retired at the time of his death. He and Mrs Jackson lived in a large house just outside Chorleywood in Hertfordshire. The estate agent who dealt with the sale told me that it had six bedrooms and a bathroom to go with each of them. There was a stable block and a swimming pool, too.' Appleby looked envious. 'It was sold for, I think he said, one and a half million.'

'So how much did the Jacksons leave when they died, any idea?'

'Not yet, sir, I'm still working on that. The papers have yet to be filed with the probate registry and so far I've not been able to track down the family solicitor. The estate agent couldn't find his record of who dealt with the conveyancing, but perhaps Peter Jackson will be able to help. When we get hold of him.'

'Well done, John,' I said. 'Keep me posted.'

Appleby smiled as he stood up. 'Yes, sir,' he said.

I was impressed by the young detective's thoroughness. He had obviously gone to a great deal of trouble to discover as much as he could about Monica Purvis's background. I made a mental note to find out where he stood in the promotion stakes; men like him have to be encouraged.

But what Appleby had told me made me wonder what the respectable, convent-educated daughter of a man who was probably worth several million pounds was doing resorting to prostitution. If she was a nymphomaniac there were easier ways to satisfy her lust than hanging about in Shepherd Market. And how on earth did she get mixed up with a jailbird like Purvis? Despite his claim that he and Monica were estranged, I did contemplate that he might have been her ponce. Not that it's the sort of thing he would have admitted. And if he had driven her on to the streets, what hold had he over her that made resistance impossible, or at best unwise?

Thirteen

Nine days had elapsed since the murder of Monica Purvis, and three days since that of Michael Cozens. But I was no nearer finding the killer of either than I had been then. Certainly a lot of background information had been collected about Monica, but it didn't really help. All I had was a hunch that the same murderer was responsible for both deaths.

I stirred my coffee and blagged one of Dave's cigarettes.

'What's on for today, guv?' he asked.

'I think we ought to have another go at Charlie Purvis,' I said. 'I'm sure that little bugger knows more than he's telling.'

'But you said that we hadn't got enough to hold him on.'

'Did you ever see *The Blue Lamp*, Dave?' I asked.

'Seen hundreds of 'em, guv. Every nick's got one outside.'

It was a typical Dave Poole smart remark. 'I'm talking about the film, you dimbo,' I said.

'Oh, that. Yeah, seen it half a dozen times, I should think.'

'Well, in that case you may remember that the villain, played by Dirk Bogarde, gave himself up at Paddington nick because the Old Bill were looking for him. But the CID threw him out and that made him even cockier than he was to start with. But he slipped up eventually. At least, I think that's how the story went.'

Dave adopted one of his infinite-patience expressions. 'What's that got to do with Charlie Purvis, guv?' he asked.

'It may just be, Dave, that if we talk to him often enough, he'll get cocky because he'll think we're floundering.'

'Well, we are, aren't we?'

I finished my coffee and walked through to the incident room, almost colliding with Colin Wilberforce on his way out.

'Ah, I was coming to see you, sir.' Wilberforce always wore the earnest expression that one would have expected to find on the face of a bank clerk. 'Peter Jackson telephoned about ten minutes ago. Lothian and Borders Police got hold of him late last night, just as he and his family arrived back from Spain. He's flying down this morning to see you.' He flourished a scrap of paper. 'Arrives at Heathrow at eleven fifteen.'

I glanced at my watch: it was half past nine. 'Get a car out there to pick him up, Colin,' I said, 'and bring him straight here.'

Perhaps now, I thought, I would start to get to the bottom of why Monica Purvis, daughter of a rich property developer, should have turned to prostitution.

It was almost lunch time when Peter Jackson was shown into my office. He was thirty years of age – Appleby had told me that – and was tall, clearly fit, and suntanned, probably as a result of his holiday in Spain.

'Mr Jackson, I'm Detective Chief Inspector Brock,' I said, shaking hands. 'Would you like a cup of coffee?'

'Thank you, that would be very welcome.'

I put my head round the door and shouted for two coffees. 'Do take a seat,' I said, turning back.

Jackson sat down in the one armchair that my office boasted and looked around, gazing briefly at the piles of paper, the charts and the group photograph of the course I'd attended at the Detective Training School years ago. 'I rather thought that you'd be at Scotland Yard,' he said, obviously unimpressed by the cramped accommodation that chief inspectors were allotted.

'Believe it or not, we've actually got more room here,' I said, sitting down behind my desk. After a suitable pause, I added, somewhat diffidently, 'May I offer my condolences on the death of your sister.'

'Thank you. Can you tell me exactly what happened? I must say it was a terrible shock when we arrived home last night to find a policeman waiting for us with the awful news.'

As fully as possible I told Jackson all that we knew, but I omitted the more gruesome features of her death; such gory details would serve only to distress him further.

Jackson remained silent for a while, during which time a DC appeared and placed two cups of coffee on my desk.

'I just don't understand it,' said Monica's brother eventually. 'A prostitute, you say?' He was obviously having a struggle coming to terms with the sordid circumstances of his sister's death.

'Yes, there's no doubt about that, I'm afraid. I've interviewed several women who solicited in the Soho area and who knew her and worked alongside her, so to speak.' I chose not to mention that she had been arrested on several occasions.

He shook his head in apparent disbelief and stared at the floor. 'I blame her husband,' he said suddenly. 'A bad influence if ever there was.' Looking up, he asked, 'Have you met him?'

'Yes, I have. I've interviewed him.'

'He'd been in prison, you know,' he went on. 'Yes, of course, you *would* know, wouldn't you. I thought she was still working at the airport.'

'She was sacked from that job eighteen months ago, Mr Jackson. Bad timekeeping, apparently.'

Jackson forced a smile. 'Monica was never a very good timekeeper,' he said. He leaned forward to take his coffee from the edge of the desk. 'It was her marriage that finished her as far as my father was concerned.'

'Oh?'

'When they were engaged, she took Purvis out to Chorleywood to meet our parents. I have to say that they were . . .' Jackson paused, searching for the right word. 'Unimpressed. The man was clearly a good-for-nothing. What she saw in him I'll never know.'

Exactly the words that Sylvia Moorhouse had used about Charlie Purvis. 'You met him, then?'

'Oh yes, I met him.' Jackson almost spat the words, making no attempt to disguise his loathing for the man. 'Monica used to get some sort of concessional flights and she brought him up to Edinburgh. Just the once. I think she wanted my blessing.'

'And?'

'I tried to be friendly with the man for Monica's sake, but I'm afraid we didn't hit it off. He had no manners, none of the common courtesies. Eventually I took her to one side and told her that if she married that oaf she would be making a dreadful mistake. And it looks as though I was proved right.' For a moment or two Jackson stared at the highly polished toecap of his shoe before glancing up again. 'Father cut her out of his will, you know.'

'No, I didn't know. As a matter of fact, one of my officers has been trying to obtain details of your parents' wills, to see if they bore any relevance to my investigation.'

'I can tell you about the wills. My parents were killed in a car accident, on their way up to see us. It was very upsetting for the whole family. My family, I mean. The children had been so looking forward to seeing their grandparents, but it ended in tragedy. The kids could never understand why they didn't arrive. We've had our fair share of policemen knocking at our door, Mr Brock, I can tell you.'

'I can believe that,' I said, 'but you were going to tell me about the will.'

'Yes, of course. My parents had each made the standard type of will. You probably know the sort of thing: if they died within twenty-eight days of each other, the rest of the legatees would benefit immediately. In the event that left just me, more or less. There were small bequests for my wife and the children, an annuity for their housekeeper and moderate amounts to one or two of my parents' favourite charities. Oh, and there was a trust fund set up to cater for the children's education. But when all that was wrapped up, I inherited some eight million pounds.'

'And your sister got nothing?'

'Exactly so. And I felt disinclined to make her a gift after the way she had upset our parents. She never kept in touch with them or me, you know. Not a Christmas card, not a birthday card. She didn't even send the kids a present and she was their only aunt. Hers was a very selfish attitude. But I put the blame entirely on Purvis; he seemed to have some hold over her. She was never like that before she met him, had always been a sweet and rather innocent girl. I just don't know what happened.' Jackson stared beyond me and out of the window. 'Looking back now, I suppose I should have made some effort, then perhaps this tragedy wouldn't have happened. But I could never get over the fact that she still remained faithful to Purvis even after he was sent to prison. He got involved in some robbery – about three years ago, I believe – and we thought, my parents and me, that she would divorce him then. But no, she traipsed up and down to Parkhurst prison to visit him.'

That was yet another interesting contradiction. Purvis had said that she never once paid him a visit while he was inside. But he'd also said that he knew nothing of Monica's family. In the circumstances, I didn't find that surprising. 'If you don't mind my asking, Mr Jackson, was Monica a Catholic?'

'Yes, the whole family is. As a matter of fact, Monica went to a convent school in Berkshire. Why, is that relevant?'

'I don't know, but policemen have this habit of collecting snippets of information. Sometimes they come in useful, you know. Incidentally, did your father ever tell Monica that she'd been disinherited?'

Jackson gave a grim smile. 'Oh yes, there was nothing deceitful about my old man. He'd made his money by good, vigorous trading. Always told the truth and never pulled any punches. Yes, he sent for Monica, on her own, not long after she'd taken Purvis to see them and told her straight that if she married him, she'd get nothing.'

'What was her reaction?'

'One of contempt, according to my father. She told him that she couldn't care less. Said something about money being his god and that there were other things in life. Odd that, because my father never worshipped money. He made a lot of it but he knew how to enjoy it. And he was generous, too. Not surprisingly, he was very upset at her attitude. More upset than I'd ever seen him before. He was doing it for the best, at least what he saw as the best. I think he was trying to save her from a disastrous marriage, but it didn't do any good. Mind you, I think he'd've relented and restored her to his will if she'd got shot of Purvis, but I think Purvis was still in prison when my parents were killed. The old man thought that if he left Monica anything, Purvis would spend it all. And he was probably right.'

I didn't bother to tell Jackson that Purvis was already out

by then, but I was learning more about Monica's character by the minute, not that it was likely to help. 'Was she at your parents' funeral?'

'No, she couldn't bloody well be bothered to turn up. Said something about being on duty. But you say that she was no longer working for the airline by then.'

'That's correct. It was, what, nine months ago that your parents died?'

'Yes, in October last year, on the M1. Apparently it was pouring with rain and the visibility was poor. My father's eyesight was not very good anyway, but he was always pig-headed about it. Said that he could see perfectly well. I told them that they should fly up and I'd've picked them up from Edinburgh Airport. But he had a love affair with that damned Bentley of his and insisted on driving it everywhere, no matter how far it was.'

'Do you happen to know whether Monica had any friends, Mr Jackson? Close friends, I mean.'

Jackson slowly shook his head. 'None that I can think of,' he said. 'To be honest I had very little to do with her in recent years. I suppose she was friendly with some of the girls she was at school with. Such friendships tend to endure, in my experience, but I can't give you any names.'

'Are you going to be in London long?'

'A day or two. I've got some business to attend to while I'm here.'

'Perhaps you'd let me know where you're staying, just in case there's anything I need to ask you.'

'Of course. I don't know where I'm putting up yet, but I'll ring you and let you know.' Jackson eased the cloth of his well-cut trousers gently over his knee and looked thoughtful. Then he raised his head. 'What about Monica's funeral, Mr Brock? I suppose I'll have to make the arrangements for that. I can't imagine that Purvis is interested.'

'Probably not, Mr Jackson. When I saw him, he described himself as estranged from Monica.'

Jackson scoffed. 'Too bloody late,' he said.

'We have to wait for the coroner to release the body, but I'll have a word with his officer and see if I can speed things up.'

119

Jackson stood up and shook hands. 'I'm most grateful to you, Mr Brock,' he said. 'I hope you catch this bastard.'

'We're doing our best, Mr Jackson.' But as I said it I had a nasty suspicion that on this occasion our best was not going to be good enough.

I had assigned DI Frank Mead a number of 'actions'. The most pressing was to attempt to discover the true identity of Mary Woods – I was convinced that the name the woman had used to open the bank account in Kilburn was false – and secondly to find her. But I held out no great hope of success, even though Mead was a tenacious and thorough officer.

There was, however, one job that I would have to do myself and that was to interview the mother superior at Monica Purvis's convent school.

Young John Appleby had already seen her, and although he was a conscientious detective, he hadn't yet the experience – nor, for that matter, the knowledge of the case – that would have enabled him to ask questions that were particularly pertinent to the murder.

I told Dave to make an appointment. He was back within minutes. 'She can't see us until after five o'clock this evening,' he said.

'How far is it?'

'About seventy miles, sir. It's somewhere beyond Hungerford.'

'Good, well, you can drive,' I said.

We left at three o'clock and fought our way out of London in the rush hour. There used to be two rush hours, one in the morning and one in the evening. But now there's only one and it lasts all day. I suppose the government would regard that as an improvement.

We arrived at the convent school at five thirty.

The mother superior was, inevitably, Irish. A large rosy-faced lady with twinkling eyes, she shook hands with a firm grip and led us into her study.

Closing the door, she rubbed her hands together. 'I daresay you wouldn't be averse to a wee drink, Chief Inspector,' she said.

'Thank you, but not for the sergeant, he's driving,' I said. Dave was not pleased. He'd obviously thought that I was going to drive the return journey.

Opening a cupboard, the mother superior took out a bottle of Bushmills Irish whiskey and poured two substantial tots. She took hers neat, but placed a water carafe next to mine on the edge of her desk nearest to me. It was, I thought, an unspoken criticism of the English.

'Well now, what can I do for you?' she asked, having fortified herself with a large sip.

'One of my officers came to see you about Monica Jackson,' I began.

'So he did, so he did,' said the mother superior. 'A fine young man.'

'But I'd like to learn a little more about Monica than he was in a position to ask.'

'Fire away, then.'

I knew that Appleby had mentioned only that Monica had been murdered. I now told the mother superior the details of Monica's death and as much about it as I had gleaned so far.

'Holy Mary, Mother of God!' said the nun, putting a hand to her bosom. 'The sins of the flesh.' She took another mouthful of whiskey. 'A prostitute, you say?'

'I'm afraid so.'

'She was a lovely girl, a bit of a hoyden, mind, but only in an innocent sort of way. At first, anyway. And her parents were delightful people; very true to the faith.' She levelled a gaze at me, but was too polite to enquire if I was a Catholic. 'Mr Jackson gave very generously to our little school. It enabled us to buy quite a lot of sports equipment for the girls.'

'Did my officer tell you that Mr and Mrs Jackson were dead?'

'Glory be, no.'

'Yes, they were killed in a car accident, last October.'

'What a tragedy. Our God works in mysterious ways, Mr Brock. But they'll be in heaven now, of that I'm sure. Perhaps it was that that turned her to her sinful ways.'

Outside in the corridor, there was a brief outburst of girlish laughter, followed by a more mature voice calling for silence. The mother superior frowned.

'No. I'm afraid she'd descended into prostitution before then,' I said, and explained about her marriage to Charlie Purvis.

'Was he a Roman Catholic?' asked the mother superior. It seemed important that she should know.

'I'm afraid I don't know the answer to that,' I said. 'My feeling is that he would have been an atheist. They were married in a register office.'

'Oh, the poor child. Such a marriage wouldn't have been recognised by the Church, you know.' In the nun's eyes there was only one church and to wed in a register office undoubtedly a sin.

'What sort of girl was she, when she was here?'

The mother superior moved her glass of whiskey to one side of her desk and opened a slim file. 'I got her records out before you arrived,' she said. She donned a pair of spectacles that had been suspended from her neck on a black cord. 'Now let me see. Yes, she did very well in her examinations. Three A-levels and a whole clutch of Os.' Dropping her spectacles, she glanced up. 'A very bright girl, brighter than the average. I had high hopes of securing her a place at one of the better universities, but she didn't want to go. Said she was tired of studying and wanted to get out into the world.' She shook her head, apparently at such youthful impetuosity. 'I tried everything. I spoke to her parents, but they had no greater success than me. Such a waste. She was determined to get a job in the airline business. It didn't seem a very promising future.' The nun took another sip of whiskey and smiled, her eyes twinkling yet again. 'And, no, Mr Brock, I'm not going to say that if the Good Lord had meant us to fly, He'd have given us wings. I think flying's wonderful. I've been to Disneyland in Florida, you know.'

'Have you indeed?' I realised, yet again, how deceptive appearances can be, and how dangerous it is to judge people by them.

The mother superior suddenly adopted a serious expression. 'I don't know whether this is important,' she began, clearly doubting if her information would be of value, 'but I recall one of the sisters reporting to me that she had seen Monica one afternoon, after school, in the town with a boy. They had come out of one of those awful fast-food places with their arms around each other. Well, that sort of behaviour is quite unacceptable and I had a few words with her.'

'I don't suppose you know who this young man was, by any chance.'

'No, she wouldn't tell me. I gathered from the sister that he was from a local school, but Monica refused to give me his name. I confined her for a week, but she wouldn't budge. I suppose it was some sort of youthful loyalty. She probably knew that I'd have a word with the boy's headmaster and that that would get the lad into trouble. It's the television, you know, Mr Brock. It gives these young people all the wrong ideas. There seem to be no moral standards any more. No honesty in relationships. No one cares about the important things in life. It's all materialism now.' She leaned forward and picked up the bottle of Bushmills. 'You'll take another?' she asked, waggling it in my direction. And then, as if to encourage me, added, 'I'm going to have one.'

'Thank you. Just a small one.'

The mother superior poured another two fingers of whiskey into my glass; perhaps she thought that *was* a small one.

'But that, I'm afraid, wasn't the end of the matter. We have inspections every so often, to ensure that the girls are keeping themselves clean and tidy. The dormitory sister found a packet of contraceptive pills in Monica's locker.'

'How old was she at the time?' I asked.

'Seventeen, Mr Brock. I know that that's over the age of consent, but contraception is a mortal sin in the eyes of the Holy Roman Church.'

'Did she offer an explanation?' I asked. Personally I thought that there could be only one explanation: she was having it off with someone, possibly the boy she'd been caught with.

'She refused to answer any questions about it. Said it was none of my business. I was shocked, not at what she'd obviously been doing, but at the change in her attitude. She'd always been such a polite young lady up until then.

I had no alternative but to get in touch with her parents and ask for her to be removed from the school. She went on her eighteenth birthday.'

'So she was expelled, then,' I said, half to myself.

'We prefer not to call it that, Mr Brock,' said the mother superior. 'She was withdrawn a few days before the end of the term in which she would have left anyway. But it made the point . . . to the other girls, I mean.'

Fourteen

There are, on average, about 160 murders a year in the Metropolitan Police District, an area of some 700 square miles of arguably one of the most crime-ridden cities in the world. And about ninety per cent of those murders are 'cleared up', as we say in the police business.

But I was beginning to get the depressing feeling that the murders of Monica Purvis and Michael Cozens were going to fall into the ten per cent category of unsolved. Not that we call them unsolved, of course. 'Inquiries are continuing' is the phrase. Scotland Yard never closes a murder inquiry. Not much. The actuality, however, is that the more days that elapse the less likelihood there is of charging someone with the crime.

In view of this disturbing but realistic thought, I decided that I was going to cheer myself up and, with any luck, cheer myself up with the assistance of Dr Sarah Dawson, rope expert and newly discovered balletomane.

'Have you solved it yet, Harry?' was her first question when I got through to her at the forensic science laboratory.

'No,' I said, 'and it's not looking promising.'

'Oh! So how can I help?'

'You can come out to dinner with me tonight.'

There was a lengthy pause at this non-professional request and I could visualise her trying to think up an excuse for not doing so. But eventually she said, 'OK. Where and when?'

Her agreement surprised me, caught me unawares. I hadn't given any thought to where I would take her. I stalled. 'Look, I'll pick you up at home, round about seven thirty. Is that all right?' I knew where she lived: it was a flat in Battersea; I'd taken her home the night that we went to the ballet with Dave, the night we met Madeleine.

'That's fine, but where are we going?'

'I haven't decided yet.'

'Well, it is important, Harry,' Sarah said. 'If you're taking me to McDonald's, I'll put on a pair of jeans, but if we're going somewhere upmarket, I'll put on a posh frock.' She chuckled, an infectious laugh that came right down the phone.

'Now would I take you to McDonald's?' I asked, injecting a plaintive note into my voice.

'It's possible,' she said. 'You forget that I know a lot about policemen.'

'Oh? Have you been out with policemen before, then?'

'Mind your own business,' came the tart reply.

'It'll be a West End restaurant. The one I have in mind does a very good whitebait,' I said hurriedly as my mind raced through my personal catalogue of decent places to eat. 'Do you, er, like whitebait?' I was making it up; right now I hadn't got a clue where we should go.

'I love all seafood,' said Sarah.

'That's good. The wine list there is impressive, too,' I said, still improvising.

'And not too expensive, I hope,' said Sarah.

'Oh, I'm paying,' I said gallantly.

'Of course you're paying,' she said. 'I'm not into this sex-equality business. I much prefer to remain superior.'

'I'm sure you'll like it,' I continued, mentally narrowing my list of options. 'The one I was thinking of has the most wonderful decor.'

'I'm delighted to hear it,' said Sarah patiently. 'Now, unless you have any more banalities to share with me, Harry, I've got a lot of work to do. See you at half past seven.' She replaced the receiver with a crash.

Sarah's agreement to join me for dinner gave me a feeling of well-being that, I was sure, would make the rest of the day seem bearable. The euphoria lasted all of thirty seconds.

'I think we've exhausted the Mary Woods search,' said DI Frank Mead, putting his head round my office door.

'Come in, Frank, and tell me the worst.'

'On a whim,' said Mead, dropping into the armchair with a sigh, 'I took photographs of Monica Purvis and Sylvia Moorhouse and showed them to the bank manager. He'd eventually tracked down the member of staff who dealt with the opening of the account. He was off sick the last time I called there, apparently.'

'And?'

'Zilch. This guy was quite adamant that he didn't recognise either of them. Mary Woods, he said, had long blonde hair. Admittedly Monica had blonde hair, but it wasn't long, and Sylvia Moorhouse we know has got auburn hair, and a right mess it usually looks. But, to be honest, I don't think this bloke would have recognised Mary Woods if I'd taken her there in person. Probably just trying to be helpful. Either that or he was terrified that he'd be called to the Bailey to give evidence. Pity it wasn't a female clerk really. They tend to notice much more about another woman than a man does. Unless he's thinking of bedding her and then he can usually only tell you about her legs and her bust size.'

'You're a cynic, Frank,' I said.

'Yeah,' said Mead.

'I wonder if it's worth putting surveillance on Charlie Purvis,' I mused.

'You must be joking,' said Mead. 'As far as I can see there isn't a shred of evidence that puts him in the frame, and we do have a budget to think about. It'd take at least twenty officers, plus a couple of nondescript vehicles and a motorcyclist or two. I couldn't cover it from my resources and if you went to SO11, they'd show you the door. As for NCIS, they'd just laugh.'

I knew that to be true. SO11, the Criminal Intelligence Branch, had only enough men to keep obo on target criminals. Charlie Purvis certainly didn't fall into that category, and most certainly he wouldn't interest the National Criminal Intelligence Service.

'Isn't it amazing,' I said. 'You'd've thought that with all this modern computer gismo that anyone opening a bank account these days could have been traced just like that.' I flicked my fingers to emphasise my point and, incidentally, my frustration. Personally I had no faith in computers. And if I needed any confirmation of that, HOLMES still hadn't been fixed.

'That's half the trouble,' said Mead. 'In the old days only the rich had bank accounts. Nowadays everyone's got one.'

After a day of frustrating paper-shuffling and abortive telephone enquiries, I arrived at Sarah's flat at twenty-five to eight. She answered the door immediately.

'You look good enough to, er . . .' I smiled at her.

'Careful,' said Sarah sternly. Her idea of a 'posh frock' turned out to be an elegant plum-coloured trouser suit that emphasised the length of her legs. Beneath it she wore a cream blouse and at her neck a single white stone on a slender silver chain. Her long, black hair shone like polished ebony, but there was no sign of the heavy, horn-rimmed spectacles she wore at work. 'Nice suit, Harry.' She looked me up and down. 'Italian?'

'German. I get them made by a little *schneider* I know in the East End.'

'What's a *schneider*?' She appeared puzzled.

'It's German for tailor.'

'Oh!' She looked up and down the street disapprovingly. 'No car, Harry?'

'I thought we'd walk through to Battersea Bridge Road and get a cab.' I do enjoy a few glasses of wine with dinner, to say nothing of the occasional cognac, and to get done for drunken driving is, these days, regarded by the police as a sacking job.

'Have you decided where we're going?' she asked as we strolled through to the main thoroughfare.

'There's a delightful little bistro in Chelsea,' I said. It was one of those intimate restaurants of the sort that suddenly appear in Chelsea, last for perhaps a year and then disappear as quickly as they came.

'Is this the one with the good whitebait?' Sarah saw a cab before I did and promptly hailed it.

'No, they were fully booked,' I lied. To be honest, I wouldn't have the faintest idea where to go in London for good whitebait.

The waiter, if one could dignify him with such a title – he was wearing a T-shirt and jeans – was about eighteen and probably a student augmenting his grant. Nevertheless, he was attentive and eager to please.

We spent the first ten minutes studying the menu and choosing what to eat. Having established that Sarah had no particular preference about the colour of the wine she drank, I ordered half a bottle of Chablis to kick off with and, to follow, a bottle of the house red on the basis that a poor house wine reflects badly on the restaurateur, at least that was the theory; I've had bad house wines in the past but I am ever the optimist.

'Why are you and your wife estranged?' Sarah paused in the act of lifting a forkful of warm stilton and walnut tart, fixing me with her deep brown eyes.

I was learning, very quickly, just how direct this woman could be. But I suppose she had a right to know about the state of my marriage; she did not strike me as someone who was willing to be a married man's plaything.

'I'm afraid we've drifted apart,' I said. Even to me it sounded lame. 'We don't get on any more. I suppose it's the job to a very large extent. Being a CID officer puts a terrible strain on a marriage.'

'Have you any children?'

'No.'

'Don't you like children?' She dabbed gently at her lips with her table napkin and gazed searchingly at me.

I did like children, very much, and my brother Geoff's two children regarded me as their favourite uncle, but as I was their only uncle that was no surprise. 'Yes, of course I do, but . . .'

'But?' Sarah, obviously intent on getting all the details, adopted a quizzical expression.

I capitulated. 'We had a little boy, Robert, but he drowned.'

'God, how awful.' Her face registered shock and she placed a hand on mine, briefly, but was too polite to probe, imagining, I suppose, that it would distress me.

But I told her nevertheless. 'Helga left him with a friend while she went to work. He was playing in the garden and fell in the pond.'

'Poor woman.'

I wasn't sure whether she meant Helga or the friend; not unnaturally the friend had been as distressed as Helga. Perhaps even more so; I was never quite sure.

'It was ten years ago,' I said. I shall never forget that day. I was a detective sergeant at an inner London station when it happened. The detective superintendent appeared in the doorway of the CID office and crooked a finger. 'A word, Harry,' he said. I thought I was in for a bollocking: I'd carried out a risky search the day before, risky because I should have had a warrant. But the guv'nor took me into his office and broke the news. Then he told me to go home and stay there for as long as necessary.

'What does Helga do?' asked Sarah.

'She's a physiotherapist. At the local hospital.'

'And where is "local", Harry? I've no idea where you live.'

'Wimbledon.'

'Helga's a nice name,' she said, trying to lighten the conversation.

'It's German,' I said. 'So's she. I had to go to hospital for a course of physiotherapy – she was at Westminster then – and that's how we met. We got chatting and I took her to a police dance that evening. A week later, she invited me to the hospital dance. Young coppers living in section houses tended to flock to such dos.' I forced a grin. 'Lots of pretty nurses just waiting to be bedded.'

I'd gone a little too far with that comment and Sarah frowned, but fortunately there was a pause in the conversation while the waiter brought her roast guinea fowl stuffed with wild mushrooms.

She stared at my plate. 'Fillet steak,' she said, shaking her head disapprovingly. 'Why is it that men are always so lacking in imagination when it comes to food? I suppose it results from grabbing a sandwich at your desk. You should take a leaf out of the Frenchman's book: two hours for lunch, no matter what.'

'I happen to like fillet steak,' I said defensively. 'And I'm not that keen on sandwiches.'

Sarah shrugged dismissively. 'So, are you getting divorced?'

The tragedy of Robert's death was clearly not going to get in the way of her finding out exactly where my marriage stood.

'I suppose so. The rift started even before the boy drowned. We were always arguing about her leaving him with other people while she went to work.' I put down my knife and fork. 'I suppose I'm old-fashioned, but I take the view that a mother should either look after her children or pursue a career. Not both.'

'I'm afraid you're bucking the trend there, Harry,' Sarah said, 'but there seems little point in remaining in an empty marriage.'

I felt like saying that it was none of her business, but her readiness to accept my offer to go to the ballet a week ago and now to dinner entitled her to a measure of frankness on my part.

'I think it will come to that,' I said. 'But what about you?' For a moment or two, I studied her. I imagined that she was a shade over thirty – but not by very much – and perhaps had hopes for her own future. 'Do you intend to get married one day?'

'One day perhaps,' she said, and then opened up a little. 'I was engaged once.' She looked vaguely into the distance, a wistful expression on her face. 'He was an army officer.'

'But it foundered?'

'In a manner of speaking,' she said. 'He was killed.'

'I'm sorry. Where, Bosnia?'

Sarah half smiled, a grim little humourless smile. 'No, he was killed on some damned silly exercise on Salisbury Plain.' And pre-empting my next question, she added, 'Two years ago.'

'God, that's awful.' Now it was my turn to place a hand on hers. 'We seem to have had more than our fair share of tragedy.' I was accustomed to violent death – it was my trade – but an accidental death of that nature was somehow more tragic than the murders that I dealt with, and I spoke from experience. 'Are you over it?'

'Yes, just about. But I think that having loved someone, and I did love him, a little of me died with him. I don't think that

131

will ever change.' She looked at her half-eaten meal and put her knife and fork together on her plate.

Our little waiter was there in an instant. 'Is there something wrong with your meal?' he asked.

'No,' said Sarah, affording him a smile. 'I'm just not very hungry.'

'How about a pudding, then?' I asked.

'No, thanks, just coffee if I may.'

There was a short conversation between Sarah and the waiter about which particular type of coffee she wanted, and I asked her if she would like a brandy or a liqueur.

She shook her head. 'Just coffee will be fine.'

I forwent a pudding and ordered a cognac to go with my espresso.

'I'm sorry, Sarah,' I said, realising that I had probably ruined her evening by raising a subject that evoked such unhappy memories, particularly after talking about little Robert.

'It's all right,' said Sarah. 'I really am over it. It's just that once in a while it comes flooding back.' She smiled. 'And the thoughts of what might have been.' She paused and then, 'I suppose you haven't got a cigarette, Harry, have you?'

I produced a packet of Marlboro and offered her one. 'I didn't think you smoked.'

'I don't usually,' she said, 'but I just fancy one now.'

Our ever attentive waiter was at her side immediately, thumbing a lighter. I was sufficiently sceptical to think that he was working hard for a tip. But I'm a pretty sour judge of character; when the bill came it included service.

Sarah accepted a second cup of coffee. 'I've enjoyed this evening, Harry,' she said. 'Thank you. And thank you for not talking shop. It makes a refreshing change to go out with a policeman who doesn't.' She stubbed out her half-smoked cigarette.

'I thought you said you hadn't been out with any policemen,' I said.

She launched a playful kick at me beneath the table. 'What I actually said was "Mind your own business".' And she laughed her infectious laugh again.

Having made such a mess of things with my probing, I felt I

owed Sarah the truth. 'Despite what I said earlier, I am actually seeing a solicitor as soon as I can,' I said. 'To start the divorce going. Helga and I have agreed to make the split permanent. In fact, she's already going out with a doctor from the hospital where she works.'

Sarah laughed. 'And you're going out with a doctor from the Forensic Science Service,' she said. 'I hope the divorce works out amicably.'

'It will. We're both being civilised about it.'

'And when did you decide to see a solicitor?' she asked. 'About ten minutes ago?'

I laughed but didn't reply, only because Sarah had got it absolutely right. She was becoming very good at seeing through me. We'd chatted throughout our meal and by the end of it I'd come to the conclusion that she would probably make a better detective than me. She had probed and questioned until she had explored most of my life, with Helga and before our marriage, and going back to my childhood and my education, such as it was, at a grammar school in Croydon. But I had managed to get little more in exchange than I could have found in her curriculum vitae.

I could only suppose that the poignant stress she had suffered from losing her beloved army officer – I didn't discover his name – had caused her to develop a shield, a carapace designed to protect her from any emotional involvement.

We walked the short walk down to Kings Road and I managed to find a taxi, no mean feat in Chelsea late on a Friday evening.

The cab delivered us to her Battersea flat and she fumbled for her keys as I followed her up to the first floor. Policemen are more aware than most of the prevalence of crime in London, despite what the Commissioner tells the Home Secretary in his annual report.

'Oh, hell!' she said as she reached the door.

I was a pace or two behind her. 'What's the matter?'

'It's been forced open.'

I took hold of her shoulders and moved her to one side so that I could examine the door. It had been jemmied,

133

and none too carefully. The woodwork around the lock had splintered and a large piece of the door-frame was hanging loose.

'Is there another way out of your flat, Sarah?' I whispered. 'A fire escape, anything like that?'

'No. This is the only way in and out.'

I put a finger to my lips and, taking her hand, led her back down to the street.

'Where are we going?' she asked, when we reached the pavement outside the building.

'Nowhere,' I said, taking my mobile phone from my pocket and pressing the SOS key to summon the cavalry. 'But if anyone's still in there, I want him captured, and I'm too old to go running after a villain on the streets of Battersea after a good meal, a bottle of wine and a large brandy.'

As I had instructed, the fast-response car approached silently, which must have upset the two macho PCs who made up its crew.

The driver got out, paused and then reached back into the car for his cap. 'What have we got, sir?' he asked, sauntering across the pavement.

'Break-in.'

'Much taken was there?' Friday night burglaries were routine for the police at Battersea.

'I don't know yet, son,' I said. 'But you and your mate are coming in with me, just in case our light-fingered friend's still inside.'

'Right.' The driver beckoned to his operator who joined us with obvious reluctance.

But the burglar had long gone.

The sitting room was small and essentially feminine in a chintzy sort of way. There were two armchairs with embroidered cushions on either side of a coffee table and half a dozen teddy bears seated primly on the top shelf of a low bookcase. I don't know why I should have been surprised at this revealing side of Sarah's character; inexplicably I'd expected that her flat would be like the laboratory in which she worked: organised and sterile.

It was difficult to tell now, of course. The bastard who'd

turned the place over, and who had probably watched us leave before breaking in, had made a mess of it. Out of pure malice he'd scored a deep scratch across the polished surface of the coffee table, probably with the tool he'd used to force the front door.

The bedroom was a shambles. The drawers in the dressing table and a chest had all been pulled out and left open – sign of a professional – and Sarah's underwear had been hurled about the room. One of her black bras was draped over the dressing-table mirror, and I gazed at it for longer than was necessary. The wardrobe was wide open and its contents had been dumped on the floor.

'Did you have any jewellery?' I asked.

Sarah gave a wry smile. 'Only what I'm wearing,' she said, holding up her arm to display her wristwatch and then touching the silver neck chain.

We returned to the sitting room. 'The television's gone,' she said, 'and he's taken the hi-fi.' There was a brittle businesslike air about her as she began picking up her collection of CDs, now spread across the floor. 'He obviously didn't like classical stuff,' she added.

'Don't touch anything,' I said, somewhat belatedly. It seemed odd having to explain the basic principles of crime-scene preservation to someone who worked in a forensic science laboratory. I turned to one of the PCs. 'Get on that thing' – I gestured at his personal radio – 'and get a scenes-of-crime officer up here, now.'

'But the CID have to decide if it's sufficiently serious for an investigation of that sort, sir.' The PC was only rehearsing Force instructions regarding the grading of crime. 'I mean, is it a major crime?'

'*I'm* a CID officer,' I said sharply, 'and I've just decided it is. This lady is Dr Sarah Dawson from the lab. She works for us and if we can't take care of our own, things really have got bad.'

The PC realised that he was on dangerous ground and there was no further argument.

It was then that Sarah saw the photograph. It was lying face down on the floor. Tenderly she picked it up. Broken glass fell from the frame as she turned it over. It was of an army officer. Slowly she replaced it on the bookcase between the teddy bears who had failed to guard it.

There were tears in her eyes as she turned to face me; the wanton damage to the image of a young man in army uniform had finally stripped away the carefully maintained façade of self-assurance to reveal a young woman who had suffered the traumatic shock of having her dearest possessions violated.

It was typical of the scum who break into other people's property that a photograph of an army officer represented all that they despised and, deep down, feared. 'Was that him?' I asked.

'Yes,' said Sarah softly, 'that was Captain Peter Hunt.' And then, as if seeking something constructive to do, 'Can I make everyone some coffee?' she asked, a little too brightly.

'Good idea,' I said and turned to the fast-response car's driver. 'Get hold of someone to secure these premises and hang on until it's done, will you. Dr Dawson won't be staying here tonight,' I added, putting an instant decision into words.

'Yes, sir.' The driver closed his incident report book and returned it to his pocket before making another call to the station on his PR. I sensed that he was none too happy at being lumbered with waiting for a carpenter. But it was one way of ensuring that the said carpenter would arrive pretty damned quick.

'Is there someone you can stay with tonight, Sarah?' I was loath to leave her alone in her present state, but I couldn't very well offer to take her home to Wimbledon. So far Helga and I had pretended not to be involved with anyone else, even though we both knew it wasn't true. And yes, I know we're estranged, but on a chief inspector's pay you can't afford to set up a second home, although I know I shall have to eventually. But let's not rush things.

'I've got a sister who lives in Raynes Park,' she said.

'Give her a ring.' I pointed at the telephone.

At two in the morning, after the SOCOs had been and gone, I delivered Sarah to her married sister's house, and gave her a chaste kiss on the cheek, just as I would have done my mother.

I walked for twenty minutes before finding another cab to take me on to Wimbledon. Helga wasn't there; I suppose her doctor-friend was on a promise.

Fifteen

Having had a bare four hours sleep, I was not in the best of moods the following morning. I made it my first job to ring Battersea nick and speak to the DI about the break-in at Sarah's flat. He had nothing to tell me yet, but promised to keep me posted. Muttering something about duty rosters and the overtime budget he reminded me that it was Saturday and that they were short-staffed. It must be hell out there.

I rang Sarah – fortunately, I'd made a note of her sister's telephone number. She said that she was quite all right and intended to return to her flat and spend the day tidying up.

Despite the fact that most ordinary people regarded today as a day off, I still had two murders to solve. Consequently I'd ordered a full team to be on duty and to hell with the overtime bill. It was always a mystery to me how those senior officers, who pontificated from their comfortable offices high in Scotland Yard, imagined that it was possible to budget for a murder you didn't know was going to happen. But do we ever?

I walked through to the incident room. There was an 'anorak' from Computer Branch in the corner trying to breathe life into the dormant HOLMES, but I resisted the temptation to tell him to take the bloody thing away. Calling him out on a Saturday must be costing the job an arm and a leg.

'I have decided to have Charlie Purvis in and give him a bit of a going-over, Dave,' I said. 'See if we can't get something out of him.'

'You're not looking too good this morning, guv'nor,' said Dave, ignoring my suggestion. 'Heavy night?'

'In a manner of speaking,' I said, and told him about the burglary at Sarah's flat.

Having let loose his stock string of profanities, he said: 'I suppose it's nothing to do with this job, is it? Could it be that someone's trying to put the frighteners on? Someone who knew that you were friendly with Sarah?'

I must admit that such a motive for last night's events had not occurred to me. 'How the hell could they know?' I asked. 'We're the ones who've been putting ourselves about, you and me, not Sarah.'

'Just a thought, guv,' said Dave.

'I doubt it,' I said, but determined that if that were the case, I'd crucify the bastard when I found him, or in the unlikely event that Battersea CID found him. 'Anyway, right now, we'll pay another visit to Purvis.'

I didn't really know what I was going to say to the guy when we got to Hilldrop Crescent, but I needed to have something positive to do. The business of Sarah's burglary was still playing on my mind and despite having the resources of the whole of the Metropolitan Police behind me, I was powerless to do anything about it. It wasn't my investigation: I just had to wait for the CID at Battersea to pull their fingers out.

But the day was to prove even more frustrating. When we arrived at Camden Town, Ephraim Murphy, the jovial black landlord, told us that Charlie Purvis had left the previous day.

'Any idea where he went?' I asked. It was a forlorn hope. Men like Charlie Purvis don't leave forwarding addresses.

Murphy spread his hands and rolled his eyes. 'No, sir. He just said he was moving on.'

'What did he take with him?'

'Just a holdall and his TV. He never had much when he came.'

'Tell me, Ephraim,' Dave put in, adopting his friendly mode, 'was Purvis ever visited by a woman while he was here?'

Murphy gave that some thought. 'No, sir, never. Not to my knowledge.'

'And did he ever spend nights away from here?'

'Yes, a few times. He said he was working.'

'Working at what?' Dave persisted. 'Did he say?'

Murphy shook his head. 'No, he didn't. He never said very much at all.'

'So what do we do now, guv?' Dave asked, when we were on our way back to central London.

'Is it a coincidence that Purvis does a runner after Mr Mead enquires at the bank about Mary Woods,' I mused, 'and on the same evening Sarah's flat gets turned over?'

Dave swore and twisted the steering wheel violently to avoid a suicidal cyclist emerging, without looking, from a side turning. 'You definitely fancy him for Monica's murder, don't you, guv?'

'Yes, I do,' I said. 'I'm not happy about the fact that he said he spent the night of the murder in bed with Sylvia, but that she says she was at home with the late Michael Cozens watching the box. Not that we can now ask the said Cozens,' I added gloomily.

'It could be the old dilemma,' said Dave.

'Which is?'

'That he was doing a different sort of screwing some place else, but couldn't prop that as an alibi because he knows you'd nick him for it.'

That, of course, was a strong possibility. Purvis was a villain and there was a good chance that he had been about some nefarious business – like burglary – on the night that Monica was killed. I laughed. 'We'll make a detective of you yet, Dave.'

'And what *about* the Cozens topping, guv? D'you reckon that's down to Purvis as well?'

'I reckon whoever topped Monica, also topped Cozens,' I said. 'We know that Cozens was having it off with Monica, and Purvis reckons he was at it with Sylvia, even though she denies it. But on that score I don't believe her. All right, he might not have been giving Sylvia a seeing-to the night of the Monica murder, but he was no stranger to her bed. I'll put money on that. You see, Dave, that little foursome were all closely associated and it's too much of a coincidence to think that someone unconnected with the death of Monica Purvis just happened along and killed Cozens, don't you think?'

'Unless Cozens was into something that had nothing to do with Monica,' said Dave, 'like drugs. Suppliers get a bit upset if their users don't pay their bills.'

140

'That's possible,' I said, 'but he didn't look like a user.'

'True,' said Dave. Detectives can usually tell, just by looking, if someone is on drugs.

'By the way, Dave, when we get back to the office, see if you can find out where Cozens was working. Might be fruitful to have a word with his boss. Sylvia reckoned it was an engineering firm somewhere out Chiswick way. Try the DSS for a start. They should have a record.'

'Right,' said Dave, somewhat tersely. 'And Geoffrey Halstead's still in the frame, is he?' he added.

'Yes, indeed he is,' I said. I was not too happy with the Minister of State at the Home Office. Even for a politician he was just a bit too confident for my liking.

On our return to Curtis Green, I did the only thing possible in the circumstances: I put Charlie Purvis's name on the police national computer as someone I wished urgently to interview.

And I didn't have long to wait. But the outcome wasn't what I'd expected.

Although the particular section of the DSS that held records of employment didn't work on a Saturday, Dave was a resourceful officer. Having spent twenty minutes on the telephone, he came up with Michael Cozens' last known place of work. It was, as Sylvia had said, in Chiswick. Dave telephoned the firm and found that, far from being an engineering company, it was a shop. And it was open today.

It was tucked away in a back street and appeared to sell second-hand pine furniture. There were no customers and only two members of staff. One was a spotty-faced youth lounging against a wardrobe.

The other, the manager – at least, that's what he said he was – glanced sceptically at my warrant card and then invited us into what passed for an office. Little more than a cupboard, it contained a badly scarred wooden desk, covered in a confusion of paper and files, and an ancient swivel chair. A filing cabinet stood in the corner but, judging by the stack of files on top of it and on the floor next to it, appeared not to be used for their storage.

'Yeah, Michael Cozens. What about him?' The manager leaned against the wall and folded his arms. He was about fifty and had a thin pencil moustache and fold-over hair that was greased flat to his head. I suspected that, on his days off, he was the sort of man who wore a clip-on bow tie and a blazer with a badge on it.

'I understand that he worked here.'

'S'right.'

'You know he's dead, I take it?'

'Yeah, read about it in the paper. Fell in the river, didn't he?'

'He was pushed in,' I said. 'Murdered.'

'That a fact?' The manager raised his eyebrows a millimetre or two. 'It happens,' he said philosophically. 'So what d'you want from me?'

'He went into the river on the twenty-ninth of July, around ten o'clock at night. So, when did you last see him?'

The manager turned to a desk diary and flicked back the pages. 'Friday the twenty-sixth,' he said. 'That's when I sacked him.'

'Why?'

'Why what?'

I don't know if he was being deliberately obstructive, or whether he was just plain thick. 'Why did you sack him?' I asked.

'Had his hand in the till, didn't he. Thieving little git. I took him on in good faith and—'

'When?'

The manager consulted the diary once more. 'The fifteenth,' he said, looking up again.

That was interesting. When we called at Bromley the first time, Sylvia Moorhouse had told us that Cozens was out looking for work, but according to this guy, he was already in employment. Furthermore he'd lied about his work: this most definitely was not an engineering firm, and that was where Sylvia had said he worked. 'You're sure about that, are you?'

'Yeah.'

'And when did you find out about the money going missing?'

'Almost immediately. He never turned up after lunch on a couple of days and I began to get a bit suspicious. When you've been in this trade for a while you don't take anything for granted. He was supposed to be a bookkeeper and part-time salesman, so I had a squint at the books. Didn't take long to find out he'd had a hundred out of the petty cash. And the entries in the books didn't tally with the takings. I'm pretty hot on doing my own checks.'

And if anyone was going to cream off the takings it would be the manager, I thought, not the hired help. 'Did he say anything when you challenged him?'

The manager laughed. 'Yeah, first of all he said it was an oversight. Then he changed his mind and reckoned he'd borrowed it and was going to put it back. Personally, I reckon it went on the horses. Well, if it happened once, it was likely to happen again, so I gave him the elbow.'

'Can you remember the dates he didn't turn up here after lunch?' asked Dave, pocketbook at the ready.

Again the diary was consulted. 'Afternoons of the twenty-second and twenty-fourth,' said the manager. 'I always make a note of these things. You have to be careful these days what with industrial tribunals and all that bollocks. So I wrote down I'd given him a written warning.'

'And did you?' I asked, more out of devilment than anything else. Frankly, I couldn't have cared less.

The manager smirked. 'Yeah, course,' he said, secure in the knowledge that if Cozens had not been the recipient of such a warning he was no longer in a position to argue.

'Those two dates were the dates of Monica Purvis's murder and the day that we interviewed him at Bromley nick, guv,' said Dave quietly.

'Very interesting,' I said.

'*That* murder?' The manager's interest was at last aroused.

'Yes,' I said. 'Cozens knew the murdered woman. He'd also been in prison for fraud.'

'I bloody knew it,' said the manager. 'You can always tell.' But then he denied his professed foresight by adding, 'I wish I'd known that when I took him on.'

'Did you get the money back?' asked Dave.

143

'No chance. Like I said, I reckon it went on the gee-gees.'

'Why didn't you inform the police?' I asked, but I knew why: the first thing that they would have done was to examine the books, and the manager wouldn't have liked that one little bit.

'Waste of bloody time,' he said, hurriedly adding, 'No offence, like. What I mean is that it would've meant going to court, losing a day's work at least. Well, all that'd add up to a sight more than a hundred quid. Just not worth the hassle, see?'

I did see. Until the courts get around to calling witnesses without causing them to hang about for days on end, all manner of villains like the late Michael Cozens were going to get away with their crimes.

'Did he ever mention a wife or a girlfriend while he was here?' I asked.

The manager appeared to give that question some thought. 'Nah!' he said eventually, 'not as I recall. Why, d'you reckon he done this girl in?'

I shrugged. 'Right now,' I said, 'your guess is as good as mine.'

The manager looked surprised at such an admission, but I've always worked on the principle that the police should give the impression of being a bit slow on the uptake. It often paid dividends.

'You said you thought he was spending money on the horses,' said Dave. 'D'you know that for certain?'

'Not really,' said the manager. 'Just a guess. It's what thieves usually spend money on, isn't it? Like they owe a bookie and can't pay, so they nick it from their employer.'

And that, I imagined, was about as much as we were going to get out of Cozens' former boss. My own guess was that Cozens had spent his money on prostitutes and that was why he hadn't told Sylvia Moorhouse that he'd got a job. If that was the case, either she didn't know that Cozens had got a job when first we interviewed her or, for some reason, had withheld that information. And the reason for that may well prove to be interesting.

It was now four o'clock on a day that had been totally

unproductive. 'I've had enough, Dave. Let's go and have a drink,' I said, when we got back to Curtis Green and Dave had parked the car.

'There's not a decent pub that won't be full of tourists mixing with the natives in search of the real London,' said Dave gloomily. There were times when he displayed a profound philosophical streak.

'Come with me,' I said.

We left Curtis Green by the back entrance, cut through Whitehall Place, across Northumberland Avenue and into that maze of streets that lie to the south of the Strand. I rang a bell high on a door alongside an unoccupied shop.

'What's this place?' asked Dave.

'A drinking club,' I said, as we were admitted by a racy-looking fellow who was on his way out. We made our way up a rickety staircase to the first floor.

'Bloody hell! Is it legal?' asked Dave, holding tight to the banister rail.

'Probably not,' I said, 'but right now I don't care.'

The woman who ran the club was called Bridie and catered for those she called her 'special' gentlemen friends; no women were allowed. Nevertheless, friend or not, anyone who misbehaved or proved unable to hold his drink was barred. For life. But curiously Bridie did not object to foul language and could probably have outdone any sergeant-major's profane vocabulary.

She was a big-bosomed, jolly woman in her late sixties. Her hennaed hair was rolled under in a style that was pure 1940s and she invariably wore a low-cut, red velvet dress that revealed most of her freckled breasts.

'Should we be in here, guv?' asked Dave, looking around nervously. 'I mean there are regulations about going into clubs and that . . .'

'You're with me, Dave,' I said. 'If we're raided, I'll take the blame.'

It was a tawdry room much in need of redecoration; the flock wallpaper was peeling in places and the bar counter, originally varnished a rich mahogany, was now scratched and stained with the rings of many glasses, and burned by

145

abandoned cigarettes. The curtains, a heavy brown velour, were permanently drawn and the only illumination came from a couple of brass wall-lights. In the corner on a wrought-iron stand was a cage containing a mynah bird whose language was among the fruitiest I had heard, most of it, I suspect, learned from Bridie, despite her cut-glass accent.

'Harry, darling, lovely to see you.' Bridie leaned over the bar – revealing even more of her copious bosom – gripped me firmly by the shoulders and planted a kiss on my cheek. She glanced at Dave. 'And you've brought a little friend. How nice. Well, introduce me.'

'This is Dave Poole,' I said.

'Lovely,' said Bridie. 'Any friend of Harry's is a friend of mine.' As she had done with me, she seized Dave's upper arms and kissed him. 'Such muscles,' she murmured dreamily. 'Now then, what's it to be?'

'Two large Scotches, Bridie, if you please, and your usual tipple for yourself.'

She turned to the row of optics, dispensed whisky and then poured a port and lemon for herself. 'How are you getting on, darling?' she asked, sliding a jug of water across the bar. She slipped a menthol cigarette into a holder and waited while Dave produced his lighter. 'Have you caught him yet?' Bridie was well versed in the criminal scene.

'Not yet, Bridie. We're still working on it.'

She signalled to me to go to the end of the bar, out of earshot of the other customers. 'There was a gent in here the other day, Harry,' she whispered, 'who let on that he knew that little slut Monica Purvis.' Bridie had no high opinion of prostitutes.

'What was he saying?'

'Reckoned he'd slept with her on a regular basis. And he was bragging about it, telling some chap what they'd got up to, bondage and all that sort of thing. Disgusting! I threw him out, pronto, and told him not to bother to come back. I'm not having that sort of filthy talk in my club and that's that.'

'What was his name, Bridie?'

'Jack Castle. He's about fifty, I should think. Something to do with the travel industry. He mentioned being in business not far from here. Other side of the Strand, I think he said.'

'Thanks, Bridie.'

Dave was obviously impressed and when Bridie had turned to deal with another customer, said, 'What d'you reckon, guv?'

'Bridie's come up with one or two good snippets in the past, Dave. She's always worth listening to.'

'So what do we do now?'

'Nothing, Dave. That is to say we have another drink and, as tomorrow's Sunday, I think we'll take the day off. Monday morning will be time enough to get on with this damned inquiry.'

Sixteen

I was in the office by half past eight on the Monday morning, feeling guilty at having taken Sunday off.

'We're getting nowhere with this bloody inquiry, Dave,' I said for about the hundredth time since we'd been called to the scene of Monica's murder. Despite my suspicions, I was no nearer discovering the murderer – or murderers – of the prostitute and Michael Cozens. I was convinced it had to be down to Charlie Purvis. But where was he? And how was I to prove it when I did find him?

The next telephone call solved the first and negated the need for the second.

Dave grabbed at the phone as it rang for the second time. 'DS Poole.' He looked up. 'For you, guv. Line two.'

'Mr Brock? It's DS Gilham, Flying Squad, guv.'

That boded ill: phone calls from the Squad always bode ill. 'Yes?' I said cautiously.

'This Charlie Purvis finger, guv. I understand you want him nicking.'

'What about him?'

'We've got him holed up in a drum in Finchley.'

'Excellent,' I said. 'I want a word with him.'

'So do we, guv,' said Gilham, 'but it's not as easy as that.'

'Oh?'

'Well, it's like this, guv. A couple days ago, we had a whisper from a reliable snout that a little team were going to do a betting shop up that way, so we set a trap. Unfortunately we sprung it a bit too soon and Purvis did a runner.' There was a pause. 'He's tooled up and he's, er, holding a hostage in a house nearby.'

'Congratulations, Skip,' I said sarcastically. I always derive a little sadistic pleasure from a Flying Squad cock-up. 'How d'you know it's Purvis?'

'We captured another one of the team and he, well, he like was sort of persuaded to give up Charlie Purvis's name.'

'I see.' I didn't enquire too deeply as to how the Squad had managed to persuade one of Purvis's co-conspirators to surrender his mate, but I knew the Heavy Mob of old. When I was on the Squad, I was always alarmed at the gung-ho approach of some of its officers. But I thought that had all changed in the new, sterile Metropolitan Police. Silly me! 'So what happens now?'

'Well, right now we've got a team of SO19 surrounding the drum . . .'

There is only one thing that frightens me more than the Flying Squad and that's members of the Tactical Firearms Group – known to us in the trade as SO19 – standing around in their flameproof overalls and striking aggressive poses while aiming at non-existent targets.

'There's a negotiator on his way from Hendon,' Gilham added helpfully. 'So it's wait and see now. I'll keep in touch, guv.'

'Don't bother,' I said. 'I'm coming up. What's the exact address?'

Gilham gave me the details. 'You can't miss it, guv,' he said. 'There's blue lights everywhere.'

Rather than relying on Dave's driving, I decided that the circumstances warranted calling on Traffic Division. I rang Command and Control, pulled rank and got what I wanted.

Sooner than I had expected, a PC, wearing the white-topped cap of a traffic officer, appeared in my office. 'Mr Brock?'

'That's me.'

'Understand you want a lift to Finchley, sir.'

'Yes. We've got a siege running up there.'

'Yeah, I heard it on the air.' The PC stifled a yawn. 'I'll be in the yard when you're ready, guv,' he added and ambled slowly out of the office as though too weary to stand for long. It did not look hopeful.

But I was surprised yet again to discover that apparently lifeless policemen undergo a rapid change when seated behind

149

the wheel of a high-powered police car. Minutes later, Dave and I were speeding towards Finchley on 'blues and twos'.

With consummate skill, our advanced-class driver threw the car around as he weaved through the heavy traffic without once endangering other road-users. In between whistling snatches of unrecognisable songs, he kept up an amusing dialogue with his partner, heavily larded with expletives, on the inadequacies of other drivers. He passed street refuges on the wrong side, cautiously negotiated red traffic lights, skirted round lumbering buses and once expertly avoided a fire engine crossing his path on an emergency call of its own: an incident that brought forth a few terse comments about the Fire Brigade's standard of roadcraft.

The house where Purvis was holding his hostage was in a street off Ballards Lane, a street that had now been sealed off by police. Blue and white tapes snaked across each end of the road and a formidable group of armed officers covered the old Victorian dwelling. An officious inspector, Heckler & Koch at the ready, appeared to be in charge of them.

'Don't know why he didn't go down the Underground, guv. We'd never have caught him then,' said the DI who was in charge of the Flying Squad team that had begun their day by staking out the betting shop. 'He must have run straight past Finchley Central station.'

A CID chief inspector from the detective training school at Hendon introduced himself as Jim Reed, a hostage negotiator. Out of range of the revolver Purvis was believed to have in his possession, he was leaning against a police car with his hands in his pockets.

'So what's the score, Jim?' I asked.

'Purvis is holed up in the front bedroom on the first floor, Harry.' He pointed up at a window. 'We established telephone contact and he made the usual demands.' He indicated a cellular telephone on the roof of the car.

'Which were?' I thought I knew what they were and Reed promptly confirmed them.

'Car and driver to take him to the airport and a flight to Spain.' Reed laughed. 'Saucy bastard.'

'Don't see the point of that,' I said. 'Doesn't he know that we've now got an extradition treaty with the Spanish?'

'No, he doesn't. He asked about it and I told him that we hadn't.'

'How dishonest,' I murmured. 'And the hostage?'

'A housewife in her early thirties.' Reed sighed. 'Couldn't have been a heavyweight wrestler who'd've beaten him to a pulp, could it?'

'Where's the woman's husband?'

'Been sent for,' said Reed. 'Works in the City. He's an accountant, someone said.'

'What's the plan, then?'

'The usual. Try to talk him out. I explained the error of his ways to him. Told him that there's no escape and that he might as well give himself up because we'll have him in the end.'

'What was his reaction?'

'A mouthful of abuse and said he wasn't going to talk to us again unless we met his demands. Then he ripped the phone out of its socket and chucked it out of the window.'

'And now?'

'And now we play a waiting game,' said Reed. 'He'll come back to us again when he gets hungry. That's when we start trading.' He fiddled with the handkerchief in his top pocket.

'What about these guys?' I gestured at the firearms officers still standing about in textbook poses.

'That's just to let Purvis know we mean business.' Reed lowered his voice. 'I just hope we don't have to use them for an assault on the place. They make me nervous.'

'Me too,' I agreed.

There was a sudden commotion at the end of the road. A man was shouting and waving his arms at one of the policemen, and gesturing towards the house. Eventually he was allowed through the cordon.

'Who's this?' asked Reed of the policeman who had accompanied the man.

'Mr Barker, sir. He's the woman's husband.'

Reed shook hands with Barker and briefly explained the situation. Then he called the firearms inspector over and the two of them questioned the hostage's husband about the layout of his house and possible ways that Purvis may use in an attempt to escape. What they actually wanted to know was how armed police could get in, but wisely Reed didn't give Barker the impression that they may have to storm the place if all else failed.

Kevin Barker did not look much like the popular conception of an accountant even though he was dressed in a smart suit, collar and tie. In his thirties with short, blond hair, he was tall, muscular and clearly very fit. He looked as though he worked out at a gym and played squash regularly. Understandably, he was very concerned about his wife.

'What's going to happen?' he asked.

'We've contained the situation, Mr Barker, and our plan is to talk the man out,' said Reed, with greater confidence than I thought the situation warranted. 'In my experience, he'll quickly realise that to harm the hostage will only make matters worse. Criminals like him often get themselves into this sort of situation without thinking, you see. Once there, they're inclined to front it out rather than lose face. It's a big thing with villains, not losing face. But after a while they come to terms with the fact that there's only one place they're going to go, and that's the nearest police station. Our strategy is to sit and wait for that moment.'

It was just as well, I thought, that Barker didn't know I wanted to question Purvis about two murders and I hoped that Jim Reed wouldn't mention the villain's name; Barker looked as though he was bright enough to make the connection with the newspaper accounts of Monica Purvis's death.

'What's he done?' asked Barker, still staring towards his house.

'He was involved in an attempted robbery on a betting shop,' said Reed.

Barker cast a nervous glance at the armed policemen. 'So what are these guys for?'

'Just a precaution, sir,' said Reed. 'Purvis is armed, you see.'

'Jesus Christ!' Barker took a bunch of keys from his pocket and started to toy with them nervously.

'Is one of those a key to your back door by any chance?' I asked.

Barker gazed at the keys as if surprised to see them in his hand. 'Yes, as a matter of fact that one.' He separated a Chubb key from the rest. 'Why?'

'It may be that we have to effect an entry, Mr Barker,' said Reed, trying not to make it sound too melodramatic.

'What, with these guys?' Barker's voice rose in alarm as he waved towards the armed officers. 'Now look here, that's my wife up there and I don't want any trigger-happy coppers rushing in waving guns about. Someone might get hurt.'

Reed nodded slowly. 'I understand your concerns, sir,' he said, 'but we do know what we're doing.'

'Yeah, I've read about it,' said Barker savagely.

Personally, I thought he was right to be worried. There had been several incidents where police had mistakenly shot unarmed people and even occasions when innocent bystanders had been hurt. But this was not the time to tell Barker that in most cases the officers concerned had thought themselves to be justified in opening fire.

Reed wisely concluded that this was not the best place for Barker to be. 'Now, sir, I'd be obliged if you returned to the end of the road,' he said. 'This officer' – he indicated the PC who had brought Barker through the cordon – 'will take you back and get you a cup of tea from our mobile canteen. I'll keep you informed of any developments.'

'Thank you,' said Barker grudgingly.

But before he had gone a few feet, the next incident in the drama unfolded. The upstairs window was thrown open and Purvis appeared holding a young woman in front of him. Even at that distance it was obvious that the girl was petrified.

'I'm not hanging about any longer, coppers,' Purvis shouted. Suddenly he spotted me and that appeared to disconcert him for a moment. But he quickly recovered. 'I've told you bastards that I want a car to the airport and a flight out to Spain. If it's not here in half an hour she gets it.' He thrust the girl hard against the window sill so that, for a moment, I thought she might topple out.

'Please do as he asks,' screamed the terrified woman.

And then they disappeared from view and the window closed.

'What the hell are you going to do now?' demanded Barker, becoming more agitated by the second. 'Are you just going to let him kill her?' His arms were forced stiffly down by his sides, his fists opening and closing.

'Try not to worry, sir,' said Reed calmly. 'It's best that you move away. We won't let any harm come to your wife.'

I thought it was a somewhat pious hope, and by his sceptical expression it seemed that Barker did too. Nevertheless, he allowed himself to be escorted back to the cordon.

For the next fifteen minutes nothing happened but then the siege was brought to a dramatic conclusion.

With a crash of breaking glass and a splintering of woodwork, Purvis came flying out of the upstairs window to land with a sickening thud, head first, on top of an ageing Austin Metro – presumably Mrs Barker's runabout – before rolling off on to the paved front garden of the Barkers' house.

There was a sudden rattling of bolts as the firearms officers got jittery but then their inspector and a sergeant stepped forward to point their weapons menacingly at Purvis's inert body.

'Impressive, aren't they?' said Dave Poole, picking at his teeth with a pin.

There was a shout from upstairs in the house from which Purvis had just fallen and Mrs Barker appeared in the gap where the window had once been. Beside her, his arm around her shoulders, was Kevin Barker. Pushing the thumb of his free hand high into the air, he shouted down at the assembled police. 'All right then?'

'How the hell did he get in?' demanded Reed of the firearms inspector. 'I thought your people had the back covered.'

'We had, sir.' But from the inspector's grim expression it was clear that someone was in for a few very unpleasant minutes. I sensed that disciplinary sanctions were being considered. 'Incidentally, sir, Purvis is dead.'

'Oh, that's bloody marvellous,' I said. Both the Purvises were now dead and so was Michael Cozens.

'I suppose you'll be arresting Mr Barker, sir,' said the firearms inspector.

'Oh, shut up,' said Reed and I in unison.

The Flying Squad DI sniffed. 'Well, I suppose you could call it a result of sorts,' he said. 'Anyone for a beer?'

Dave and I fought our way through the massed bands of the media which, somewhat belatedly, had heard about the siege and rushed to the scene. There were television cameras everywhere fighting for supremacy with press photographers. A horse-faced frump declared loudly that she was from the BBC, as though that ought to afford her some precedence.

Ignoring questions, we found our traffic car and headed back to central London.

Apart from the fact that I would be unable to question him, I was not greatly concerned about the demise of Charlie Purvis. He was just one more villain that my colleagues and I would no longer have to pursue.

What worried me was that if Purvis really had killed his wife – and perhaps Cozens too – his death would make it very much more difficult to prove that those murders were down to him.

The one thing about which there was no doubt in my mind, given the do-gooders' great concern for villains, and their indifference towards victims – and the Barkers were the victims here – was that the erudite legal minds of the Crown Prosecution Service would give serious consideration to charging Kevin Barker with murder, or with the lesser offence of manslaughter. Provided, of course, that they had a more than evens chance of proving that Barker had thrown Purvis out of the window and that Monica's widowed husband hadn't just taken a dive.

But when Dave and I got back to the office there was a snippet of information waiting. It was the sort of straw that detectives like me clutch at.

'Mary Woods, Harry,' said Frank Mead, as he entered my office and kicked the door shut behind him.

'What about her?' I asked. 'Don't tell me she's dead as well.'

Mead grinned. 'No, but we've traced what may be the passport that was used to open the bank account at Kilburn.'

I sat up and took an interest. 'Go on.'

'I got in touch with my contact at the Passport Office, but without much hope. There must be thousands of Mary Woods in the country, but when I told him the story, he came up with an idea. He checked the list of passports reported lost or stolen.'

'And?' I felt in my pocket for a cigarette, forgetting I'd given up. 'Got any cigarettes, Frank?'

'I don't smoke,' said Mead smugly. 'Anyway, a Mary Woods had reported her passport lost. And,' he continued triumphantly, 'she said she thought she'd lost it at Heathrow Airport.'

'When?'

'Just over six months ago,' said Mead. 'In fact, one week before our Mary Woods opened the bank account into which the blackmail money was paid by Geoffrey Halstead.'

'Interesting,' I said. 'Interesting that Heathrow Airport seems to be playing such a large part in this inquiry. Our murder victim worked there and it's where she met Charlie Purvis when he was on some building works. And it was there that our revered Minister of State at the Home Office picked her up for the occasional screw. And it's where Sylvia Moorhouse works.'

'There's one other thing, Harry, while we're talking about Heathrow,' said Mead. 'I don't know whether it's connected, but I picked up a report from the CID out there. They've had information from a guy who used to work in the airline business. He thinks that someone at the airport is running a fiddle.'

'I've no doubt a lot of people are running fiddles out there, Frank,' I said. 'Not for nothing is it known as Thiefrow. Is there anything in it for us?'

'Apparently it's the same airline that Monica Purvis worked for and it's something to do with excess baggage. At least that's what the DS at Heathrow said.'

'Well, well.' I sat back and rubbed my hands together. Such seemingly unconnected bits of information had solved murders in the past, but I'd never been that lucky. 'D'you think this scam's anything to do with the one that's worrying the life out of Sid Marley?'

'Could be,' said Mead with a shrug, 'although from what you said that was straightforward embezzlement. I gather that this is a bit more sophisticated. Anyway I'm checking it out and I'll let you know when I've got a few more details.'

'Leave it to me, Frank,' I said. 'Could be relevant.'

Seventeen

Depressed, I glanced at the calendar on my desk and at the red ring I had put around the twenty-second of July: a fortnight ago Monica Purvis's body had been discovered in her flat at Talleyrand Street and since then Michael Cozens had been murdered and Charlie Purvis had died. And I was no nearer solving any of it.

'Dave, you remember going to Bridie's last Friday . . . ?'

'Yes, I do,' said Dave. 'Funny sort of set-up.'

'And d'you remember what Bridie said about a certain Jack Castle who claimed to have slept with Monica Purvis?'

Dave nodded. 'Yeah, I was wondering about him, guv.'

'I think we should go and have a chat.'

Jack Castle's travel agency was in a street on the north side of the Strand. It was a tiny shop and despite its central London location gave the impression of not doing a great amount of business. I wondered if Castle had got his fingers in some other pies . . . like smuggling or drugs. But then I have a very suspicious nature.

A young woman was stocking the racks with brochures, but stopped to afford us a bright smile when we entered. 'May I help you?' she asked.

'Is Mr Castle here?' I asked.

'In here, young man,' called a voice through the half-open door of an office at the rear of the shop.

Such flattery will get you nowhere, I thought, even though it's true.

Jack Castle was a florid-faced man – about fifty, as Bridie had said – and had the upswept moustache and general appearance that cartoonists mistakenly associate with 'colonial types' and army colonels.

158

'Mr Castle?'

'*Major* Castle, actually. How can I help?'

So I was right, or rather the cartoonists were. Well, nearly. 'Detective Chief Inspector Brock, Metropolitan Police,' I said, giving him a quick flash of my warrant card.

'Ah!' Castle looked distinctly unhappy at this revelation, reinforcing my suspicions that he had much to hide. 'What can I do for you, old boy?' He crossed the office and closed the door before inviting us to take a seat.

You can stop calling me 'old boy' for a start.

'I understand that you claimed to have slept with a prostitute called Monica Purvis,' I said.

'What on earth makes you think—?'

'Did you or didn't you, Major Castle? And before you answer, I should tell you that I'm conducting an investigation into her murder.'

'Oh Christ!' Castle ran a hand round his face and gave his moustache a nervous tug.

'Well?'

'Yes, as a matter of fact, I did. But I don't know anything about her death. I mean to say, having it off with a prossy is one thing, but doing her in, well, that's not on, old boy, is it?'

'When was this?'

'God, I don't know. About a month ago, I should think.'

'Tell me about it.'

Castle spread his hands. 'My girlfriend was in Egypt with a tour – she's a courier – and I was feeling a bit fruity, don't you know, so I wandered up to Shepherd Market. I just picked the best-looking one there. She took me to some awful room over an antiques shop and five minutes later it was all over. Hardly worth it, really, and it cost me a hundred quid.'

'Did she tell you her name?'

'Only that she was called Monica, but when I saw her picture in the paper – what, a fortnight ago? – I realised it was the same girl.'

'Didn't you think it might have been helpful to get in touch with the police?'

'I don't really see what I could have told you, old boy.

In the circumstances it's the sort of thing one keeps quiet about, what?'

'Really? Then why were you boasting about it in Bridie's Bar?'

'Who told you that? Bridie?'

'Of course not,' I said. 'Bridie's the soul of discretion.' Like hell she is! 'You should know that. But there are other people who regularly use the place, and several of them overheard you claiming that you slept with Monica Purvis regularly. You were also heard describing, in graphic detail, what the two of you got up to. That doesn't accord with your story that you went with her only the once. Or was that just bravado?' I was deliberately provoking Castle, just to see if he would react. But I suspected that he was the sort of windbag who, with a glass in his hand, would make preposterous claims of sexual prowess just to look good in front of his drinking chums. But I was wrong. 'I'll remind you again, Major Castle, that I'm investigating this woman's murder.' I toyed with the idea of cautioning him, but decided against it for the moment.

Castle collapsed like a deflated balloon. 'Yes, I was seeing her on a regular basis, Inspector.'

'*Chief* Inspector,' I murmured. If Castle was going to be rank-conscious, then so was I.

'Sorry. I suppose I saw her about once a month.'

'Just her, or were there other women?'

'No, just her.'

'How many times, in total?'

'Six or seven, I suppose.'

If he was being honest about what he paid Monica, his visits would have cost him six or seven hundred pounds. Looking around Castle's office, I didn't think that his business was making enough to sustain the cost of such luxuries. But I made a mental note to ask my brother Geoff: he's in the business. 'And what exactly were these things the two of you got up to, Major, that you were boasting about?'

Castle looked down at his desk, fiddled with a pen, and mumbled something inaudible.

'I'm sorry, I can't hear what you're saying.'

With a sigh of resignation, Castle stared straight at me, the bombast vanishing. 'She used to tie me up and whip me,' he said, and then looked down at the desk again.

And yet Sherry Higginbottom, the black tom I'd spoken to at West End Central police station, claimed that Monica 'didn't do whips', and would send men wanting such 'services' across to her. Against that, of course, we'd found a whip and two sets of handcuffs in Monica's room at Talleyrand Street. We also had the statement of Simister who claimed to have negotiated with Monica for similar 'services', but said that he couldn't afford the price she'd asked. However, prostitutes have been known to keep secrets from each other.

'What did she use to tie you up with?' Please say rope. If that was the answer, it was possible that I'd found the girl's killer.

'She didn't actually *tie* me up, she had a couple of pairs of handcuffs that she used. Kept them in a drawer. For her special customers, she said.'

Hell and damnation. So near and yet so far. 'Did she ever use rope, Major Castle?'

'Not on me, no.'

I glanced at Dave, record-of-interview book open on his knee, and a look of disappointment on his face. It was obvious that, like me, he'd thought we'd found our man. It was still possible we had, of course. Most of the murders I've investigated have started off with suspects ducking and diving in their attempts to outwit the dim policeman. But any copper will tell you that it's not a smart bit of evidence turning up at the last minute that solves murders, it's thorough investigation and tenacious questioning that eventually get to the truth. Oh, I forgot the perspiration and the luck, too. 'And the whip?'

'A nasty leather thing. Hurt like hell.' Castle gave an embarrassed half smile.

Even with my experience of investigating the depths of depravity, I am still amazed at the sort of sexual perversions that some men seem to find both pleasurable and gratifying. 'As a matter of interest, where were you during the evening of Monday the twenty-second of July?'

'Good God, I don't know, old boy,' exclaimed Castle. 'Hold on a moment.' He turned to a desk diary and flicked through its pages. After what was clearly an anguished pause he hesitantly admitted having been with a girlfriend.

'Back from Egypt by then, was she?' Dave asked.

'Er, no. Different girlfriend.' Castle was beginning to look decidedly uncomfortable, probably because he knew what would come next.

'Name and address?' Dave waited, pen poised over his book.

'Oh, I say, is that absolutely necessary? I mean she's married.'

'Name and address?'

For some reason I could never fathom, Dave always looked at his most menacing when his pen was hovering as he waited for an answer that was slow in coming.

Castle capitulated and gave us a name and address. 'But you will be discreet, won't you?'

'Perhaps you'd better give us her phone number, then we can speak to her right now.' Dave knew the dangers of collusion: given a moment to himself, Castle would probably have rung her to concoct an alibi.

Reluctantly, Castle furnished us with the woman's office phone number.

Dave stepped out into the street and rang the number on his mobile.

'Yes,' he said, returning to Castle's cramped office, 'she confirms that you were with her all evening and spent the night in bed with her at a hotel.' He paused. 'And I got the distinct impression that she's not at all happy with you for broadcasting what she called "private arrangements". As a matter of fact, I think she may be phoning you very shortly.'

'Well, for God's sake, what d'you expect?' said Castle, glancing nervously at the telephone as if it may explode at any minute.

'Never mind,' said Dave. 'I expect your other girlfriend'll be back from Egypt soon.'

And we left it at that. Another blow-out. And probably another destroyed relationship.

But Dave, who hates loose ends, made an inquiry of the Ministry of Defence, just for the hell of it. He later told me that Castle had been a *sergeant*-major, not a major, and had been court-martialled and dismissed from the army for dipping into the sergeants' mess funds.

It's a sordid world in which we coppers operate.

Next morning, as a consequence of finding myself in a temporary investigative cul-de-sac, I decided to take an interest in the scam at Heathrow, even though I thought it was unlikely to be relevant. But you never know with a murder inquiry.

Needless to say, the detective sergeant at the airport who had dealt with the matter was out of the office, but then he would be, wouldn't he? However, Dave's usual gentle approach persuaded the administrative assistant, CID support unit – they do love their titles, the police civil staff – to disclose the name and address of the man who had reported it to the police. Fully expecting him to reside in Aberdeen or some similarly inaccessible place, I was delighted to discover that he worked in an office just off Trafalgar Square. It was encouraging.

Dave and I walked the length of Whitehall, suffering the usual number of interruptions from tourists wanting to know the way to places I'd never heard of, or museums I didn't know existed. And no, I didn't know why the Life Guards wore red tunics and the other lot blue ones.

The informant, as we say in the police, was a Mr John Smith – honestly! – and he was the marketing director of some obscure company that sold something I didn't bother to enquire about too deeply on the grounds that it was not pertinent to my inquiry.

'I understand that you made a complaint to the police at Heathrow Airport regarding what you believed to be a fraud,' I said, once the necessary introductions had been made and the obligatory offer of coffee accepted.

'It wasn't a complaint really,' said Smith. 'More of an observation.'

'I see.' Clearly I was dealing with a pedant. 'Then perhaps you'd be so good as to tell me what aroused your suspicions.'

'You're taking it seriously, then. I mean, a chief inspector *and* a sergeant . . .'

'We take all such matters seriously,' I said piously, but decided not to tell him that I was actually investigating a murder. I didn't want to inject too much excitement into his mundane life. 'What exactly was it that caused you to make this, er, observation, Mr Smith?'

'Some years ago, I used to work for an airline,' Smith began, 'as a long-haul steward, but quite frankly the unsociable hours got to me.'

'I can imagine,' I murmured. It must have been hell travelling to exotic sun-drenched places and spending stopovers lounging by a swimming pool in the company of gorgeous, bikini-clad stewardesses. Give me night duty in the Mile End Road any time.

'About a fortnight ago I went to Berlin for a sales conference, and I had a load of display stuff with me. I knew I'd have to pay an excess baggage charge, but that didn't bother me; after all, the company pays.' Smith allowed the trace of a frown to cross his otherwise bland features. This was clearly an important matter to him. 'It amounted to ten kilograms and they wanted to charge me seventy pounds. Having been in the airline business, I knew that this figure was negotiable so I argued the toss. Eventually the supervisor turned up and we haggled a bit. As I said, the company was paying, but I am a director so, in a sense, it would have come out of my bonus.' He smiled apologetically at such avarice. 'However, she finally agreed a figure of four pounds a kilo and I finished up with a bill of forty pounds instead of the original seventy. Then she said that she'd take the money straightaway, to save me queuing at the cashier's desk.'

'Is this unusual, then?' I asked, wondering if he was eventually going to tell me why he was so concerned about it.

'No, it happens quite often. Check-in agents do have a certain discretion in the matter of excess baggage,' said Smith, missing my point, 'but it was what happened next. She produced one of those hand-held swipe machines for credit cards. I know I've been out of the business for a few years now, but I must admit I was a little surprised because I'd only ever seen them in France before.'

Really? Smith obviously didn't frequent the Italian restaurant that I used.

'Go on,' I said, hoping that he would soon get to the crux of his *observation*.

'Well, I didn't think too much about it until I came to put in my expenses. The slip, and I have it here' – Smith produced the credit card voucher with a flourish worthy of a magician – 'showed that the payment was made to some obscure passenger handling company. Personally I thought that it should have been made out to the airline that was carrying me.' He handed me the slip. 'There may be nothing in it, of course, but it did seem a bit strange.'

'May I keep this?' I asked, waving the credit-card slip gently in his direction.

'Of course.'

I handed the small piece of paper to Dave. 'Can you describe the supervisor who dealt with you, Mr Smith?'

Smith looked thoughtful for a moment or two, probably trying to frame the description in the police-like prose he had seen so often on television, and which he imagined was the way the police really operated. *Oh that we did!* 'I would guess that she was about twenty-something with frizzy red hair and was, er, quite well built, if you take my meaning.' He gave an embarrassed smile, as though guilt-ridden that he should have noticed the woman's figure. But my estranged wife reckoned that blokes like him were the worst: all hands at the hospital Christmas party, she used to say.

'You mean she had big knockers?' asked Dave bluntly, looking up from his notebook and speaking for the first time in the interview.

'Er, yes,' replied Smith. I got the impression that he had taken an instant dislike to Dave.

'I suppose she didn't give you a name?' I asked, even though I was certain, from his description of her, that the check-in agent he had described was Sylvia Moorhouse.

'I think she probably did, but I don't remember it.'

'Could it have been Moorhouse? Sylvia Moorhouse?'

'Possibly, but I've got an awful memory for names,' said Smith.

Perhaps that's why he called himself John Smith.

Back at the office I gazed at the slip that Smith had given me and finally decided that anything involving Sylvia Moorhouse was worthy of further investigation.

'Dave, get a warrant so that we can investigate this handling company.' I handed him the credit-card voucher.

Dave placed it firmly on his desk and studied it for some moments. 'It's financial, guv,' he said eventually, tapping it with his forefinger.

'I can see that, you prat,' I said. I had a feeling that Dave was about to duck out of trotting up to Bow Street magistrates court to swear an information. 'So what?'

'Needs a circuit judge's warrant for that.'

'So get one.'

Dave returned the voucher. 'Can't, guv. Got to be an inspector. "Special procedure" warrant, is that. Police and Criminal Evidence Act, Part Two, Section—'

'All right, all right,' I said, retrieving the vital piece of paper. Life was much easier in the old days when you just got on and did the job without all this poncing about.

I managed to find a sympathetic judge at Middlesex Guild-hall Crown Court who happily signed the warrant without question, and we paid a visit to the credit-card company of which there are now all too many.

I'd only got as far as introducing myself when the managerial type to whom we'd been directed, said: 'We're not allowed to discuss clients' financial affairs, if that's what you're going to ask.' He was clearly determined to stand on the principle of client confidentiality in the face of what he saw as a blatant police fishing expedition.

I laid the warrant on his desk.

'Ah!' I got the impression that it was not the first such document the manager had seen, but he read it assiduously nevertheless. 'So what can I do for you?'

'You can start by telling me who the account holder is,' I said. Deep down I enjoy prising information out of people who are reluctant to give it.

The manager turned to his computer and tapped a few keys.

Then he spun round in his chair and gave me the name of the handling company that was on the voucher.

'That much I know,' I said patiently. 'It's the principals of that outfit that I'm interested in.'

'It's a Sylvia Moorhouse,' he said, 'and a Monica Purvis.'

'What address d'you have for Sylvia Moorhouse?'

The manager read out the Bromley address. 'D'you want Monica Purvis's address too?' he asked.

'She's dead,' I said.

The manager frowned. 'Are you sure?' He was obviously irritated that we had cast doubt on the accuracy of his records.

'Positive,' I said. 'That's why I'm investigating her murder.'

'How very unfortunate!' I wasn't sure whether the manager was talking about her predicament or mine. Or even his. 'We'll need to see a copy of the death certificate,' he said, obviously desperate to tie up loose ends. I could visualise him waking up in the middle of the night worrying about it.

'I'm sure you can obtain one from the General Register Office at St Catherine's House,' said Dave helpfully. 'Incidentally, what's the account worth?'

'Worth?'

'Yeah, what's the average monthly turnover?'

'Oh, I see,' said the manager, and turned again to his computer. After keying in a few further details, he came up with an answer. 'Very little, actually, but I suppose a ball-park figure would be about a thousand a month. More often it's less, say seven hundred.'

Knowing Dave's dislike of platitudes, I frowned at him before he could acidly enquire which particular ball park the manager had in mind. Now that we had got the guy in a reasonably responsive mood, I didn't want him upset by one of my sergeant's acerbic comments about clichés and the bastardisation of the English language. Even though we'd got a warrant.

'Thank you,' Dave said and scribbled a note in his pocketbook. 'And where does the money go from here?'

'It's paid monthly into a bank account in Hounslow, in the

167

joint names of Sylvia Moorhouse and Monica Purvis,' said the manager, and then corrected himself by adding, 'The late Monica Purvis, that is.' He frowned again: we'd obviously ruined his day.

Eighteen

Dave grabbed at the phone. 'DS Poole.' He looked up and made a wry face. 'It's Sid Marley, guv, that ex-copper who pretends to be a security officer at the airline where Monica worked.'

'Yeah, I remember.' I picked up my phone and flicked down a switch. 'Brock.' I listened to what Marley was saying with a fairly heavy measure of scepticism. Eventually I replaced the receiver and sat back in my chair. 'I don't believe it,' I said.

'What don't you believe, guv?' Dave was accustomed to my little guessing games.

'Marley reckons he's found our murderer for us.'

'Bully for him,' said Dave calmly. He was not easily panicked into thinking that crimes of violence were that easily solved, particularly by the likes of Sid Marley.

'Get a car, Dave,' I said. 'We're going to Heathrow.'

It took an hour to reach the airport, but I didn't tell Dave what Marley had told me, mainly because the ex-copper had not been specific about his information, merely saying that he had something of importance that would 'break the Monica job for you'. He was obviously making the most of his brief return to police work. Anyway, I didn't want to excite Dave while he was driving and preferred that we both approached such evidence as Marley thought he had with open minds.

We found an illegal parking space right outside Terminal Three. Dave put the police logbook on top of the dashboard, threatened a nearby traffic warden with instant arrest if by some oversight the car was towed away, and followed me to Marley's office.

'I had to call in the local Old Bill this morning,' Marley began, lighting a fresh cigarette from the stub of the old one.

I could see that he was going to make the most of this little drama. 'Really?'

'I think I told you, when you were here last, that for some time now we've had cash going adrift. I've got an idea it's some scam that one of the check-in girls is running.' Marley chuckled. 'Some people still pay in cash, believe it or not,' he added.

I knew what sort of scam it was, and it had nothing to do with people paying in cash, but I wasn't about to tell Marley and have him buggering up my investigation into that. For all I knew, he may be involved, and right now there were more important things to deal with. 'Yeah, go on,' I said patiently. I could see that Marley was not to be hurried through his moment of glory.

'Well, it's a bit iffy, like, and I haven't worked out how they're doing it yet, but I'll get there, believe me.'

'I'm sure you will, Sid,' said Dave caustically. 'Eventually.' He shared my view that Sid Marley couldn't detect a bad smell, let alone a crime.

'We did a quick audit this morning, on the hurry-up, like, and found a monkey missing, so I got the local lads to search the staff lockers, see, looking for bundles of cash.'

'Good move,' said Dave. 'And did you find this five hundred quid?'

Marley's face assumed a crooked smile. 'Not exactly,' he said.

'Not what you'd call a result, then,' said Dave with heavy sarcasm. He was clearly becoming as impatient as I was with Marley's procrastination.

'I remembered what you told me about the Purvis job, see.' Marley stood up, brushed cigarette ash from the front of his jacket and crossed the office to a filing cabinet. Opening the top drawer, he took out a bottle of Scotch – which he placed on top – and a large, transparent plastic bag. 'There's a pair of trainers and a cufflink in there,' he said triumphantly, putting the package on his desk. 'Still know how to look after exhibits,' he added.

I stared at it. 'What the hell are *you* doing with those?' I asked. 'Why didn't the local law take possession of them?'

I could immediately see problems with continuity of evidence when we got to the Old Bailey. *If* we got to the Old Bailey, that is.

'Reckoned it didn't mean anything to them, despite me telling them this stuff might be of interest to you,' said Marley. 'They muttered something about illegal seizures.'

'Useless bastards,' I said, and determined to have someone's guts for garters.

'Don't worry, I made sure no one put their prints on the cufflink,' Marley added hurriedly.

'I should hope so,' I said. 'Now then, are you going to tell me whose locker these were found in?'

'Sylvia Moorhouse's,' said Marley.

'Did she admit to them being hers?'

'Haven't asked her. She's not here. Day off, see.'

That was a bonus. The thought of the damage that Marley could do by interrogating my murder suspect frightened the life out of me. Without opening the bag, I studied its contents. There was a cufflink bearing the single word YES and a pair of trainers one of which, I sincerely hoped, would match the imprint found at Monica's 'workshop' in Talleyrand Street. 'Well I'm buggered,' I said.

'Thought you would be,' said Marley, grinning like a Cheshire cat. He crossed to the filing cabinet and fingered the Scotch bottle. 'How about a celebratory snifter then?'

'Thanks for the offer,' I said, 'but we've got work to do. First of all, Dave here will take a statement from you and then you can give me the number, rank and name of the leery officer who obligingly searched your staff lockers for you.'

'I don't want to get anyone into trouble,' said Marley, gazing longingly at the whisky bottle, but evidently deciding against drinking alone. At least not until he was completely alone.

'You've changed your tune,' I said. Since our first meeting I'd drawn Marley's police record of service. His annual appraisal reports indicated that he'd been a not very resourceful detective sergeant at an outer London station for most of his time in the Job, and had acquired a reputation for being a hard-drinking bully, not unusual among the inefficient. He'd eventually been 'invited' to retire with twenty-seven years

171

service or face disciplinary proceedings for being drunk on duty. But now, of course, he was no longer in the Job and it wouldn't do to upset the police at the airport for fear that he ever needed the occasional favour in the future.

'Yeah, well.' Reluctantly Marley gave me the number of the PC who had found the trainers and the cufflink. He'd obviously decided that it wouldn't do to upset me either.

The business of Marley's brief written statement done with, Dave and I drove through the tunnel to the airport police station where I told the duty officer – in a way that made it apparent that I was not in the best of tempers – that I wished to interview one of his PCs. Right now.

The youthful inspector told a constable to radio the PC and call him in. 'Is there a problem, sir?' he asked. Obviously adept at summing up a tense situation, he was probably wondering that if there was to be any fall-out, any would fall on him.

'That depends,' I said. 'When my commander reads the statement that DS Poole has just taken from Sid Marley in conjunction with the one he's about to take from your PC, he may well consider that disciplinary action is appropriate.' It was no idle threat: the commander was a stickler for the rule book.

'Ah!' In the circumstances, the inspector had clearly opted for economy of speech. Apart from which he had probably worked out that anything he said could be taken down in evidence et cetera, et cetera . . . The spectre of a charge of lack of supervision hangs over all of us with rank.

'Afternoon all. Somebody want me?' The PC was not a callow youth whose actions – or lack of them – could have been put down to inexperience, but an overweight man in his mid-forties. His type was instantly recognisable from his confidently jovial manner, and he wore his helmet a shade too far back on his head so that he looked like an escapee from *The Pirates of Penzance*. He was the sort of policeman known in the Job as a uniform carrier.

'I'm Detective Chief Inspector Brock,' I said. The name obviously rang a bell, a positive carillon most likely. The PC licked his lips and looked less jovial. 'Seen these before?' I produced the exhibits bag containing the trainers and the cufflink and waved it gently in front of him.

172

'Er, I think so, sir.' The wheels were working slowly: retribution appeared imminent.

'And did Mr Marley tell you that these exhibits may be of interest to me?'

'Well, he did mention something about it, sir, yes.'

'A former police officer with twenty-seven years service – most of it in the CID – suggests to you that these' – I waved the bag again – 'could be important evidence in a murder inquiry, but you decided not to take any action. Have I got that right?'

The PC glanced at his inspector but found no comfort in his superior's stony expression. 'We all know Sid Marley, sir.' The PC laughed nervously. 'I know he used to be in the Job, but you have to take what he says with a pinch of salt. He came up with some story about the girls on the check-in desks nicking money, but we never found any. No call for police action as you might say.'

I imagined that that phrase was one of the officer's favourites. 'But it didn't cross your mind that a telephone call to my office may have resolved the matter one way or another?'

'It was only a pair of old trainers and a cufflink, sir,' whined the PC.

'Yes, and that pair of old trainers and that cufflink may well be vital evidence in a double murder inquiry,' I said. There was nothing like rubbing it in. 'My sergeant will now take a statement from you regarding this matter.'

'Excuse me for interrupting, sir,' said the inspector diffidently, 'but if the officer is to be reported for a disciplinary offence, he's entitled not to make a statement at this stage. That's his right.'

I sighed. The inspector was obviously a man who had a broad grasp of the regulations but not the small print. 'I'll tell him what his rights are, Inspector,' I said. 'He will make a duty statement for the purposes of continuity of evidence, and if this case goes pear-shaped at the Bailey because of the cock-up he's made, he'll probably be looking for a job.' I turned to Dave. 'When you take the statement, Sergeant, make sure that nothing is included that may inhibit an investigating officer from pursuing any disciplinary inquiry that may arise out of

173

the matter.' Although I didn't think that was very likely, you never knew which way my commander was going to jump.

As we made our way back to the Bath Road, Dave asked, 'What now, guv? A visit to Sylvia Moorhouse?'

'Not until we've had the lab check the trainers against the imprint found at the scene, Dave. If we don't get a match, the cufflink won't be worth two penn'orth of cold tea on its own.'

When you've been a CID officer for as long as I have, you learn to live with disappointments. Often apparently unshakeable evidence turns out to be useless. However, speed was vital. If Sylvia got to the airport before we got to her, and found the trainers and the cufflink missing, she'd probably do a runner.

'Make straight for the lab, Dave.'

I logged our exhibits at the forensic science laboratory at Lambeth and asked for a quick opinion, like now.

While a fingerprint officer examined the cufflink, a scientist compared the sole of the trainer with the photograph of the imprint found near Monica's body. After some time he nodded sagely. 'On a cursory examination, Mr Brock, I'm pretty certain that there's a match,' he said eventually. 'Certainly, the seven-shaped cut tallies, but I'll need to carry out further tests. For traces of blood, obviously.'

'Obviously,' I said. That was the best I could hope for from a forensic scientist. 'But safe enough to make an arrest,' I mused.

The scientist smiled. 'You're the detective, Mr Brock,' he said.

'I wasn't asking you,' I said irritably. 'I was thinking aloud.'

At that point the fingerprint officer returned. 'There are no marks on that at all, Mr Brock,' he said, returning the cufflink.

'So now do we go to Bromley, guv?' asked Dave.

'Yes, Dave,' I said. 'Now we go to Bromley, but softly-softly. We'll put the excess baggage fraud to her first of all and see what she has to say about that.'

*　　*　　*

One would have thought that the arrest of a young woman on suspicion of the scam she'd been running with Monica – to say nothing of the girl's murder, or at least some involvement in it – would have been a simple matter. It wasn't.

When Sylvia Moorhouse answered the door, she was wearing a black tracksuit and trainers, and her hair was tied back into a ponytail.

'Oh, not again,' she said. 'What is it now?'

'May we come in?' I asked.

Sylvia shrugged and held the door wide. 'I've just come back from keep-fit,' she said. 'I was about to have a shower.' She glanced at her watch. 'And I'm going out shortly,' she added, 'so I don't have much time.'

I wouldn't bank on it, I thought. I couldn't have been more wrong.

The three of us stood in the hall. 'Ms Moorhouse,' I began, 'I have reason to believe that you, with others, have been involved in defrauding the company for which you work at the airport—' But I got no further. Whether it was that allegation, or the sight of the plastic bag containing the trainers and the cufflink, I don't know, but sure as hell it produced a reaction.

Dave and I were standing between the woman and the open front door, Dave a pace or two to my rear. Suddenly Sylvia leaped past me and seized Dave's right arm. The next thing I knew was that she had somehow thrown him with what must have been a classic judo hold. Dave cannoned into me, knocking me back against the wall, and Sylvia went through the still-open front door like a rocket, and into the street.

'Guilty knowledge, guv,' gasped Dave, scrambling to his feet, his words interspersed with desperate efforts to get his breath back.

I do like an officer whose sense of humour prevails in the face of adversity. 'Well, don't stand there moaning,' I said, 'get after her.'

Affording me a baleful look, Dave rushed out of the house, closely followed by me, just in time for us to see Sylvia's trim figure disappearing at speed round the corner of her road, ably demonstrating that her keep-fit classes had done just that.

175

'It's no good, guv,' Dave said, 'we'll never catch her.'

'I don't know how you managed to let her escape like that, Dave,' I said, following the example of all senior officers: when something goes wrong, thrash around for someone else to blame.

I sat down on the stairs and wondered what the hell we should do next. Years ago, when I took the promotion examinations, there was always a cunning problem called 'the knowledge and reasoning question'. The examiners invented a set of unlikely and extremely complex circumstances and invited the examinee to come up with a textbook answer. They could never have visualised what had just happened to Dave and me in Bromley: two able-bodied detectives seen off by a slip of a girl in her mid-twenties.

'I think it'll be a waste of time, Dave, but we'll have to get someone to keep obo on this place. Not that I think she'll be coming back.' I stood up and stretched. 'Got any cigarettes?'

Dave shook his head slowly in an expression of censure and then produced a packet of Silk Cut. 'What now, guv? Back to the office?'

'Not yet. While we're here, we may as well have a look round. And a bit more thoroughly than last time.'

It was a typical three-up-two-down semi and there was little to interest us. It was apparent that Sylvia Moorhouse was not the best of housekeepers: dirty clothing and bedlinen abounded, and the whole place was in need of a good dusting. But such failings are of no value in a murder investigation.

Nineteen

'If that business with the excess baggage really is a scam, Dave,' I said, 'it's brilliant.'

'It's got to be bent, guv. Why else would Sylvia do a runner?' said Dave, tapping his teeth with a government-issue ballpoint pen. 'She knows we've been back and forth to the airport, and she probably thought that Sid Marley had shopped her.'

'I could handle an extra grand a month,' I mused. 'But the trainers and the cufflink are an even better reason for taking off.'

'She might not have known anything about them,' said Dave. 'After all, we didn't put it to her, did we? That Marley had found them in her locker, I mean. What d'you reckon? Another word with him?'

I pondered that suggestion, but not for long. 'Not before we've made a few more inquiries about him,' I said. 'Supposing he'd stumbled across this fiddle – and stumbling across it'd be about right knowing his detective ability – and instead of doing his job as a security officer decided that he'd lean on the two women for a cut of their fiddle?'

'Sounds right,' said Dave. 'So who do we talk to?'

'For a start, someone who might know about his financial and marital state,' I mused.

'Like someone who was in the Job with him, you mean, guv?' asked Dave, and instantly wished he hadn't.

'Good thinking. He was more or less chucked out of the Job two years ago, that much we know. See if you can find someone – a skipper or a DC – who was working with him and see what they have to tell us.'

'I thought you were going to say that,' said Dave, and sighed.

Dave Poole was probably the best telephone detective I've ever come across. Within half an hour, during which time he'd made about seven calls, he'd tracked down two detective sergeants and a detective inspector, all of whom had served with Sid Marley in the two or three years immediately prior to his enforced retirement.

'Well known as a womaniser and a drunk,' Dave began, referring briefly to his notes, 'which comes as no surprise. Spent a lot on booze and the gee-gees, and wasn't above borrowing from his mates – assuming he had any – and for being a bit tardy about paying them back.' He looked up and grinned. 'His wife left him about five years ago and screwed him for every penny. One of the DSs I spoke to reckoned he was even forced into making over half his pension to her for life, which means he won't have much of that left to spend on his drinking or the horses. Plus he put some bird in the club and she got a paternity order against him which doesn't run out for another eleven years. The general view is that that little bit of fun was what finally caused his missus to walk out.'

'Sounds a likely runner for sharing in the profits of this scam, then,' I said. 'He must be practically on his uppers.'

'And there was one other thing, guv. About the time of his marriage break-up, Complaints Investigation Bureau were running an inquiry on him for allegedly copping back-handers from a massage parlour on his ground. Something to do with tipping them the wink when the Old Bill was taking an interest. He must have got wind of it though, because it didn't come to anything, but where there's smoke and all that . . .'

'Is that it?'

'Not quite. Apparently he's now shacked up with an ageing air hostess who he shares a flat with somewhere in Hounslow.'

'Well, she can't be very choosy,' I said. 'What's he getting paid now? Any idea?'

'That's easy,' said Dave. 'Last time we saw him, I just happened to catch sight of his pay slip which he'd sort of accidentally left lying around on his desk. After deductions, he's pulling down just over a grand a month. He's getting taxed on his pension as well, including the half he's made over to his former wife.' He gave a dry laugh. 'Then there's the maintenance he's paying to his ex for their two children and the paternity for the kid he had by the bird who caused the divorce. But he does get concessions on airline tickets so's he can go to places he can't afford to go to.'

'You're a cynical bastard, Dave,' I said.

'Yeah, I know, guv. I've had a good teacher.'

Given Marley's parlous financial state, my gut reaction told me that he was almost certainly involved in the excess baggage scam that Sylvia Moorhouse was working, and that to talk to him about it would be counterproductive to say the least. The top priority therefore was to find Sylvia because, once the chips were down, she was likely to shop Marley. I hoped. That, however, didn't remove the fact that the trainers and the cufflink had been found in her locker. But found by Marley. And that worried me.

'Any suggestions that he was a planter, Dave?' When we talk of planters in the Job we're not talking about upright young men who'd spent their formative years nurturing tea in India or rubber trees in Malaya. We're talking about unscrupulous detectives who were not above 'finding' incriminating evidence on prisoners' persons that the prisoners didn't know they possessed until that very moment.

'No,' said Dave, 'but on the basis of his form so far, I should think it's a racing certainty.'

And I thought so too. But proving that he planted the trainers and the cufflink in Sylvia's locker would probably be very difficult. On the other hand it was within my experience – having carried out a few investigations into bent coppers – that the loud-mouthed bullies were usually the first to hold up their hands. And Marley was a loud-mouthed bully.

'I've just had a thought, guv,' said Dave.

'You be careful, Dave. Harm can come to a young man like that.'

'How did Marley know about the trainers? We didn't tell him and it wasn't released to the press. There was only that bit about trying to trace the missing cufflink. And that idle sod

179

of a PC at Heathrow didn't know either. We hadn't even put anything about trainers on the PNC.'

I stared at Dave. 'Christ!' I said. 'I'd completely forgotten that. Why in hell's name didn't you mention that when we were at the airport yesterday?'

'Because it's only just occurred to me,' said Dave, somewhat ruefully. 'Anyway, the chances are that Marley would've come up with an instant answer. Bit out of character, I know, thinking on his feet, but we've got plenty of time to put it all together. After all, he's not going anywhere, is he?'

'I wouldn't be too sure of that, Dave,' I said, thinking of one of the cells at Charing Cross police station.

Nevertheless, it had become a matter of some urgency that we talked to Sid Marley again. But I decided that we would only discuss Sylvia Moorhouse and where we might find her. Bearing in mind what Dave had said, we would need more time to screw Marley down if he was involved in the murder of Monica Purvis, and giving the impression of getting him on our side might just engender an overconfidence that would eventually sink him. Perhaps. It would be interesting, I thought, to see his reaction to the flight of Sylvia. Guilty knowledge produces some interesting behaviour. Or is 'body language' the in-phrase now? I must try to keep up to date.

The languid young blonde who had been sitting on Marley's desk on the occasion of our first visit was now occupying his chair behind it, but she was no longer quite so languid. In fact she appeared somewhat harassed. Of Marley there was no sign.

'Can I help you?' she asked, managing to convey the impression that she didn't really want to.

'Detective Chief Inspector Brock and Detective Sergeant Poole to see Mr Marley.'

'He's not here,' said the girl. 'I'm Debbie, his secretary.' She stood up, teetered round the desk and perched on its corner. 'And I'm trying to cope with everything. Know what I mean? He never rang in or nothing. I dunno where he's gone.' She flicked long blonde hair out of her eyes. 'He should've been here,' she added as an afterthought.

I imagine that Marley had hired Debbie more for her physical attractions than for any secretarial skills she may possess. She was tall and slender, long-legged and short-skirted, and her tight-fitting sweater was reminiscent of those worn by the film stars whose photographs appeared on the cover of the *Picturegoer* magazines that my old man used to drool over when I was a kid. But having spent his entire working life as a motorman on the Underground's Northern Line, I suppose he needed something to brighten his otherwise uneventful days. He'd really have enjoyed today's explicit top-shelf porn literature.

'Any idea where he is?' I asked.

'No. He just didn't show up this morning. Sorry about that.'

So was I. 'Do you have an address for him?'

'We're not supposed to give out staff addresses,' said Debbie. 'Sid's very particular about that.'

I'll bet he is. 'It's important that I speak to him immediately,' I said. 'I'm carrying out a murder inquiry and Mr Marley's a vital witness.'

'Oh!' said Debbie, but still appeared reticent about parting with Marley's address.

'I'm sure you wouldn't want him to be arrested and hauled up in front of a judge at the Old Bailey for contempt of court,' I said, gilding the lily outrageously.

That did it; they must have had something going, him and Debbie. But how did a chain-smoking, drunken wreck like Marley manage to pull a girl like her? Leaning back slightly, she flicked open a book on the desk and promptly told us where Marley lived, which was, as Dave had said earlier, in Hounslow, although he hadn't known precisely where.

To be honest, I had no hope of finding Marley at home. Something told me that he'd decided it was time to put some space between himself and his erstwhile employers in the shape of Dave and me.

Our visit was not without profit, however. Although Marley was not there – as I had anticipated – his live-in lover was. On the way, Dave had made a quick call on his mobile and discovered that the electoral roll showed the registered voters to be Sidney Marley and a Shirley Marley. Shirley *Marley*, eh? Interesting.

'Mrs Shirley Marley, I presume?' I asked of the overweight, peroxide blonde who answered the door. The moment I set eyes on her, I knew that she and Marley were meant for each other. She may well have been an air stewardess in her prime, but from her appearance that must have been some time ago. I reckoned that she was at least forty-eight, and that was being charitable. Very charitable.

'That's me, darling.' Shirley had a cultured voice that was slightly slurred around the edges, and in a pretence at coy embarrassment, she closed the neck of her fading blue candlewick dressing gown with one hand. The other held a glass that I suspected contained gin and tonic – and probably more gin than tonic – even though it was not yet eleven o'clock in the morning.

Most of the airline girls I'd come across were elegant, and fastidious about their appearance and make-up. And even those who weren't exactly raving beauties usually managed to make the best of themselves. But Marley's lady friend had failed on all counts.

'We're police officers. Friends of Sid,' I lied. 'Is he about?'

'Not at the moment. But do come in.' She turned, leaving the door ajar. At least she still had the walk, and sauntered up the short hall with the sort of poise that tends to characterise air stewardesses.

The sitting room was a tip and I surmised that housework was not *la femme* Marley's strongpoint.

'Any idea where he is? It's important that we speak to him. We've got a job running together, you see.' It was a half truth: I saw no point in telling her that I was thinking about nicking him.

'No idea, I'm afraid, darling.' Shirley flopped down in a cheap armchair and listlessly waved a hand to indicate that we should sit down too. 'He didn't come home last night. No phone call, nothing, but with his job you never know where he's likely to be. Last time he went off, he was in Spain for a week, something to do with a fraud he was looking into, so he said. But if you believe that, you'll believe anything. He reckoned that one of the three-fours was having the airline over by fiddling the duty-free. Personally, I think he was having one of the three-fours over.'

'One of the three-fours?' queried Dave.

'Yes, darling, it's what they call the cabin staff who do the in-flight serving. Used to do it myself when I was flying.'

'Is it possible to fiddle the duty-frees?'

'No chance,' said Shirley. 'At least, not with the number two we had, and the customs were always waiting to pounce.' She made a wry face and shrugged. 'Would you boys care for a drink?' She waggled her empty glass and smiled. There was pink lipstick on her teeth. Probably left over from yesterday.

'No, thanks. It's a bit early for us,' I said, vicariously including Dave in my refusal.

'You won't mind if I do, will you?' Shirley heaved herself into an upright position and ambled across to a side table laden with bottles. I wondered if they were duty-free. 'Have you tried the office?' she asked over her shoulder as she dispensed her second – or maybe fifth – gin and tonic.

'Yes, we've just come from there.'

Shirley sat down again and took a sip of her drink. 'Can I pass on a message if he happens to ring?'

'Not really. And you've no idea where he might have gone?'

'Not a clue, darling, but that's the airline business for you. Just the same in my day. Always getting fucked about.'

Dave looked up with a frown on his face. Although a master of obscene language himself – when the occasion demanded it – he found it unpalatable coming from a woman. And somehow Shirley's cultured tones made it sound even worse. 'Have you been married to Sid long?' he asked.

Shirley switched her gaze to Dave and laughed. 'Oh, we're not married, darling. I just use his name. It stops the neighbours talking.'

Sweet old-fashioned thing. As if anyone gave a toss these days. 'When he shows up perhaps you'd ask him to give me a call,' I said, standing up and handing Shirley one of my cards. 'It is rather urgent.'

'Of course. Sure you won't stay for a drink?'

183

'Quite sure, thanks.' And I was in no doubt about what else would have been on offer if Dave hadn't been with me.

'Where to now, guv'nor?' Dave asked when we were back in the car.

'Heathrow again, Dave. We'll have a word with one of the airline's bosses, see if he knows anything. But I've a nasty suspicion that Marley's done a runner.'

'I've no idea where he's gone,' said the director into whose office we were eventually shown, 'and I'm bloody annoyed about it. He's certainly not on official business.' He paused. 'And it's not the first time he's disappeared without a word. Anyway, what did you want to see him for? Perhaps I can help.'

Avoiding the matter of the trainers and the cufflink, I explained about the baggage-handling racket that Sylvia Moorhouse was perpetrating, and loosely implied that Marley might be involved.

The director became incandescent with rage. 'That's most certainly not an official arrangement,' he spluttered. 'The bastard's defrauding us.' The thought that his airline should have been the victim of a long-term swindle at the hands of a trusted supervisor *and* the very security officer appointed to detect such frauds appeared to leave him utterly bereft of any faith in human nature he may have had to start with.

'We have no direct evidence to link Marley with the scam,' I hastened to point out, 'but there's no doubt about Sylvia Moorhouse's involvement. And Monica Purvis was in on it, too. Hence my interest, given that she was murdered.'

'So that's why she left,' mused the director.

'*Left?* I thought she was dismissed for bad timekeeping.'

'Absolute rubbish,' said the director. 'I was surprised when she handed in her notice. She was a good worker and we were considering her for flying duties. Anyway, who told you that she'd been sacked?'

'Marley did. He told us that she was dismissed eighteen months ago. And it was confirmed by Moorhouse. However, to get back to this baggage fraud. Didn't you think it strange that your company wasn't receiving any revenue for excess baggage?'

'But we were,' said the director. 'I can check the figures if you like, but—'

'It's not relevant at the moment,' I said, shaking my head, 'but it seems to indicate that Moorhouse, and possibly Marley, weren't being too greedy. From the figures I've seen, they probably confined their fiddle to five or six occasions a week, but put the majority of charges through the airline's books so as not to arouse suspicion. Incidentally, Marley said something about cash going missing. D'you know anything about that?'

'It's news to me.'

'A few days ago, the last time we were here in fact, Marley claimed that he'd done a spot check and found that five hundred pounds had gone missing.'

'No chance,' said the director. 'Anyway, it's not Marley's job. That's what we've got an accountant for and he doesn't miss a trick. He'd have known.'

'He didn't know about the excess baggage fraud though,' said Dave thoughtfully.

And that was the most we could get. When we left, Marley's boss was muttering darkly of suitable punishment for his errant security chief and Sylvia Moorhouse, and possibly even the accountant. But as far as the absentee Marley was concerned, I got the distinct impression that the director was thinking in terms of hanging, drawing and quartering him. When he found him, that is.

We returned to Curtis Green, deflated.

'I have a feeling, Dave,' I said, 'that Marley planted the trainers and the cufflink in Sylvia's locker, and invented the story about cash going missing so that he could con the Old Bill at the airport into doing a search and making the discovery. Unfortunately he got lumbered with a PC who wasn't interested. It would have looked much better, from Marley's point of view, if we'd got a call from the police at Heathrow rather than from Marley.'

'I can just imagine the scene, guv,' said Dave. 'A tip-off

from an ex-copper who would have told the PC he could have done himself a bit of good by finding vital evidence in a murder case.'

'Yes,' I said, 'and he'd probably have told them not to mention his name because he was doing the PC a favour. But what he was really trying to do was to lumber Sylvia with incriminating evidence that he knew she wouldn't have read about in the paper.'

'Yeah, but he wouldn't have read about it in the paper either,' said Dave, 'so how did he know if he didn't top Monica himself? I think he's just put himself in the frame.'

'So do I, Dave.'

'What now, guv, lunch?' asked Dave hopefully.

Somewhat belatedly we went to our usual Italian restaurant and had a spaghetti bolognese.

'The only thing we can do is put him on the computer – flagged up as wanted for interview – and wait, Dave,' I said as we strolled back to the office. 'Until we find him and Sylvia, we're stuck.'

'Perhaps they're together somewhere and milking the account out of a cash dispenser,' Dave said.

I stopped abruptly and a German tourist cannoned into the back of me.

'*Entschuldigen Sie!*' said the German, as though it were his fault, and raised his hat.

'*Tut nichts*,' I murmured, allowing the German to think it really was his fault. I stared at Dave for a moment or two. 'Why didn't I think of that?' I asked.

'Because you've got me to do it for you, guv,' said Dave, with a perfectly straight face.

'In that case, we'll start with the bank at Hounslow where this money's lodged.'

'We'll need a warrant for that,' said Dave.

'We've got one,' I said.

'That was for the credit-card company. We'll need another for the bank. Bank managers tend to know about these things. You'll probably find that a whole series of lectures at bank training schools is devoted to the subject of circuit judges' warrants.'

We hastened to Middlesex Guildhall and got another warrant.

Faced with that singularly unimpressive piece of paper, bearing my favourite judge's signature, the bank manager offered us any assistance he could. 'What d'you want to know?' he asked.

'For a start the names of the account holders.' I was fairly certain who they would be, but I had to make sure. They might have set up a holding company from which the money was siphoned off into another account. Fraudsters are crafty people.

The manager turned his VDU so that we couldn't see it and tapped in a few details. 'In the joint names of Sylvia Moorhouse and Monica Purvis,' he said a few moments later, and then gave us the two addresses that were known to us.

'Monica Purvis is dead,' I said. 'I'm investigating her murder.'

'Yes, I know,' said the manager, obviously better informed that his credit-card counterpart. 'It's on the computer.'

'Must be true, then,' murmured Dave.

'And have there been any drawings from cashpoints?' I asked.

The manager keyed in another question. 'In the last fortnight, two hundred pounds a day,' he said.

'D'you know where those cashpoints are?'

'Of course.' The manager looked offended. 'Most of the drawings were from a dispenser at Heathrow Airport, but the last two – yesterday and today – were from a machine at Farnham in Surrey. Incidentally, one attempt was made to draw on the card issued to Monica Purvis, but we cancelled that the moment we heard of her death.' He gave a wry smile, probably at the thought that someone should even try.

'When was that? And where?'

'Heathrow Airport, Terminal Two, on Wednesday the twenty-fourth of July.'

Well, well. Two days after Monica's murder. It looked very much as though the murderer – or murderess – did take Monica's card at the time of the killing. Or maybe had taken it some time previously. I made a mental note to check whether

187

the card had been found among Charlie Purvis's possessions after the Flying Squad had cleared up the mess they'd made.

'There was a drawing by cheque, too,' the manager continued. 'Two thousand pounds payable to a Sidney Marley on the seventeenth of June.'

'Wonderful!' I said, and meant it. What a careless bastard. Anyone who knew what he was about would have insisted on cash, not left documentary evidence in the form of a cheque. Any CID officer on the take knows that a bribe paid that way can be traced, and Marley, as an ex-CID officer and airline security chief, should have known it too. But from what I'd heard, he'd been a useless detective and an even worse security officer.

'One last question,' I said. 'What's the balance of the account now?'

The manager glanced briefly at the screen. 'Fifteen thousand pounds, give or take.'

'Mostly take,' I said, but the subtlety of that remark was obviously beyond the bank manager's humour threshold.

Twenty

'Well, now we know that Marley copped a cheque for two K from the baggage scam, Dave, we've got something to hold him on,' I said. 'When we find him,' I added, peering out of the incident-room window in the direction I thought Farnham might lie.

'What we don't know is whether Sylvia's with him,' said Dave.

'That's true,' I said, hoping that it wasn't. 'He might somehow have got hold of Sylvia's cashpoint card and be using it.' And then, remembering what the bank manager had told me, I glanced at DS Wilberforce, the incident-room pundit. 'Do we know if the Flying Squad found Monica's card in Charlie Purvis's possessions, Colin?'

'No, they didn't, sir.'

'So, I wonder if Marley's got it,' I said. 'If we now find it among his property, he'll have a lot of explaining to do, given that an attempt was made to use it two days after Monica was murdered.'

'On the other hand, Charlie Purvis might have topped his wife and nicked the card,' said Dave, leaning back in his chair and putting his hands behind his head.

'Maybe, but there's no way of proving it now. Anyway, not even I can take a dead man to court.'

'Really, guv'nor?' said Dave with a sarcastic grin.

'Any idea where Mr Mead is, Colin?' I asked.

'In his office, I think, sir.'

And so he was. 'Frank, do we know anything about Farnham?'

'Yes. Nice little town in Surrey, about ten miles from Guildford. They have a very good beer festival there every

189

April, but housing's pretty expensive. Why, thinking of moving?'

'Do we know of any connection between Sylvia Moorhouse, Sid Marley and Farnham?' I asked patiently, ignoring Frank's lame attempt at humour.

'Not to my knowledge, Harry. Want me to find out?'

I explained my interest and Frank set to work immediately.

An hour later he put his head round my office door with the glad news that Sylvia Moorhouse was with her brother in Farnham and gave me his address.

'How the hell did you find that out?' I asked. It seemed that what Dave had said about Frank Mead having some good snouts was true.

'Took a chance on a risky shortcut,' Frank said. 'Got one of the woman officers to ring up all the Moorhouses in the Farnham phone book and ask for her "old school friend Sylvia" who she hadn't seen for years. On the fourth call, bingo!'

'Did she actually talk to Sylvia?'

'No, she was out.'

'Excellent,' I said.

'That it, then?' Frank stood up.

'Yes, apart from our going to Farnham to detain her before she remembers she didn't have an old school friend who was likely to ring her up at an address that she didn't know she was at.'

It was eight o'clock in the evening when we arrived at Sylvia's brother's house. As well as Dave Poole, I took a woman detective with me – one who'd represented the Metropolitan Police at karate – just in case Sylvia cut up rough again.

'Mr Moorhouse?' I asked when a man answered the door.

'Yes.'

'We're police officers. We'd like to talk to Sylvia.'

'Police? Whatever's wrong?'

Either Sylvia hadn't explained the reason for her sudden visit, or her brother was a good actor.

'If we may come in, sir . . .'

Sylvia was in the sitting room, watching television, and leaped up as we entered, a hunted look on her face. Her brother stood in the doorway, a bemused expression on his face.

'It's no good running again, Sylvia,' I said, not that she had anywhere to run, short of jumping through the closed, double-glazed window. 'I think you know what I want to talk to you about.'

The reactions of people whom the police suspect of a crime are as varied as they are perverse. 'I haven't done anything wrong,' stammered Sylvia. She glanced at her brother. 'Really, Jamie, I've done nothing.'

'Well, in that case,' I said, 'you've nothing to worry about. But I'd like you to accompany me back to London.'

'There must be some mistake,' Sylvia's brother spluttered. 'You can't just go about arresting people without any proof.'

I wondered briefly if he was a lawyer. 'I'm not arresting her, Mr Moorhouse,' I said, even though I didn't owe him an explanation. 'In fact I'm hoping that your sister will be able to help us with our inquiries.'

Jamie Moorhouse scoffed at that. 'Yes, and I know what that means,' he said. 'Why d'you want her to go back to London? Can't you ask your questions here?'

'There are various items I need to show Ms Moorhouse, and places I want her to see,' I said curtly, 'and they're at Heathrow Airport.' I turned away. The last thing I intended to do right now was to get involved in an argument with a relative who was showing all the signs of being a know-all. 'But if she doesn't come voluntarily, I *will* arrest her.' *And you can have that with me, sport.*

The forty-mile journey to Charing Cross police station passed in total silence. I had warned both Dave and the woman detective that no questions were to be asked of Sylvia Moorhouse, but that notes should be taken if she volunteered a statement. In the event, she said nothing.

Even though it was late, I decided that I would talk to Sylvia immediately, and having waited for the custody sergeant to puff himself up with sufficient self-importance to go through the routine of completing all manner of paperwork, Dave and I were eventually closeted with Sylvia in an interview room.

Dave undertook the business of switching on the recording machine, telling it the time and the place and who was there – and explaining to Sylvia that she would be given a copy of the tape – and finally asking her if she wanted a solicitor. To my surprise, she didn't.

'When we called at your house the day before yesterday to discuss a certain fraud at the airport,' I began, 'you assaulted my sergeant and fled. Would you care to explain that?'

Dave slid a scrap of paper across to me. On it was written 'CAUTION!' I presumed he meant that I should administer the official caution, but I preferred to interpret that single word as advice that I should proceed carefully. Anyway, as I've mentioned before, I never could remember the wording and I'd lost my little card with it all on.

'What would you have done?' demanded Sylvia truculently.

'I'm not talking about me, I'm talking about you, Sylvia,' I said.

'Well, what did you think I was going to do? You turn up at Bromley making wild allegations about some fraud or another. Well, don't forget that I know how you lot stitched up Charlie Purvis. Of course I ran away.'

I produced the credit-card slip that John Smith had given me. 'D'you recognise this?' I asked.

Sylvia took it and studied it. There was no sudden gasp, no telltale signs of guilt. 'What about it? It's just a voucher for excess baggage.'

'Issued by you and credited to an account held jointly by you and the late Monica Purvis.'

'I've nothing to say.' It was obvious that Sylvia Moorhouse was possessed of more steel than I had given her credit for.

'Very well. Sylvia Moorhouse, I'm arresting you for defrauding the airline for which you work by diverting monies that were rightfully those of your employers. Do the business, Dave.'

Sylvia displayed a bland indifference while Dave was administering the caution, but when he'd finished she leaned forward, a purposeful expression on her face. 'Sid Marley was in on this, you know,' she said.

'You mean he was in on it from the start?'

'Not likely. No, he caught me using the machine one day, but instead of reporting me for it, he put the squeeze on Monica, silly little cow, having guessed that she was involved too. When she told me, I sent him a cheque on the account where we'd put the money from that. Just on the off-chance, like.' She gestured briefly at the voucher and laughed. 'Like a prat he cashed it and I knew we'd got him.'

I decided to change tack and put the plastic bag containing the trainers and the cufflink on the table in front of her. 'These,' I said, 'were found in your locker in the staff room at Heathrow Airport on Monday last. One of the trainers exactly matches the shoe print found at the scene of Monica's murder' – I know the guy at the lab wasn't sure, but I was – 'and this cufflink, embossed with the word YES, appears to be the partner of one marked NO that was also found at the scene.'

'So what?' Far from being discomfited by this damning evidence, Sylvia raised her chin slightly. 'I've not seen them before and I didn't put them there,' she said.

'Any idea who would have done?'

'Sid Marley, I should think. He's the only one that I know of who's got pass keys for everywhere, including the staff lockers.'

'Why should he have done that?'

'Perhaps you'd better ask him,' said Sylvia, 'but it's pretty obvious, isn't it. He wanted it to look as though I'd killed Monica.'

'Why should he want to do that?'

'To cover his own tracks, I suppose.'

'Are you suggesting that Marley killed Monica?'

'You're the detective,' Sylvia said sarcastically. 'You tell me.'

'Why you in particular? Why not try to implicate someone else? Someone who wasn't known to him.'

Sylvia shrugged. 'Probably because he tried coming on to me once. But I wasn't having any with that scumbag, so I hit him. I s'pose he wanted to get his own back. I don't know. He tried with all the girls. Christ knows what they see in him, but whatever it is, I didn't see it. He's even screwing his secretary, Debbie. I don't know how he gets away with it.'

'You say he came on to you. Would you care to tell me the circumstances?'

'Can I smoke?'

'If you wish,' I said, and slid an ashtray towards her.

'Like I said, he tried it on with me.' Sylvia took a lighter from her handbag and applied the flame to her cigarette, slowly enough to give herself time to think. 'But I wasn't as soft as Monica.' She turned her head and blew a plume of smoke into the air. 'She let him screw her whenever he wanted to, but I wasn't having any of it.' And then she began to open up. 'When Marley first found out about the fiddle we were running, he put the squeeze on Monica. He picked on her knowing that she was a friend of mine and because, I suppose, he thought she was the weakest of us two, and he said that he'd shop us to you lot unless she had sex with him. So the stupid bitch did. But that wasn't enough for him and he tried it on with me. I reminded him that he'd cashed the cheque I'd sent him and that the minute I felt like it the bosses would know that he was in on it too. And I told him there was no way I was going to jump into bed with him.' She stubbed out her half-smoked cigarette and looked up, an expression of disgust on her face. 'Can you imagine doing it with that drunken bastard?'

'Not really,' I said, tongue in cheek.

'Anyway, that wasn't good enough for him. He got me in a corner in the staff restroom one night duty when there was just the two of us. He pushed me against a wall, put his hand up my skirt and made a grab for my boobs.'

'So what happened?'

'I grabbed him in a wrist lock, kneed him in the balls and threw him across the room. He was off sick for a week.' Sylvia smiled at the recollection. 'I've been doing judo classes for quite a while now.'

I glanced sideways at Dave but he wasn't smiling, and I wondered if there really was any truth in the stories that Madeleine beat him up from time to time.

'And you think that this is why he tried to implicate you in the murder of Monica Purvis?'

'Seems a pretty good reason to me.'

'And you had nothing to do with her death?'

194

'Of course I didn't. She was my friend.'

'Despite the fact that she was having it off with your lover Michael Cozens?'

Sylvia shrugged. 'So what? I was having it off with Charlie.'

'When I suggested that to you before, you were adamant that you'd never slept with Charlie Purvis.'

Sylvia smiled defiantly. 'So I lied,' she said. 'Anyway, Monica was getting laid by Geoffrey Halstead.'

'Who?' I decided not to show that I knew about this.

'Oh, come on, copper. You asked me about a guy called Geoffrey when you came to see me once.'

'Yes, and you said you didn't know much about him. A snooty type you called him, and when I asked if he and Monica were having an affair, you said you didn't know.'

'Yes, well, she didn't want it broadcast, but he was a politician, a minister, I think.'

And so it came to that. There was just not enough evidence to charge her with the murder of Monica Purvis, even though the trainers and the cufflink had been found in her staff locker at the airport. Her story about Marley trying to rape her – because that's how she'd tell it in court – coupled with the proof that he'd been stupid enough to accept some of the proceeds from the fraud, would almost certainly convince a jury that he'd planted that evidence out of sheer malice.

I had expected Sylvia to implicate Marley in the swindle and she'd done so. Not that I needed her testimony, but the fact that she claimed that he'd planted the trainers and the cufflink in her locker was, in my view, an attempt to extricate herself without giving me any hard evidence that Marley had committed the murder.

We were going to need more proof. The case against her had to be beyond all reasonable doubt and I didn't think it was. Not yet anyway.

I charged her with the fraud and she was released on bail to await an appearance at Bow Street court.

But the next morning, I found that the kaleidoscope had been shaken yet again.

A somewhat crestfallen Colin Wilberforce greeted me when

195

I arrived at Curtis Green. 'I should have spotted this before, sir,' he said, producing a buff-coloured file.

'What is it, Colin?'

'It's Charlie Purvis's criminal record, sir.'

'I've seen that.'

'Yes, but I've just noticed the details of his last conviction, when he was put down for three years for a robbery he said he hadn't committed.'

'They all say that. So what's so special about it?'

'Sid Marley was the arresting officer, sir.'

In view of that revelation it was obvious that our top priority now was to find Marley. If it turned out that he had framed Charlie Purvis for a crime he had not committed, I would definitely want to lay hands on him. The one thing that gets right up my nose is a bent copper. And I had no reason to believe that Marley had gone bent only *after* he'd left the Job.

I went back to my office and kicked the door shut. Clearly I had to work out how to find Marley in a way that was more positive than just putting his name on the police national computer. Even so, I could not see that stitching up Purvis was any reason for murdering the man's wife.

The phone buzzed and I snatched it up. 'Brock.'

'Mr Brock, it's Geoffrey Halstead. I'd be most grateful if you could spare the time to come and see me, sooner rather than later. I don't wish to discuss the matter on the telephone.'

I was surprised by Halstead's conciliatory tone. 'Certainly, sir,' I said. 'When would be a suitable time?'

'Now if you can, Mr Brock.'

Dave and I walked across to the Home Office and were shown into Halstead's office without delay. The minister stood up and shook hands before indicating that we should sit down in the small, informal area at the opposite end of the office from where his desk was situated. A tray of coffee appeared almost immediately.

'I'm afraid I've had another blackmail demand, Mr Brock.' Halstead reached over to a side table and drew a single sheet of paper from a folder. 'It'll have my fingerprints on it, of course, but I don't know whether you'll be able to do anything with it.'

I took hold of the note by a corner, but had little hope of finding the prints of the blackmailer on it. If it had been sent by who I thought, he would have been careful enough to avoid providing me with any incriminating evidence. It was exactly the same as the previous note I'd seen, complete with what I believed to be the deliberate mistake of writing 'your' instead of 'you're'.

'When did you receive this, sir?'

'This morning. But this time it arrived at my home address. Previously they've come here to the Home Office.'

It wouldn't have been difficult to find out the minister's home address: a simple following job would have revealed that. 'And you've no idea who might be behind this?' I asked. 'You see, sir, I'm really struggling with this inquiry, linked as it is to the murder of Monica Purvis.'

There was a long silence during which Halstead leaned forward and took a sip of his coffee. Carefully replacing his cup and saucer on the small table that separated us, he looked up. 'Does the name Marley mean anything to you, Chief Inspector?'

'Yes, it does.' But I wasn't going to give too much away. After all, this man Halstead was still a suspect in my book, although I'd've given him fairly long odds.

'Some time ago Monica Purvis told me about this man Marley. Apparently he's some sort of security official with the airline that she worked for. She told me that he had threatened her.'

'Did she say why?'

'Apparently he accused her of being mixed up in some sort of fraud that was going on in the company – which she denied – and demanded that she should have sex with him or he would report her. That's what she said, anyway. Then she said that she'd told Marley that she would tell me all about it if he didn't stop. I think she hoped that I could do something. A damned foolish thing for her to do in my opinion: Monica knew what my position was and that our, er, liaison had to be kept a secret. I was, after all, very generous towards her.

But I think she had this silly idea that I might leave my wife for her.'

'Did you ever consider that course of action, sir?' I asked. 'Or give her the impression that it was in your mind?'

Halstead gave a hoot of derision. 'Good God no! People like me don't marry prostitutes.'

I wouldn't be too sure about that, you pompous bastard, I thought. Men of apparent substance had been known to marry a tart before now. 'Of course not,' I said.

'I have to say it came as a shock when you told me she was married, and to a man who was serving a prison sentence.'

'Charlie Purvis is dead now, of course.'

'So I believe. An unfortunate business up at Finchley so I'm told.'

'And Sylvia Moorhouse?' Implying that I knew more than I did, I floated the name just to see what his reaction would be.

'What about her?' Halstead looked uneasy.

'When I mentioned her name previously, you appeared not to know it, or that of her common-law husband Michael Cozens.'

'I'm afraid that wasn't quite true, Mr Brock. She was one of the girls at the airport with whom I dealt from time to time.' Halstead paused, searching the expensive wallpaper of his office as if seeking the right words. 'She and I had a brief fling.'

Oh well! Halstead wasn't the first politician who couldn't resist a woman who flattered him, and I suppose that's what she'd done. 'Would you care to tell me about it?'

'I travelled through Heathrow one day when Monica was off duty. Sylvia Moorhouse went out of her way to smooth the usual problems of travelling by air and we had quite a chat. She made it fairly obvious that she was available and, like a fool, I took her up on it.'

'Which hotel this time, sir?' asked Dave. 'One of those you took Monica to?'

'Er, no, a different one. In Guildford as a matter of fact.'

'And did she pay the bill?' I asked.

'Yes, she did, but I reimbursed her, of course.'

'With a little bit extra presumably,' I murmured.

Halstead didn't like that. 'I gave her a present, yes,' he said huffily.

This man's whoring must have been costing him a fortune, especially when the blackmail was included. 'But you didn't continue the affair?'

'No. She was after more than just a night's fun. She tried to persuade me to abandon Monica and . . .' Again Halstead broke off, thinking how best to phrase the next part of his admission. 'She wanted me to make it a permanent arrangement.'

'What sort of permanent arrangement?'

'I think she wanted me to set her up in a flat. Something like that. I hadn't been with her for very long when I'd worked out that she was a scheming woman.'

Well, well, a flash of shrewdness for once. 'When did she suggest this?'

'Just as we'd finished making love.'

'And I presume that that sort of arrangement didn't form part of your plans.'

'It certainly didn't. Having casual sex with a woman is one thing, but having a permanent mistress is not a good idea in my position.'

'So what did you do? Kick her out?'

Halstead gave a humourless little laugh. 'I played one off against the other. I told her that I much preferred Monica, and that Monica was much better in bed than she was. A bit ungallant, particularly as we'd just spent a pleasant hour between the sheets, but I really needed to disentangle myself from what I saw as a dangerous situation.'

Ye Gods! It may be ungallant in your book, mister, but it's certainly a bloody good way of making a vicious enemy of a woman. 'And how did she react to that?'

'She was furious. Threw a tantrum. I didn't realise she was such a strong woman. It was almost as if she had a black belt in judo, the way she came at me.'

'She does have a black belt,' I murmured.

'Good God! Really?' Halstead shook his head. 'I'd just taken a shower and when I returned to the bedroom she came at me like a tigress. Forced me down on the bed and, well, she . . .'

'I think I get the picture,' I said.

'When she'd finished, she asked if I still thought that Monica was better than she was.'

I couldn't resist posing my next question. 'And was she?'

'Well, yes, as a matter of fact, she was.' Halstead had the good grace to smile. 'But it didn't make any difference. I could foresee awful complications if I'd kept on with her.'

'There is one other thing,' I said. 'When you paid the blackmail demands, I understand that you did so with cheques made payable to a Mary Woods.'

'How did you know that?' Halstead seemed surprised that I had found out.

I was tempted to say 'because I'm a detective'. 'I made inquiries at the bank.'

'Oh, I see,' Halstead said. Nevertheless he seemed quite perturbed that I had done so.

'It would have saved me a lot of time if you had told me that in the first place.'

'I'm sorry, Mr Brock. Of course, I should have done so, but this whole thing has been such a strain . . .'

'Did you ever meet a Mary Woods, or have anything to do with a person of that name?'

'No.' The strain that Halstead had mentioned was clearly etched on his face.

But I still couldn't feel any sympathy for him. He was a victim of his own sexual appetite and his own stupidity.

Twenty-One

I gave Colin Wilberforce the seven-page statement that Dave had taken from Geoffrey Halstead about his involvement with Monica Purvis and Sylvia Moorhouse, and told him to file it.

Colin put it in one of several filing trays that were in a strictly regimented line along the front of his desk. 'A couple of things, sir. I had a call from Shirley Marley about half an hour ago. She said that a girlfriend rang her last night. Apparently this girl – she's a stewardess – had checked into one of the Gatwick hotels that her airline uses. She claims to have seen Marley and a blonde all luvvy-duvvy in the bar. She reckoned that they were staying there.'

'Which hotel?'

Colin smiled and handed me a slip of paper bearing the hotel's address. 'That one, sir.'

'D'you think Shirley Marley knows why we want to talk to him, Colin?'

'I don't think she cares.'

'Nor hell a fury . . .' muttered Dave.

'What was the other thing, Colin?' I asked.

Colin fingered another piece of paper across his desk. 'Got the result of the DNA test on the cigarette-end, sir.'

'Cigarette-end? What cigarette-end?'

'The one found at the scene of Monica Purvis's murder.'

'What's the good news, then?'

'The lab reckons there's sufficient to make a comparison,' said Colin. 'When you've got a sample to compare it with, that is.'

Stopping off at Bow Street court to obtain a warrant for

Marley's arrest – it was best to play it safe – I set off with Dave for the hotel at Gatwick. I had also taken the precaution of arranging for Frank Mead to search Marley's flat at Hounslow. And I suggested that he took a woman officer with him so that he would not be left alone with Shirley Marley. The outcome of Frank being one-to-one with her could seriously prejudice our case, to say nothing of his career. And, for that matter, his marriage.

Having persuaded the hotel duty manager of the importance of catching Marley unawares, we induced him to open the door of Marley's room with his pass key.

We were confronted by a leggy blonde of about twenty-nine attired in nothing but a G-string. Sid Marley was lying on the bed wearing a pair of revolting Y-fronts. True to the traditions of the worst B-movies the blonde covered her breasts with her hands, squealed and ran into the bathroom.

Marley, however, did not seem at all perturbed by our arrival. 'Well, well, well,' he said. 'Paying house calls now, are we? Must be urgent. So, how can I help you, gents?'

I let Dave execute the warrant just so that Marley wouldn't feel important enough to be arrested by a detective chief inspector.

'Sidney Marley, I have a warrant for your arrest on a charge of conspiring with others . . .' Dave finished telling him what it was alleged that he had conspired to do, namely the baggage scam, and then cautioned him.

'You'll have to go some to make that one stick, guv'nor,' said Marley, addressing me but still not moving from the bed.

'Who's the girl?' I asked, nodding towards the closed bathroom door.

'Trudy Watson, not that it's anything to do with her.'

'You'd better get dressed then, Sid,' I said. There was no reason to be formal: he was an ex-copper, after all. 'And we'll go back to London.'

'Yeah, righto,' said Marley, and rolled off the bed. He walked across to the bathroom and put his head round the door. 'I've got to go back up the Smoke, Trude, love,' he said. 'Something's come up. If you'll settle the bill, I'll square up with you later. You can make your own way back, can't you?' And with that he abandoned Trudy Watson, probably for ever. I know for a fact that he never settled up with her.

We booked Marley in at Charing Cross nick, charged him with the offences relating to the baggage scam and then took him through to the interview room.

'I'm not answering any questions,' he said. 'Because now you've charged me you're not entitled to ask any except to eliminate—'

'I don't propose to,' I said, cutting across his sketchy knowledge of the law, 'at least not about the conspiracy. I want to talk to you about the murder of Monica Purvis.'

'Talk away,' said Marley, lighting a cigarette. 'But there's nothing I can tell you other than that I found the trainers and the cufflink in Sylvia Moorhouse's locker.'

'Sylvia Moorhouse alleges that you planted them there.'

'Well, she would, wouldn't she? She doesn't like me, that girl.'

'Is that because you tried to rape her in the staff restroom?'

'Is that what she said?' Marley scoffed. 'She was begging for it, but I turned her down. Don't do to have it off with the staff.'

'Then why did she knee you in the crotch and throw you across the room, as a result of which you were off sick for a week?'

Marley laughed outright at that. 'I should coco,' he said. 'Slip of a girl like that and she reckoned she threw me across the room. Anyway, it's her word against mine. Why? Thinking of charging me with attempted rape?'

'If you were so averse to having sex with the staff, Sid, why did you have it off with Monica?'

'I should be so lucky. Bit of all right she was.'

But at that point the interview was interrupted by the arrival of Frank Mead. 'A word, Harry?' He managed to contain his elation until we were outside the interview room. 'We took possession of his laptop computer.'

'And?'

203

'You're going to love this,' said Frank. 'He had the black-mail letters on his hard disk. One for before Monica's murder, and one for after.' He handed me a couple of printouts: they were identical with the letters that Geoffrey Halstead had received.

'Nice one,' I said. 'Incidentally, did you find Monica's cashpoint card there?'

'I'm afraid not, Harry.' Mead was obviously disappointed. So was I. 'However, I did get this statement from Shirley Marley,' he said, handing me a typed copy. 'She's well pissed off with him, I can tell you.'

I glanced through it and smiled. 'Isn't she just?' I said.

Time to confront Marley with these latest pieces of evidence. 'Who opened the account at Kilburn that the money was paid into from you blackmailing Halstead, Sid?' I didn't waste time telling him how we knew.

But Marley wasn't giving up that easily. 'Don't know what you're talking about,' he said, and lit another cigarette from the stub of the one he'd just finished.

I tossed the letters on the table in front of him. 'Detective Inspector Mead has just executed a search warrant on your flat at Hounslow, Sid. He found your laptop and those' – I gestured at the letters – 'were on your hard disk.'

Marley shrugged. 'That's that, then,' he said.

'D'you want to tell me who opened the account?' I asked, after Dave had cautioned him.

'Sylvia Moorhouse, and if you spin her drum you'll probably find the blonde wig she wore when she pretended to be Mary Woods.'

'Did you nick the real Mary Woods's passport?'

'No, I found it at the airport.'

'And you decided to blackmail Halstead . . . just like that.'

'Not really. He's some big wheel at the Home Office appar-ently, and Monica tried to put the arm on me by threatening to tell him that I was coming on to her. All lies, of course. But I guessed that he and she were having it off so I did a following job when he left the Home Office, and finished up at some hotel in the sticks. They were at it all right. It was too good an oppor-tunity to miss so I thought I'd screw him for a few grand.'

I was amused by that: he readily admitted to blackmail – albeit once the chips were down – but still denied having had sexual intercourse with Monica. 'How did you recruit Sylvia?'

'She was more than willing. She'd fancied Halstead for a long time. In fact I think she screwed him once, but she really resented Monica having got her claws into him, so when I put it to her that we could make a few bob, she jumped at the chance. She really hated Monica, not only for hanging on to Halstead, but because Monica took Cozens off her as well. Randy little cow that Monica.'

'Is that why she went on the game?'

Marley shrugged. 'Maybe. I don't know. There's easier ways of getting a man than hawking your mutton round Soho, isn't there?'

'Are you suggesting that Sylvia murdered Monica?'

'Search me, but don't forget I found the trainers and the cufflink in her locker.'

'You'd better have a look at this, Sid,' I said, changing the direction of my interrogation and handing him the copy of the statement that Frank Mead had taken from Shirley Marley. 'She confirms that you were off sick for a week with severe bruising of the testicles at the time Sylvia Moorhouse claims to have kneed you in the crotch.'

Marley glanced through the statement and laughed. 'That's a load of balls,' he said.

'I came to that conclusion too,' I said mildly, but the subtlety of my comment clearly eluded the ex-copper.

'Anyway, a wife can't give evidence against her husband.'

'She can actually, Sid, but she's not your wife anyway. You're not married to her.'

'Bloody cow,' said Marley.

'That aside, I shall seek the authority of a superintendent to take a swab of your saliva,' I said, 'in order that I may have a comparison made of your DNA.'

'Comparison with what?'

'A cigarette-end found at the scene.'

'Well, you can whistle for that,' said Marley. 'I'm not giving any samples and you can't compel me to.'

Somehow I knew that would be his rejoinder, but he was only half right. 'You are aware that your refusal may be put in evidence at any trial and the jury will be invited to infer what they will from such a refusal, aren't you?'

Marley laughed. 'Yeah, I know all about that. I used to be in the Job, remember? But you've got to have a trial first. And if you're thinking of charging me with Monica Purvis's murder, you'll need a bit more than what you've got.' He stubbed out yet another cigarette. 'And don't think of using those,' he said, pointing at the overflowing ashtray, 'because it'll be inadmissible.'

But Marley was thinking only of *intimate* samples, and his response was typical of an overconfident ex-policeman who had failed to keep up with changes in the law. I've met a few of them over the years.

Somehow we had to obtain more evidence if we were to make a charge of murder stick. But perhaps it *was* Sylvia Moorhouse who had killed Monica. According to Halstead's account of Sylvia's 'rape' of him, she was certainly strong enough to have overpowered Monica. Or perhaps it was Charlie Purvis who'd killed her. Or Michael Cozens. Or even Geoffrey Halstead.

But I still had one other card up my sleeve. 'That's not a problem,' I said. 'In that case I shall seek the authority of a superintendent to take a sample of your hair, nail-clippings or scrapings. And if necessary, take them by force. And that *will* be admissible.'

It was done within the hour and the samples were sent off to the lab. But I determined that Marley would be kept in custody until I'd interviewed Sylvia Moorhouse again.

'You didn't ask him how he knew the trainers were relevant to the inquiry, guv,' said Dave, once Marley was in the cells.

'Neither did I,' I said. 'I think we'll leave that until the trial and let prosecuting counsel ask him. That ought to make Marley's eyes water.'

The next morning, I sent Frank Mead to re-arrest Sylvia Moorhouse, now back in Bromley, and charged her with blackmailing Geoffrey Halstead.

Frank found the blonde wig that Marley told us might be there. And he also found a passport in the name of Mary Woods. Both had been wrapped in cling film and concealed in the loft, which is why Dave and I hadn't found them the day that Sylvia did a runner. But of Monica's cashpoint card there was no trace. I reckoned that whoever had taken it had destroyed it by now.

'Marley threatened to report our little fiddle to the police,' said Sylvia. 'I was frightened that he might just do that so I went along with his plan to blackmail Halstead. I didn't want to, but . . .' She shrugged.

I didn't bother to dispute that. She was bobbing and weaving now and this latest story – with its implication that she was frightened of Marley – didn't really accord with her original statement, a statement in part confirmed by Shirley Marley, that she'd assaulted him when he'd tried to have sex with her. *And* she'd sent him a cheque from the baggage scam account so that he would be implicated.

It amused me that a cocksure ex-policeman like Marley was so greedy – or so hard up – that he put himself in the frame by cashing the cheque when he could have used it as evidence against Sylvia and Monica. But then there was no doubt in my mind that Sid Marley was as bent as a corkscrew. And, like so many bent coppers, he thought he could beat the system.

But despite what Marley and Halstead had said, I was not wholly convinced that Sylvia was innocent of any involvement in Monica's murder. 'I put it to you that on the night of Monday the twenty-second of July you went to Talleyrand Street in Soho and murdered Monica Purvis for no better reason than she was having an affair with Geoffrey Halstead.'

'Why should I do that?' Sylvia did not seem at all concerned that I was clearly thinking of charging her with murder.

'Because you fancied him. You saw him as someone of power and influence, and if you could have broken up his marriage and had him for yourself, you'd have been delighted. You even went as far as having sexual intercourse with him. However, the truth of the matter is that Halstead told you that Monica was a much better sexual partner, and you couldn't accept that.'

'You seem to forget that I was at home in Bromley the night that happened, watching the television.'

'So you said.'

'Michael confirmed it.'

'Michael Cozens is dead.'

'He wasn't when he confirmed it,' said Sylvia sarcastically. 'On the other hand, I might have been in bed with Charlie Purvis,' she added, defiantly raising her chin. 'Anyway, you can't prove I wasn't. Not now.'

I gave up on that for the time being. 'Let's talk about the murder of Michael Cozens.'

'If it was murder. Personally I think he got pissed and fell in the river. End of story.'

'What about the copy of *Hansard* that we found in Michael's car?'

'I put that there,' said Sylvia.

'Why?'

'It was Sid's idea. He said that as Michael had been in prison, it would look as if it was him who was blackmailing Halstead. I think he intended to send you an anonymous letter pointing the finger at Michael.'

I shook my head and smiled. That was typical of Marley's muddled thinking. 'You told me that Monica had been sacked for bad timekeeping, but she hadn't, had she?'

'I could hardly tell you she'd left to go on the game, could I?'

That was pretty rich, I thought. Here was a woman who screwed around herself – and I was sure that the stories about orgies at Bromley were true – but jibbed at admitting that her work colleague had become a professional whore. 'Why *did* Monica Purvis turn to prostitution, Sylvia?'

'That's easy: she was greedy. She reckoned she could earn as much in a day getting laid as she earned in a month at the airport. She was a calculating little bitch was Monica. Always putting herself about, if you know what I mean, eyeing up the passengers, *and* getting some takers. She even let Sid Marley have her, not that it did her much good. Frankly I think she was a nympho. She'd been doing it part-time anyway, whenever she had an evening off. But after Charlie got put inside, she packed in her job at the airport and went full-time up Soho. After all, he wasn't in a position to argue, was he? Not that he did anyway because when he came out he acted as her ponce. Always had an eye to the main chance did Charlie Purvis.'

That was all very interesting, and I'd been right about Charlie Purvis acting as Monica's ponce, but it didn't push the inquiry any further forward. 'It's my intention to get authority from a superintendent to take a saliva swab from you,' I said.

'What's that for?' For the first time since her arrival at Charing Cross police station, Sylvia appeared apprehensive.

'In order that I can have a DNA comparison made with a cigarette-end found at the scene of Monica Purvis's murder.'

There was a long pause. And then Sylvia said, 'I think Sid Marley killed her.'

'Why d'you say that?'

'Marley was forcing himself on Monica fairly regularly, but she hated it, really hated it. Well, who wouldn't, the nasty, smarmy bastard. He kept telling her that if she didn't let him screw her, he'd report both of us over the fiddle we were running.'

I glanced at Dave. We'd both spotted yet another contradiction.

'Then he asked for a bigger cut,' Sylvia continued. 'I reminded him that he'd cashed the cheque for two thousand I'd sent him and that he'd be dropping himself in it, but he laughed that off, saying that we couldn't *prove* he'd cashed it. He said that as an ex-copper, he knew the law.' Sylvia paused to light a cigarette. 'But it got so bad that the poor little bitch packed her job in and I was left to carry on the fiddle on my own. You could say that Marley more or less forced her into prostitution.'

I wasn't convinced of that attempt to wriggle out of any liability. From what I'd heard and, indeed from what Sylvia had said previously, it was a voluntary decision on Monica's part.

'But Marley still wouldn't leave her alone,' Sylvia went on, 'and he tracked her down to her place in Talleyrand Street. He was up there about twice a week, having it off with her for free. So Monica and me came up with a plan. I told Marley that the next time he screwed her, I'd say I'd seen him and that we'd report him to the police for rape, and they'd have to believe it because there were two of us. Well, you know what happens to rapists when they get banged up, and being an ex-copper as well . . .'

Sylvia was dead right about that. The going rate for rape is about seven years, but I couldn't visualise Marley hacking more than about six months in the nick before he topped himself.

'So I reckon he killed her and then put that stuff in my locker so's he'd do for both of us in one go.' Sylvia sat back, crossed her legs and drew heavily on her cigarette.

I had to admit that it all sounded very plausible, but it was getting beyond me. Clearly it was something that the Crown Prosecution Service would have to sort out, God help us!

And that, for the time being, was that. A murder inquiry, nearly three weeks old, and all I'd got were two arrests: for fraud and for blackmail. But I wasn't much closer to solving the murder.

Back at my office there were two messages waiting for me. One was from the DI at Battersea to say that he'd got nowhere with the break-in at Sarah Dawson's flat. His only hope was that he might get a cough when some villain was nicked in the distant future. Then he'd 'take it into consideration'.

The second message was from the Yard to say that the other set of fingerprints found in Michael Cozens' abandoned car were those of Sylvia Moorhouse. And just to make my day it added that those fingerprints did not match any found at the murder scene in Talleyrand Street.

But my investigation into Cozens' death was immediately brought to a shuddering halt by a telephone call from Dr Henry Mortlock, the Home Office pathologist, who chose that moment to tell me that Michael Cozens had not necessarily been murdered after all.

'You see, Harry, I've been thinking about it and consulting with professional colleagues. The consensus is that he could have fallen in the river by accident.'

'But you gave me some spiel about vagal inhibition and

how there was no water in the lungs and that must have meant—'

'I know, I know. But given that Cozens was drunk, and the post-mortem indicated that he was, he would have been shocked – I use the term clinically – at striking the cold water. That would account for the absence of water in the lungs. In layman's terms, it was probably the shock that killed him.'

'And that, I presume, would be your evidence at a trial if ever we charged anyone with Cozens' murder?'

'I'm afraid so, Harry,' said Mortlock.

I suppose I should have been pleased that one of the murders I was investigating had been converted into an accidental death, but somehow I felt cheated.

I told Dave what Henry Mortlock had said but he just laughed.

In the meantime, I decided to look into the arrest of Charlie Purvis. 'Where was Purvis charged by Sid Marley for robbery or whatever, Colin?'

Colin Wilberforce busied himself for a few minutes before coming up with the answer. It was, needless to say, a police station on the very fringe of the Metropolitan Police District. But then it would be, wouldn't it?

The duty officer, an inspector, was not at all happy to see us. When a detective chief inspector from a Scotland Yard department turns up talking about an arrest that took place some years previously, the automatic reaction is that a disciplinary inquiry has been set in motion. Policemen – and policewomen, for that matter – have an instinct for taking cover and saying nothing.

However, having finally managed to convince the inspector that I was investigating a murder and that the arrest of Charlie Purvis – the victim's husband – was possibly relevant, we got what we wanted. Or I thought we had.

Among other examples of maladministration, the inspector told us that when the time came to transfer Purvis's property from the police station property store to the prison, certain items were missing. Namely a pair of trainers.

There had been an inquiry, but nothing had been resolved. It had, said the inspector, been put down to sloppy paperwork.

Surely to God it couldn't be this easy, not after all the painstaking work that had gone into this inquiry. Could it be that the evidence I needed had been on my very own doorstep all along? Or had it?

My money was on Sid Marley having taken them. But why, and why so far in advance of a murder in which they played so significant a part?

But then common sense kicked in and I remembered a lecture – given by the commandant of the Detective Training School, an experienced detective chief superintendent – that I was privileged to hear during my basic CID training. 'Look at what you've got,' he had said, 'and no more. Never jump to conclusions. The job of a detective is to make a molehill out of a mountain, not the other way around.' And he should have known. He had successfully investigated one of the most difficult murders in recent history, one that was clouded with all manner of inconsequential and misleading evidence, much of which turned out not to be evidence at all.

But were the missing trainers the ones we now had in our possession? That was the real question.

If they were, it still posed a number of problems: there was no way of proving that Marley had taken them and, furthermore, no way I could prove that one of them was identical with the trainer that had left an imprint at the scene of Monica Purvis's murder.

Even so, I decided that that constituted enough of a coincidence to warrant charging Marley with Monica's murder. Convictions have, after all, been secured with less evidence than that.

Twenty-Two

I cobbled together a preliminary report and showed it to the commander. I knew that he didn't understand it because after putting on his half-moon glasses and riffling through the first few pages, he told me to leave it with him. That usually meant that he wanted to look up his dictionary and some of the law books in his bookcase that I suspected were there to impress us lesser mortals.

It was three hours before he sent for me. But he still wasn't prepared to make a decision. 'Well, what d'you think, Mr Brock?' he asked.

'I think it's worth giving it a run, sir, although I'm not sure that the Crown Prosecution Service will wear it. Doesn't exactly meet their criterion of a fifty-one per cent chance of succeeding at court.'

'Mmm, yes, I see what you mean,' murmured the commander, probably not seeing at all. Mind you he wasn't totally incompetent: he could write a blistering memorandum, but he'd probably learned how to do that at the Police College at Bramshill. 'Well, see what they say.' He pushed the report across the desk and prodded it with a forefinger. 'Incidentally, you've spelt "misappropriation" wrong on page four.'

'It is only a draft, sir,' I said. I always put in a deliberate mistake: it tended to take the commander's mind off the dodgy bits.

To my utter astonishment, the lawyer at the Crown Prosecution Service, having skimmed through the final report at top speed, grinned and said, 'Oh, why not? Let's go with it, Mr Brock.'

'What, Marley *and* Moorhouse? I don't think the evidence

against her is very strong,' I said. After all, one does have to be fair in these matters.

'Despite the trainers and the cufflink being found in her locker,' mused the lawyer, 'I think we can charge Marley with the murder of Monica Purvis and use Moorhouse for the prosecution.'

The murder trial took place six months later at the Old Bailey's Number Two Court. And to no one's surprise Marley pleaded Not Guilty.

In the course of my few hours in the witness box, I emphasised that Marley had not been made aware that a pair of trainers played a significant part in my investigation, neither had it been disclosed to the press.

When Sylvia Moorhouse gave evidence, with greater confidence than I had anticipated, the jury listened closely, particularly to the part – accompanied by crocodile tears – where she described how Marley 'got me in a corner and tried to rape me'. Defence counsel had a go at her in cross-examination, but wasn't able to do much to shake her testimony.

Shirley Marley had been summoned to give evidence, but turned up drunk. Prosecuting counsel decided that it was too much of a risk to call her and we had to do without her evidence of Marley's week of sickness following Sylvia's assault on him. But it didn't seem to matter.

The telling evidence, however, was that given by the forensic scientist who had compared the DNA of Marley's hair with that of the cigarette-end found at the scene of the murder, and declared them to be a positive match.

In a desperate attempt to repair the damage caused by the scientific evidence and the damning accusations of Sylvia Moorhouse and me, Marley's counsel – somewhat reluctantly, I suspect – put him in the box.

It was a pathetic fiasco. True to his character, Marley whined and ducked and dived. He admitted having been at Talleyrand Street, but not on the night of the murder. He must have left the cigarette-end on a previous occasion, he suggested unconvincingly. He accused Sylvia Moorhouse of having got it in for him, but couldn't explain why, other than to say it was because he was a security officer, and no one liked security officers.

When questioned by prosecuting counsel about how he knew that the trainers were of significance, he blustered and bumbled, and muttered something about having heard it somewhere, but there was little that his own counsel could do to help him in re-examination.

In his closing address, however, Marley's counsel muddied the waters sufficiently about the trainers and the cufflink to ensure that the judge made a big thing of them in his summing-up.

'Much has been made, ladies and gentlemen of the jury,' he said, 'about the pair of trainers that were allegedly missing from a police station, the police station to which Charlie Purvis was taken after his arrest by ex-Detective Sergeant Marley.

'There has been a suggestion by the Crown that Marley took the trainers at the time of Purvis's arrest and that it was one of those trainers that left the imprint at the scene of the murder. But is there any proof that it was one of *those* trainers that left the imprint? It is a question, ladies and gentlemen, of continuity of evidence, and in this case there is no such continuity. Setting aside the cufflink for the moment – such cufflinks are so widely available as to set their evidential value at nought – it would appear that the method of recording prisoners' property at the police station in question was so slipshod' – at that point the judge glanced at me, as if I had been personally responsible – 'that no one can be sure that they were ever there at all. And there is certainly no evidence that they were ever in the possession of ex-Detective Sergeant Marley between the time of Purvis's conviction for armed robbery and when Marley claimed to have found them in Sylvia Moorhouse's locker.

'You must consider, therefore, that perhaps they never left the late Charlie Purvis's possession until much later. Given what you have heard about the relationship between Charlie Purvis and Sylvia Moorhouse, it may well be the case that Purvis gave those trainers and that cufflink to Moorhouse and she put them in her locker at Heathrow Airport for safe-keeping.

'But that does not make Marley the murderer. Whether

Purvis was responsible for his wife's death can now only be a matter of conjecture.

'Had that been all there was to this case, however, I would have suggested that there was a sufficient inconsistency in the chain of evidence to warrant your considering whether the case against the accused is proved *beyond all reasonable doubt*.

'But, ladies and gentlemen, that is *not* all. I invite you to ask yourselves whether Marley put the trainers in Sylvia Moorhouse's locker in an attempt to throw suspicion on her. Moorhouse, you will recall, alleged that Marley indecently assaulted her as what she saw as a prelude to rape. If that is true, and if it is true that Moorhouse, as she claims, defended herself by violently assaulting Marley, it may well be that Marley's pride was wounded, and he sought revenge.

'But more to the point, you heard Detective Chief Inspector Brock tell the court that the information about the trainers and their relevance to the murder was deliberately kept from the public. So how did Marley know of their importance when he affected to have found them? You may have found his explanation unconvincing.'

And so, on the slimmest of circumstantial evidence – and despite not being able to show any really credible motive – the jury convicted Marley of the murder of Monica Purvis. But that's police work for you: some you win, some you lose. This time we'd won.

Fresh from receiving a life sentence, Marley appeared in the dock once again, this time with Sylvia Moorhouse alongside him. They pleaded Not Guilty to both counts on the indictment: demanding money with menaces from a certain Mr X (whom only the prosecution, the defence and the police – and of course, Marley and Moorhouse – knew was Geoffrey Halstead, a Minister of State at the Home Office), and defrauding the airline for which they both worked.

This time we had very firm evidence of the two crimes: John Smith told the court of the transaction that had first alerted us to what was going on; the bank manager of the Kilburn branch testified to the cashing of the cheque that Sylvia Moorhouse had sent Marley; Frank Mead told of finding the incriminating letters on the hard disk of Marley's computer and, not least, there was Marley's own admission.

Included in my contribution was what could only be regarded as a ragbag of circumstantial evidence, some of which was ruled either inadmissible or irrelevant by the judge. But you have to try. Haven't you?

I told the stony-faced jury that, at the outset of the inquiry, Sylvia had said she didn't know that Monica Purvis was having an affair with Mr X. But when I started to relate details of Mr X's conversation with Sylvia, and that he'd had an affair with her too, the judge put the kibosh on it. God knows why. Well, I do actually: it was hearsay. But I'm a firm believer in putting all the evidence in front of the jury and letting it make up its own collective mind.

In the end, inevitably, both were convicted. Marley received eight years for the blackmail and four years for the fraud, to be served concurrently with his life sentence for the murder, and Sylvia got four years and two years.

'Well, Dave, that's another one under our belts,' I said, when we'd retired to the Magpie and Stump for a glass of much needed sustenance.

'D'you think Marley really did murder Monica, guv?'

'I don't know, Dave, but the jury thought he did, and that's good enough for me. But I suppose you think that Sylvia should have gone down for it too.'

Dave Poole's black face split into a huge grin as he rolled his eyes, and parodying the sing-song accent of his West Indian ancestors, he said, 'Well, boss, you can't win 'em all.'